SUICIDE MISSION

"The NVA will know you're coming and that there are only four of you."

The team was in a state of shock. Sullivan had apparently lost his mind.

"How?" Warner asked, afraid of the answer.

"We leaked the intelligence to their agent already. He's expecting you," Sullivan said. It crossed Warner's and Pate's minds to resign right there. Bonn was digesting the impact of what he heard. Tan simply stared at Sullivan in disbelief. Telling the enemy your intentions was not in his comprehension.

"The idea," Sullivan said, "is that the NVA will wait to bag you all in one jump when you make contact. They think you're coming in to find out what happened to Team Delta. It's perfect cover."

"It's also suicide," Bonn said.

SPECIAL OPERATIONS

Frank Camper

A DELL BOOK

Published by
Dell Publishing
a division of
Bantam Doubleday Dell Publishing Group, Inc.
666 Fifth Avenue
New York, New York 10103

ISBN: 0-440-20302-3

Printed in the United States of America
Published simultaneously in Canada

November 1989

10 9 8 7 6 5 4 3 2 1

KRI

Dedicated to the memory of my father,
whose battlefield was the Pacific
and whose weapon was a submarine

"First, welcome to Special Operations," Sullivan announced, as if he were giving a rehearsed speech. "You will be part of Operation Thirty-five, specifically the deep penetration of Laos for intelligence-gathering purposes.

"I must instruct you at this time that everything you will do is *top secret,* and that the release of information of any kind concerning Operation Thirty-five is a treasonable and court-martial offense."

AUTHOR'S NOTE

A glossary of the military terms, slang, and acronyms used in this novel appears at the end. All the letters and numbers translate into the language of life and death.

SPECIAL
OPERATIONS

1

Specialist 4 Christopher Allen Bonn; LRRP ambush site, II Corps

Bonn sat back invisibly in the trees, holding his carbine, waiting, watching. The jungle trail before him was dappled in sunlight through the leaves overhead, and insects lit on wisps of weeds.

Under the fronds and ferns he was just another shadow in the dark spots, his eyes hidden below the brim of a grenade pin–decorated soft hat, his tiger fatigues streaked with irregular black stripes edged with shattered green and brown patterns. Like the three others on the team with him, he wore his rucksack and all his gear, every strap buckled, every cord tied, ready for anything.

They had taken the position off the trail a day before, after discovering fresh footprints on it. Only a few minutes ago what seemed like voices had drifted in on the wind from downhill. They were close.

The calm before the kill possessed Bonn, his senses animal sharp, his body controlled by instinct.

Then he heard it with clarity beyond doubt.

People were coming down the trail.

He thumbed his weapon safety off and switched the fire selector forward to rock and roll, just as four Asian soldiers cleared the bend in the trail. Bonn held perfectly still.

The team leader opened up when the men came into the center of the ambush. The roar of three CAR-15s and Bonn's carbine was earsplitting.

The moment of surprise was eternal for the dying, the

leafy branches they fell into snapping and spinning as the men were flung off the trail by the storm of bullets. Dirt exploded around the twitching bodies until the ambushers' magazines hit empty. The silence that followed the gunfire was like air rushing in to fill a vacuum.

Scrambling out of the foliage, the team leader and the radio operator rushed the bodies, quickly examining the bloody pockets for documents, staining their fingers.

The radio operator saw that the man he was kneeling over still breathed. He shoved the muzzle of his CAR-15 into the gasping soldier's ear and pulled the trigger; the entire body jerked with the impact of the shot.

The team leader left delayed death for the comrades of the slain Vietnamese who would find the corpses. He pulled the pin on a white phosphorus grenade and slipped it under the weight of a dead arm, so the safety lever wouldn't spring off until the body was moved.

Bonn took point and led the team to a gully near a clearing, and the radio operator made contact with an extraction helicopter.

After a week out on the long-range reconnaissance patrol hunter-killer team, nineteen-year-old Chris Bonn was tired, nervous, and dirty. He crouched with his team in the shelter of the gully, watching the treeline around the clearing over the sights of his carbine, waiting for the helicopter.

When there was time to think about such things, he usually thought about going home. He even planned for it, but he was too good at what he did. The war was absorbing him. Destiny had found Bonn, and he didn't even know it yet.

Specialist Four Joseph Pate, Sniper, IV Corps

Pate's eyes were gray, and there was no compassion in them.

He swept the opposite riverbank through his binoculars in a methodical pattern. It was two hundred meters from where he lay to where he looked, and it was not simply distance.

To Pate it was range.

He wore an olive drab bandanna tied pirate style on his head, and his lean face was smeared with dark greasepaint. By his side was a bolt-action Remington rifle, its once-glossy stock and barrel now dulled black and green, and frayed burlap was twisted around its large telescopic sight.

The handloaded cartridges in its magazine were tipped with heavy soft-nosed bullets that could stagger the bulk of a deer. They almost destroyed a human being.

His spotter and security man lay within arm's reach, blended low into the roots and foliage. He carried an M-14 rifle so they could share their 7.62 mm NATO ammunition if necessary. Pate knew the man likely wouldn't go back out with him again. Few did. His reputation as a sniper who almost wouldn't return without a kill was justified. He would stalk a target, if that was what it took, or endure virtually any hardship waiting for prey.

They had been out of water since dawn. The mission was supposed to have been only an overnighter, but Pate wouldn't quit. All their canteens were empty. Filling them required crawling down to the river, which meant possible exposure, and Pate wasn't about to let that happen. To take his mind off his thirst, he stuck a fresh unlit cigarette into the corner of his mouth. Several crumpled but unburned ones were discarded beside him in a little hole he'd scooped in the soil.

The river was clear and shallow. The smooth rocks on the bottom reflected the sunshine as it bounced in the ripples of the water.

The hot delta day seemed to last forever, and Pate longed to dive into that cool water. His camouflaged fatigues were grimy, his heat rash burned, and the dazzling sun had given him a throbbing headache.

Instead, he stayed put, spying on the sandbar and lower banks through the heavy field glasses. Suddenly his heart jumped. A man had stepped out of the shadows under the jungle of trees along the water's edge.

Pate ranged the figure instantly, pulling the stock of his rifle in tight to his shoulder, and saw it was a man with a gun. The weapon hanging on the farmer's shoulder signed his death certificate for him.

The cross hairs met in the high center of the man's chest. Pate relaxed, let the cigarette fall from his mouth, exhaled, and slowly pulled the trigger. The recoil of the high-powered rifle was like a kick in the armpit. When Pate regained his focus through the scope, the man was lying faceup in the sand, his feet kicking feebly and hands clutched to his ragged black shirt.

Chambering a fresh round, Pate wondered what the man had been doing in the open like that. He pocketed the empty brass cartridge case and hoped the man had not been alone. The day was beginning to show some promise.

Sergeant A. E. Warner; First Air Cavalry, An Khe, II Corps

The bullet that had knocked Warner out the day of the ambush and saved his life had perfectly clipped the point of his chin and dropped him like an uppercut from a prizefighter.

What he'd seen in those few moments before the bullet hit him had been enough to last a lifetime.

The M113 track ahead of the truck he'd been riding on had hit a mine and exploded. The infantrymen crowded on its deck were thrown into space, falling out of the air to thud like sandbags on the road, and the driver of his truck had run over some of them.

Up and down the convoy, mines and B-40 antitank rockets slammed and smashed at the vehicles. Fuel tanks were burning. Trucks were run into ditches. A captain in a jeep sat headless, his hands still holding a rifle across his knees.

Warner was new to Vietnam that day, only a few weeks in country, a twenty-year-old specialist E-4. He'd been riding with his company on what was supposed to be a routine convoy in a secured area. The bullet that knocked him out left him appearing bloody and very dead, so when the North Vietnamese overran his part of the convoy and killed the survivors of the mines and rockets and raking machine guns, Warner had been ignored.

Later the medics had sewn up the little split under his chin, and he had received a Purple Heart and promotion to buck sergeant. The drugs and treatment took away the pain and swelling in his face, but nothing could cure the terror in his heart.

Unacknowledged and suppressed, Warner's fear of death and pain quickly became debilitating paranoia. His official job now was squad leader in an infantry platoon, but he had desperately maneuvered and been sent to the rear to work at base camp.

He felt that his subordinates hated him and that his superiors distrusted him. He was not far from wrong. His pale complexion and shallow features inspired no confidence, and his habit of talking *at* people and not *to* them destroyed friendships before they began.

He considered his chevrons his only ally but saw no chances for advancement in rank for himself in base camp. His desire to escape his unit and gain the rocker stripe that would make his buck sergeant's grade respectable had finally become a possibility.

It was in the form of a call from the First Field Force at MACV asking for volunteers. It was for something called the Special Operations Group.

"What do they do?" Warner had asked the personnel officer, who had previously had a private talk with Warner's company commander and knew transferring Warner away, anywhere, was a silent priority.

"It's all hush-hush," said the officer. "I do know that Special Forces has something to do with it, and it's run right out of General Westmoreland's headquarters. My guess is they need support troops."

"Can I make any rank?"

"Those green beanies get the best of everything. They've got channels to slap stripes on you we just don't have. You'd really have a lot of opportunity with this SOG unit. Probably live in a Saigon hotel and wear civilian clothes and all that good spook stuff."

"How do I volunteer, sir?"

"An interviewer is coming around. They like recon people, so I'm carrying you as part of our recon platoon."

"Thanks, sir!" Warner said, and meant it. The officer smiled.

Lieutenant Phoc Tan; Second Vietnamese Ranger Division, IV Corps

Tan put his boot sole on the back of the man's head and pushed his face into the dirt. The man writhed inside his barbed wire binding, begging incoherently.

"Who attacked the village with you, *monkey*?" Tan barked. "Where are they *now*? If you lie to me, I will cut off your ears and feed them to the *pigs*!" He kicked the man in the side of the head to emphasize the statement.

It was not a bluff. He did not have to resort to that. He was known throughout the delta for his adherence to his word.

Tan was in his middle twenties, tall for a Vietnamese, and imperially slim. He used his ruling-class social demeanor and Hue University education to intimidate the unschooled soldiers and rice farmers. He demanded respect and obedience as his due and received them.

When he began an interrogation, prisoners could see the specter of death in his face, so he was rarely given misleading information. It was also rare that his victims lived to tell the tale of his technique.

Three young men, all wrapped in rusty barbed wire, lay at his feet. They were plainly scared to death. A few ARVN soldiers watched idly from the shade of a hut, and some women and children stared silently from farther back.

Tan listened as the man babbled names and places through his swollen lips, writing them down in a small pocket notebook, until he was satisfied.

Tan pulled his bayonet from its scabbard, the bluing worn off the blade from innumerable sharpenings, and grabbed the VC suspect by the hair.

He lifted viciously, jerking the man's face upward, and slashed across the exposed throat, opening the flesh to the neckbone. Blood and air mixed, gurgling, as the severed trachea expelled the contents of the lungs.

Tan stood knowledgeably aside so the strong spurts of blood, as the heart beat its last, would not ruin his tailored uniform.

"Shoot the rest of these dogs," Tan ordered the soldiers as he walked back to his jeep and driver. He had an appointment with the major for which he was late. It probably concerned more trouble about the prisoners, as usual.

The carbines cracked as Tan rode away.

2

Camp Enari, Pleiku Province, Fourth Division,
LRRP Company

Bonn lay on his cot in the sweltering heat of the afternoon. The camp lay becalmed, the sides of his tent rolled up to catch any errant breezes.

He had been with the long-range reconnaissance patrol company for nearly half a year now, and his job was beginning to fit him like the faded black-striped tiger fatigues he wore.

Even when he was out of the jungle, Bonn moved as if he were slipping from shadow to shadow. His short brown hair had been bleached almost blond by the sun, and his skin was burned brown; but maturity had not yet hardened his face.

Even though he spoke softly, it was a mistake to think him unaggressive. The blood of five men was on Bonn's youthful hands.

He looked at his watch, a dull-finish stainless steel Bulova Accutron Astronaut model, to see how long it was to chowtime. Most of the other men were buying glittery Seikos at the base camp PX. Bonn had ordered the Accutron because it was claimed to be the most accurate watch in the world. The Astronaut model was actually designed for and used by the NASA space program and had secondary dial faces to record elapsed time into mission, date, and stopwatch functions, features also useful on patrols.

Bonn was a believer in good equipment. Everything he used to stay alive was carefully considered. He had a leather-handled Air Force issue survival knife with a hammer butt, parkerized finish nonglare blade, and sawtooth keel. A sharpening stone was tucked into a special snap-closed pocket on its sheath. He considered big, bright-bladed knives too much of a reflection hazard, and their impressive size only extra weight.

He carried a Korean War era armory-rebuilt folding-stock full-auto M-2, a .30 caliber carbine. The M-16 rifles were certainly too dirt- and carbon-sensitive to trust fully. The compact CAR-15 variant, with its short barrel and telescoping stock, was handy; but his carbine always fired, and it was his weapon of choice.

Bonn kept his fatigues repaired, the rips sewn and buttons replaced, and he had packing for a mission down to a science. Each pocket and each pouch of his load-carrying equipment and uniform were always filled with just the right items. He equated attention to detail and professionalism with survival.

In that stifling dry day in the central highlands of Vietnam, Bonn had only one worry on his mind. He wondered if he had made any technical errors during the morning's ambush.

Ninth Division Base Camp, IV Corps

Pate jumped off the chopper in the driving delta rain, a large plastic bag protecting his weapon. He waded to the Tactical Operations Center and stepped in on the duckboards. He grinned and held up one finger.

The S-2 intelligence officer brightened when he saw the sign. "How did it go?" he asked.

"One round, one kill," Pate said, mimicking the slogan of the sniper school. Water pooled under him as he opened his shirt and leaned against the wall.

"I dropped this gook across the river and waited for three hours for somebody to do something, but nothing happened," Pate explained.

The officer recorded the information on the report. "No one even tried to get his weapon?"

The sniper shook his head. "Nope, would you?" he asked.

Pate walked to the coffeepot and poured himself a cup as the paperwork was finished, watching the rain leak through the sandbag roof and spot the plywood floor. He was tall and spare the way frontiersmen were supposed to have been, and he spoke with a southern drawl. He had the inner toughness people get from being poor all their lives.

The officer extended his arm and offered Pate a cigarette from the pack. The sniper took one and hung it in his lips but didn't light it. He had once been a heavy smoker, but smoking was impossible in the field. It was visible at night and could be smelled anytime. No mere cigarette was going to deprive him of a kill, so he'd quit, except for the habit of sometimes putting one in his mouth unlit.

"By the way," the officer told Pate, "I just got a distribution from MACV. They want some volunteers from our LRRP and sniper units. Says the qualifications should be recondo or sniper schools, ranger, tracker, et cetera. You interested?"

Pate frowned. "What for? What kind of missions do they pull?"

The officer shrugged. "It doesn't say. It's for SOG, that Special Operations Group. Probably sneaky pete trips into Cambodia or someplace like that," he said.

"Any money in it?" Pate asked.

The officer shrugged again. "You'd get a chance to go to jump school, so you'd probably get some jump and TDY pay at least," he said.

"Yeah, what the hell," Pate said somberly, "I'll do it. Maybe it'll get me the fuck out of these rice paddies."

Second Ranger Headquarters, ARVN, IV Corps

The major sat behind a desk in an air-conditioned office. Tan reported to him and saluted briskly. The major did not return the salute or beckon him to sit.

"Tan," the major began, "I have received another complaint against you by the American intelligence commander of the Ninth Division. He claims you've killed several of their detainees during questioning. He has sent this report to Saigon as well."

Tan did not blink. "Sir, the Americans do not understand—" he said, but the major cut him off with a raised palm.

"That is of no importance here," the major said coldly. "What is important is that you have caused me trouble one more time with Saigon. Those insolent people from the government will be in my affairs, investigating everything, and I will not have that happen!" Tan stood impassive, waiting.

"I have a transfer for you," the major informed Tan. "The Americans in Nha Trang need an interpreter who can pass a U.S. Army top secret security clearance. You are going, since you can speak English."

"Sir," Tan protested, "I do not have such a clearance."

The major allowed himself a smile. "You do now. I have seen to it. Now go pack your equipment. Your orders are being prepared today."

Tan saluted, spun on his heel, and left the room. He walked straight across the compound to his tent and pulled the flap closed behind himself. He fully undressed, hanging his uniform on a broomstick nailed between two ammunition crates that served as his closet, and washed in cool water from the tin basin that was his sink.

The major was related to a deputy minister in Saigon. Tan knew he sold food, equipment, and sometimes even weapons that he took from military stocks on the black market. The major was a petty, corrupt little king in his own fiefdom. He didn't seem to care if the war was being won or not, as long as he could steal what valuables the Americans provided.

What an amazing lot the Americans were, Tan thought. They had come in on the coattails of the defeated French and flooded Vietnam with riches, even committed their own men to war, and some of them were dying. Not as many as the Vietnamese, of course, but enough. Yet even with such an investment of blood and treasure, they ignored the realities of war. They almost played at it, adhering to civil rules and self-imposed restrictions that gave so much advantage to the enemy. As individuals some of the Americans could be reasonable and intelligent. As a whole they were childish, overeager fools.

Tan did not have to be a soldier. He could have avoided the army altogether, using his father's connections within the government, and stayed as a student in the summer house in Hue or lived in the family villa outside Saigon.

When he had married, he had only just received his diploma. A postgraduate course would have secured his professorship. His wife, a beautiful, artistic young girl from a good family, had encouraged him to stay in school. He paused for a moment at his framed photograph of her, the portrait taken just before they had wed. She had given it to him as a special present. He loved her with the kind of love that hurts the heart.

He slowly packed his old brown suitcase, leaving out only the clothes he would wear. The last thing he put away was the photograph of his wife, dead two years now from a Vietcong terror attack. Her life was a debt on which he never stopped collecting.

First Air Cavalry Division Headquarters, An Khe

Sergeant Warner smoked nervously as the tiger fatigue–clad Special Forces lieutenant read his 201 file. He watched the man's face for some giveaway expression but could find none.

"Looks okay, Warner," the officer finally said. "Guess

you've seen a lot of action with the Cav." Warner simply nodded his head and stubbed out the half-finished cigarette.

"We need good noncoms," the lieutenant said. "You'll be going to Recondo school and then on down to the jump school in the Philippines to get your wings. Does that suit you?"

"Jump school, sir?" Warner asked.

"We require all our recon team people to be jump qualified. You'll like it," the officer explained.

Warner thought very fast. He lit another cigarette to stall. The wrong answer could ruin everything right now, and he was ready to do anything to get out of his outfit.

"Great," Warner said. "Should be fun."

Nothing the officer had said seemed encouraging. Recon teams sounded too much like combat again. Still, one opportunity usually created another. All he had to do was play along until something better came up. Even jump school was better than the infantry and another ambush.

That night Warner drank so much in the NCO club he had to be carried back to his tent. He was dumped on his cot and spent the night mumbling in his sleep and dreaming ugly nightmares about parachutes.

The next morning he was sick, but nobody cared.

Camp Enari

Filling sandbags was more monotonous than hard, and shirtless, Bonn sweated with the small crew of laboring LRRPs drafted into the effort to add a new wall to the already impressive division headquarters fortress complex.

His mind was adrift, far away from the repetition of shoveling, filling, tying, and heaving the burlap bags. *It was his favorite daydream, the one that sustained him, a dream he could see and feel. It always began with his picking Linda up on a bright summer Saturday morning, his red convertible Monza so highly waxed it mirrored the sun, its top down, engine tuned, and gas tank full.*

Linda would come out of her house wearing a white terry-

cloth beach jacket over her ocean green bathing suit, carrying a gym bag full of suntan oil and towels. She was almost seventeen, with thick auburn hair, stand-up breasts, firm dancer's thighs, and trusting blue eyes. She always made Bonn take a deep breath when he saw her like that.

The drive to the ocean would be fast and fun, the Monza running like a racer, the radio giving them guitars and drums and high school songs. At the beach the asphalt parking lot would be too hot to walk on barefoot, the smell of sea spray and grilling hot dogs would swirl on the breeze, and the ice chest sodas were so cold they hurt your teeth. Jukeboxes on sandy footprinted wooden promenades boomed rock and roll, and the sky was cloudless.

In the warm surf, waves would wash over Linda, streaming her hair across her face as she laughed. In the water, out deeper where no one could see, he could secretly touch her, and the splashing children and beached sunbathers were all unknowing.

What could go wrong in paradise?

"I've got your orders for Recondo school," the headquarters company first sergeant informed Bonn, bringing him back to Vietnam. "The group you're in will start the next training cycle in a week. We'll hold you off any missions until you leave."

"Great," Bonn grunted, stabbing his shovel into the sand again. "I'll just pull your shit details until then."

The sergeant checked the angry reply on the tip of his tongue and walked away, wondering why the LRRP company had to be attached to him. They thought they were such goddamned hotshots.

As soon as Bonn had the chance, he returned to his tent and wrote the letter to Linda he'd been planning that morning.

1 Oct. 67

Sweetheart,

    I've got orders now to go to Recondo school in Nha Trang. I hope I can learn enough there to keep me alive these next six months. It's a Special Forces course, so it ought to be pretty good.

The line companies are still taking casualties, but our LRRP platoon is doing okay. We've got a good bunch of guys here and a better kill ratio than anybody in the division.

Only 187 days left to go.

I really miss you. When I get back, we'll spend my whole leave at the beach. How are things at school? What are you taking now as a senior?

Don't worry about me. I'm coming home.

Love,
Chris

3

*Recon Phantom Flight, thirty thousand feet over
Northern Laos*

Reconnaissance aircraft are usually lightly armed or not
armed at all. The flight of four camouflage-painted RF-4B
Phantoms, camera- and electronics-equipped versions of the
F-4 fighter-bomber, carried no weapons.

A protective flight of fully armed escort fighters was on
the way to meet them for a morning's incursion from Thailand over Laos into North Vietnam. The rendezvous point
was some distance still inside enemy territory. Late linkups
were possible since the big ground-to-air missiles and MIG
fighter cover were concentrated over the cities and military
target zones.

Resistance going to or coming from the targets was rare,
even though the U.S. Air Force and Navy jets often used the
same in-out air corridors and even stuck to fairly predictable
schedules.

Everything seemed to be okay and on schedule to the
flight leader of the RF-4Bs. The sky was clear above low-
level rain clouds, and a special electronics bomber with a
sophisticated array of sensing and jamming equipment was
due to join them shortly, flying high overhead like a watch-
ful angel.

Then one of the backseat radar and electronics operators
switched on his radar, beginning his checklist as they over-
flew the border of North Vietnam.

The blips appeared on the Phantom's radar screen with

no warning. "Bogeys coming from the north and moving fast," the backseat said to the pilot, urgency in his voice.

"Any target radar on *us*?" the pilot asked quickly.

"I can't tell yet," the REO answered. "I'm getting nothing consistent on the ECM."

"Playboy Leader, this is Four," the pilot called. "I've got bogeys on my scope moving in from due north and on a direct intercept with us. Are you monitoring any missile battery radar? Over."

"Negative, Four. But I also have your bandits now. Do we have EB-sixty-six cover yet, NKP?" the flight leader asked his airfield at Nakhon Phanom in Thailand.

"Roger, Playboy, you are under the umbrella. He confirms bandits but says you are not being radar-tracked, over."

"I've got a visual! MIGs! I've got a visual!"

"Where are they?"

"Evade! I see two of 'em! Air-to-airs incoming!"

"Playboy Leader, what is your situation?"

"Dave's hit!"

"Any chutes, goddamn, do you see any para—"

"Roll, roll!"

"Two, missile coming up on your tail!"

"I'm punching out—"

"Outturn it! Stay on the inside!"

"Playboy Leader, this is NKP, say again your—"

"NKP, Playboy Leader's down!"

"Who is this?"

"We're hit—"

"Say again your situation."

"There was no radar warning! They're all over us!"

"Playboy flight, say again your situation. Playboy flight, this is NKP. Please say again your situation, over."

Nha Trang, Recondo School, Fifth Special Forces Group

Tan left the twin-engine C-123 cargo plane and walked across the heat-shimmering runway. It had been years since he had visited Nha Trang. He hailed a cyclo and asked the driver to take him to the American Special Forces compound.

Nha Trang had changed a great deal, he realized, since the Americans had come. Once there had been only the sleepy coastal city here, and now it was truck convoys, roadside vendors, barbed wire, and sandbags.

He was pleased to find the camp near the beach, the sand and surf reminding him of Vung Tau and the swimming holidays he had known there as a child.

Tan paid the cyclo driver and showed his orders to the gate guards. They admitted him past the boldly painted Fifth Group insignia on the sign beside the gate.

He asked his way to the operations building and to a desk marked IN PROCESSING. "Excuse me, sir," Tan said to the American lounging at the desk, "I am to be reporting here now."

The specialist took Tan's papers and looked them over. "Uh . . . sit down, I'd better get the colonel," said the clerk. Tan dropped into a wooden chair and noticed that the rest of the clerks in the room paid him no attention at all.

"Hey, Lieutenant Tan"—the specialist summoned him from a hallway—"come this way, the colonel will see you now."

Tan entered the indicated office and found himself alone with a balding middle-aged American officer. Tan stood at rigid attention and saluted smartly. The colonel smiled and pushed aside a pile of paperwork. "Sit down, Lieutenant Tan," he said.

Tan recognized the need for pleasantries and tried to respond to the officer's warmth. "Thank you so much, sir. I study English very hard to speak well," he said politely.

"What have your duties with the Second Rangers been?" the colonel asked, lighting his pipe.

Unaccustomed to direct conversation in English, Tan pieced his sentences together carefully as he spoke. "I work sometime with the Ninth Division, question VC they capture. I go with my army in ranger unit, have operation. Kill VC," Tan explained.

"Why did you want to leave Saigon and join us up here?" the colonel inquired. "The missions you'll go on might take months to complete. It's dangerous work."

"I must fight VC and help my country," Tan said, his sincerity bridging even the language gap. "I kill Communist."

The colonel thought that over for a moment and closed the file. "I'm glad to have you here, Tan. We always need good linguists. We'll get you billeted and started off as soon as the next group finishes up, and I personally want to thank you for volunteering." He stood and held out his hand, and Tan took it, saluted again, and left the office.

As Tan was shown to the barracks, he wondered why Americans always gripped his hand so hard.

Warner was reporting in as Tan reached the transient barracks. He received a routine processing and was directed to the transient barracks as well. Tan had slipped his suitcase on a shelf over his bunk and left the prefab building by the time Warner was dumping his gear on a cot.

A clerk in the operations building picked up Warner's folder. "Here's another one of those Special Ops people," he mentioned to his buddy at the next typewriter. "You gotta hand it to those guys; they sure have a lot of balls."

Warner decided to pass up chow and went in search of the local NCO club. He found it and dug in there, leaning on the bar and trying to work down the supply of 3.2 beer on hand in the refrigerator, smoking cigarette after cigarette, grinding them out with his boot on the floor.

Drinking helped. It made tomorrow seem far away. It was also easier to get along with himself when he was drunk. He didn't feel his failures so keenly. He'd always been hard on himself, more damningly critical than anyone else, even his father—or his teachers, even his scoutmaster. They couldn't just let him alone. They pushed him to be the best, and he'd had to lie and cheat on his tests to make them think he was good enough.

They were a hypocritical bunch, making their love and favor dependent on his performance. It made him ill and nervous; it made him worry all the time. They were fakes, treating him like that, so he'd faked the fakes, made them think he was smarter, better, worthy. He lived every day with the fear they'd find him out.

Away from home for the first time at college, away from the pressures, he'd been unable to maintain his grades. He couldn't go home, so he'd joined the Army. Now he was really in trouble. He was where he could be *killed*. It was too much. He was desperate. He drank, looking for mercy in the alcohol.

Tan ate a meal outside the gate and came back to camp before the gate curfew. He passed the NCO club by accident on his way to his barracks and, wanting a drink, looked in, wondering if he should go inside. The place was jammed with GIs, their music loud and incomprehensible, and he could see no familiar Asian faces. He entered cautiously.

The bartender served him a beer with no problems, so Tan drank, watching everyone else down the bar and at the tables scattered around the room.

The air was full of cigarette smoke and harsh, jabbering English. Tan noticed the American standing next to him was finishing three beers to his one, doing some serious drinking. The soldier wasn't talking to any of the other Americans, and he wore a sour look on his face. The patch on his jungle fatigues was one of the United States First Air Cavalry, and the sergeant's stripes sewed to his sleeves were high and prominent.

An inner sense told Tan the man was scared. Scared soldiers are nothing new in war, but it was different in this case. It was almost like the streak of weakness Tan could discern in some men at the beginning of an interrogation.

Warner looked up long enough to see the Vietnamese standing by him. The Vietnamese was a wiry, compact man, with close-cropped black hair and fine features. *Goddamn dink,* Warner thought, *can't get away from them! I shouldn't even be here,* he pondered gloomily. *Screw this goddamn school.*

New Pleiku Air Force Base, II Corps

"You any good with that thing?" the Huey crew chief asked Pate as they refueled, looking at the long bolt-action rifle with the big telescopic sight that Pate carried so casually. It was easy to imagine that he was going after squirrel with it, instead of people.

"Yeah," Pate said, hoping the man would drop the subject.

"I've always wondered about you snipers." The crew chief pressed. "What's it like when you're on operations?"

"It's just a lot of waiting," Pate said. "Sometimes you get lucky, sometimes you don't."

"How far can you hit accurately?" the crew chief asked, determined to find out more.

"Fartherest I've shot and hit a man is about a thousand meters," Pate said, not stretching the truth.

"Jesus Christ!" the man exclaimed reverently. "How many gooks you killed?"

Pate gazed across the landing field, allowing a dramatic pause. "You wouldn't want me to brag, now would you?" he finally said, a sardonic smile pursing his lips.

The reply impressed the air crewman more than a given figure would have. The door gunner finished the fueling and waved everybody back on board, and in no time they were airborne and speeding westward toward a Special Forces camp deep in the mountains, right on the border of Cambodia.

Pate rested against the bulkhead, noticing how different the country was, comparing the delta with the hilly, rugged terrain of the central highlands. It impressed him only that the fields of fire were much shorter in most cases.

He was thankful for the difference in the temperature, however. The heat in the delta paddies irritated him badly, and he hoped the change up in the highlands would do him good.

SOG Team Delta, Laotian Panhandle, North Vietnamese border

The trail junction near the village was deserted and quiet. Checking his watch once more, the team leader crept out of the underbrush and looked down each branch of the trail again. There was nothing moving.

He edged back into the concealment and cursed softly, damning the idiotic error that had put him where he was. Behind him, one of his best men, a veteran Nung, was still bleeding. The best effort of the team medic was only forestalling death.

Only three days into the mission one of the new men had accidentally shot him. Laos was not a place to be making mistakes, and certainly not on a mission of this importance.

The border of North Vietnam, and the site of the objective they had been sent to recon, were less than a day's walk away. The dying Nung knew the country well, having served on a previous mission in the same area, watching trains for a four-month period.

If the Nung died, the team would lose its chief scout. The team leader had only one chance, and he was taking it. A friendly agent, who was listed as active and ready to help, lived in the village. If the agent could get some medical supplies and provide them with refuge while the Nung recovered, the mission might be saved. It was a chance that had worked for other teams.

But the agent was late. He was supposed to walk the trail every day at 1400 hours, and it was almost sundown. The team had placed the sign that assistance was needed, a strip of colored cloth tied high in a tree, which had been taken by someone earlier in the day. That should have been the first part of the contact; now they needed the second.

A noise on the trail alerted the team. It was a stick being

rapped against the trunk of a tree, three beats fast, three beats slow.

It was a signal. The team leader crawled to the trail again, looking for the man making the noise. He saw someone standing alone in the open. It was a short, stocky Laotian dressed only in a loincloth. His mouth was partly open, and a large prominent gold tooth shone proudly between his lips.

The team leader struck the tree beside him in the same manner and was surprised to see the agent turn and run. *"Hey, what the hell—"* the team leader muttered.

The ambush erupted, tracers flashing past the trees, the foliage thrashing as if it were a hurricane wind, whipped by the tremendous firepower concentrated onto the team.

When the NVA platoon charged into the underbrush, it encountered no opposition.

The agent was given his reward on the spot. When he finished counting the roll of currency, it totaled more than he would have made from the other side in a year.

Special Forces "A" Camp, Five Tango, II Corps

Pate saw the camp from the air first, as his ship approached to land. It was a crudely triangular fort, a throwback to strongpoints a thousand years old, walled with earthworks and barricades.

The Huey landed inside the camp, blowing dust over everything. Pate jumped off with his rucksack and rifle, and the ship flew away, back over the mountain.

A bare-chested man, wearing bleached-out tiger fatigue trousers and a threadbare flop hat, trotted over to meet Pate.

"Hi, I'm Captain Don Sullivan, CO of the 'A' team here. You must be Spec Four Joe Pate from down south," Sullivan said. They shook hands cordially, and Pate felt an instant liking for the tall young officer.

"Some place you got up here," Pate said. "Looks like Dogpatch."

"It's not much, but it's home," Sullivan said. Montagnard

soldiers loafed about, pigs and chickens wandered loose, and the guards in the shaded towers along the walls seemed to be half asleep. Pate smiled wryly.

"C'mon inside and let's have a beer," Sullivan said, ushering Pate toward a tin-roofed shed that formed a patio of sorts outside the main bunker. They sat at a table improvised from a giant commo wire reel turned on its side. Sullivan took two beers from a small refrigerator tucked under a sandbag shelf. The steady beat of a generator could be heard from somewhere behind the main bunker.

"What kind of cannon you got there?" Sullivan asked, reaching for Pate's Remington.

"That's my own," Pate said. "I had my granddaddy mail it to me. I didn't like those M-fourteens we used at sniper school. My scope's better than the Army one, too."

Sullivan aimed the rifle out in the distance. "This might be a good unit, but you can't interchange your scope with a Starlight the way you can an ART," Sullivan commented.

"Don't need to," Pate said. "I can hit 'em where they are, day or night."

Sullivan propped the weapon against the table. "Shoot seven-point-sixty-two NATO?" he asked Pate, who nodded.

"I got my own ammo, too," Pate said. "I don't trust the Army stuff. My granddaddy loads it for me and mails it over."

"Military ammo is match grade, Pate! It should be the best," Sullivan said defensively.

"Try grouping it at twelve hundred meters sometime," Pate said bluntly, finishing his beer.

Sullivan's eyebrows arched. *"Twelve hundred* meters! Hot damn, wait till I get you out on ambush, we'll shoot NVA clear over into Cambodia!" he exclaimed.

"I guess I'm the first one here," Pate said.

Sullivan retrieved two more cold beers from the refrigerator. "Yeah. They're putting your team together now. We'll have time for your course at HALO school and some OJT in the mountains before your team reports in. Anyway, I *really* want to see you shoot."

"Glad to, sir," Pate replied, "glad to."

"How'd you find out about Special Ops?" Sullivan asked.

"My S two. What's this SOG outfit all about, anyway?"

"You mean you don't know?"

"Nobody will explain. Everything's top goddamn secret."

"I like your style, Pate. I'm surprised you're not SF. We're the guys who're not supposed to know what we're volunteering for. I can tell you this much. Special Ops is just what it says it is. Operations outside the norm."

"Who's on my team?"

"I don't know yet. I've received an allocation for four of you. Didn't even know your name until yesterday. We only get this stuff on a last-minute need-to-know basis."

"What's the mission?"

"No orders yet. I don't have anything to do with that. I'm just supposed to provide a place for you to group up, equip, and brief."

"Who really runs this show?" Pate asked.

"Saigon. Every Special Ops mission is individually authorized from the Pentagon."

"Are you in SOG?"

"I couldn't say if I was, but I'm cleared for it. I used to be with Project Delta. I took an 'A' team just after the reorganization into the C and Cs."

"Delta? C and Cs? What's that?"

"Delta was LRRP-type missions. C and C means command and control. They're the op headquarters."

"Guess I've got a lot to learn," Pate said.

"Don't sweat it. Nobody but the Pentagon knows it all, and sometimes I wonder about them," Sullivan said, and they both laughed.

4

Recondo School

Bonn entered Reconnaissance-Commando school with the attitude it could teach him little he did not know about jungle warfare after months of firsthand practice.

He discovered how wrong he was.

There was advanced map reading and land navigation, and he did triangulation and back azimuths until they were second nature. He studied topographic maps and side elevation plans and learned to draw them, so that the flat map sheets became three-dimensional to him at a glance.

He had north, south, east, and west forever replaced in his mental reference with degrees and minutes and seconds off the rotating dial of his compass face.

He was lectured on how to recognize real intelligence in the field and how to interpret it, beginning with such basics as "If they're traveling with packs and canteens, you know they're a long way from camp" and ending with oddities like "Ants won't remake a trail after someone has stepped on it. They'll move around and start a new one. Look for this when you're tracking."

In communications classes Bonn learned about radio relay and the techniques used in long-distance communication and handled the special radio sets that were built for deep-penetration teams.

He made jungle antennas and strung them in the treetops, using only common wire, and as the instructors said, they worked. Static, skip, meter band, and jamming became realities to him.

Artillery support and air strike direction was presented to the students by actually doing it, until guiding a jet in on a target by voice alone was easy going, even if the student was so near the target that the bomb jarred his teeth.

The medical and survival instruction was particularly more complete than the basic courses he had received in stateside training. Doctors ran the courses he had received in lifesaving techniques designed especially for isolated situations.

Bonn used blood expansion kits, arterial clamps, and trachea tubes, the experience broadening him, bringing out an assurance that if he had to, he could save a life.

Even simplified dental techniques were covered. Few things can incapacitate a man as much as a toothache, and he found out how to deaden exposed nerves and relieve abscesses.

When patrolling itself was taught, he listened harder than at any other time in the school. It seemed that if a team followed all the rules set down for a recon team operating alone, it couldn't, absolutely *could not*, be caught. Only those who compromised died.

They examined and fired the Soviet-bloc Kalashnikov AK-47. Its short wooden buttstock, pistol grip, heavy curved thirty-round steel magazines, and unfamiliar sights felt very foreign to Bonn.

The riflelike full wooden stocked Simenov Karbine Semiautomatic, which everyone called the SKS carbine, had a ten-shot magazine and a blade or spike bayonet, depending on the variation, hinged under the barrel. It fired the same 7.62 mm × 39 "Russian Short" cartridge as the AK-47.

There was also the simple pistol grip-fitted, tubelike B-40 rocket-propelled grenade launcher. The rocket was larger than the tube, and only its shaftlike motor and folded stabilizing fins were inserted into the front of the launcher. The B-40 was supposed to be mainly a close-range antitank weapon, but the enemy had the reputation of shooting it at almost anything.

Bonn fired the Chinese-made copy of the Russian Tokorev pistol, which looked like an old .32 Colt automatic, and handled a row of light, medium, and heavy enemy machine guns, from the squad model assault RPD to the big 12.7 mm muzzle-braked antiaircraft weapons, equal to the U.S. .50 caliber.

To liven it all up, there was plenty of physical conditioning. They ran, they climbed, they carried, they rappeled off towers, so that not a moment was wasted. At night, if they were not on duty, they studied the manuals or cleaned equipment or just collapsed and slept. The course was fast-moving, information-packed, and exhausting. Bonn loved every minute of it.

Recondo school was a graduate class of veterans honed to the final edge, ready to be turned loose back into the jungles.

Command and Control North (CCN), Special Operations Group, Da Nang

"Team Delta is six hours overdue with their SITREP, sir," the radio operator remarked, consulting his log. The OD walked over to the bank of remotes and long-range sets.

"When did they last report?" he asked.

"We got 'em at eighteen hundred hours yesterday," the operator read, flipping back a page.

The officer looked at the wall map. "Is that position we have marked on them accurate?" he inquired, pointing at a flag high on the panhandle of Laos.

"Yes, sir," the radioman confirmed. "That was plotted after their report yesterday."

The officer decided to let it go for the moment. "It won't be the first time somebody has reported in late," he said. "If we don't get something by twenty-three hundred, let me know."

The operator nodded and resumed listening through his headset, reading a paperback novel.

Nha Trang

Tan got away after hours from the school and swam in the warm blue South China sea every chance he got. It was one of the few times he could forget the war and relax.

The course was impressing him with its efficiency and attention to detail, and even with the language barrier he was learning a tremendous amount.

One day while Tan was floating peacefully in the surf just off the beach a GI noticed the SAT CONG tattoo burned deeply on his chest and asked what it meant.

"Means kill Communist," Tan explained, grim-faced. "Means kill *all* Communist."

Tan had noticed Warner in the classes and had marked him as a potential failure. Whatever was being done, Warner barely seemed to have the intellect or the stamina necessary, but he always managed to stay in the group, if at the bottom of it.

Sometimes he drank more than he should have at night, paying for it the next day in nausea and weakness. It only caused the instructors to bear into him all the harder.

Among other problems, Warner was a heavy smoker and a restless sleeper. Both were serious drawbacks on recon missions. He didn't have the discipline not to smoke unless he was constantly supervised, and when asleep on patrol, he exhibited the sins of thrashing about, moaning, and occasionally talking in his sleep.

Warner had a history of sleep disorders. As a child he would sleepwalk with his eyes wide open, talk, and answer back if talked to—a behavior that frightened his parents, who nevertheless didn't take him for any medical treatment in hopes he'd grow out of it. The same was true for his bed-wetting, which lasted for years. The bed-wetting and sleep-walking did diminish in time, but not his somnambulant talking. In times of stress he would cry in his sleep. Otherwise he might blurt out coherent words, even whole sentences. He knew he did it, and it caused him even more stress. He always worried about what he might reveal. Warner couldn't even trust himself.

Bonn was excelling. His classmates knew it, and the school cadre knew it. Because of his ability, he had received a recommendation of which he was not yet aware.

A man with a civilian haircut, dressed in jungle fatigues, his eyes hidden by sunglasses, stood in the shade of a wooden shed and watched the trainees climbing a scaffold and rappeling off the top.

Bonn came off and dropped in short jerks, his gloved hands gripping the nylon line, his feet straight out, twisting to allow his boots to hit the ground at the last instant and releasing his snap link as soon as possible.

The practice was for exiting a helicopter into a jungle too dense for the ship to set down. Satisfied with his conclusions about Bonn, the observer approached the group of men Bonn sat with as they took a break.

The trainees were soaked with sweat and darkly tanned, their combat gear lying in piles where they had dumped it to cool off.

"How are you men doing?" the observer asked informally. A few soldiers grunted replies. His clean pores and light skin revealed he did not live in the dust or the sun as they did, but there were concentration lines on his face even though he was in his early thirties.

Bonn could see himself in the lens reflections of the sunglasses. The man looked directly at him and asked, "How long do you have left in country?"

"I've been here since June," Bonn said. "You an officer?"

The man smiled again. "No, don't worry about that," he said. Bonn wondered if the man was a reporter.

"Well," the stranger said, "nice talking to you. Take it easy," and turned and walked away in the direction of the headquarters building. His jungle boots were new.

A whistle blew, and a Special Forces instructor ran across

the drill field, yelling, "*Formation!* Let's go *formation!* You lazy legs move it! Show them how, Airborne!"

A cheer went up from one group, and a countercheer broke out. Bonn clambered to the assembly, conversation forgotten.

In the HQ, Bonn's file was pulled and examined very thoroughly for the second time that day, and an interview arranged.

After chow and the evening briefing, Bonn lay on his cot in the cooling twilight. The training was over for the day. He considered going for a swim or resting and waiting for the movie that would be shown in the mess hall. There was a lot to be said for the green beanies, he mused; they sure knew how to live.

A soldier looked in the door. "One of you guys named Bonn?" he asked.

Bonn sat up. "Yeah, that's me," he said.

"They want you in the operations building," the orderly told him. "I think you got a message or something."

Bonn buttoned his shirt as the orderly waited outside. They walked to the long operations building, and the orderly pushed the door open. It was air-conditioned inside.

Captured weapons and flags decorated the room. All the clerks were gone. "Wait here," the orderly said, and knocked on a closed office door, opened it, and went in, leaving Bonn alone in the deserted operations room.

They got the AKs and flags to give the place a hard-core look, he noticed with amusement, *and they have air conditioning!*

The orderly entered the room again. "Major Allgood will see you now," he said.

Major Allgood was sitting behind his desk, which was covered with papers and coffee cups. He was a tall black man, seemingly too young for the gold leaf pinned to his collar.

As Bonn stepped into the room, he saw the stranger he had met earlier that day sitting off to one side on a folding chair. He was smiling his used car salesman's smile at Bonn, a clipboard and file folder in his lap.

"Come in, come in." Allgood beckoned. "Sit down, Chris. Want a cup of coffee?" Bonn sat on another folding metal chair, noticing the weathered green beret and camouflage-taped M-16 slung on a coat rack behind Allgood.

"No, thanks, sir, no coffee," Bonn said, crossing his legs nervously.

"How about a soda then?" Allgood offered, standing, and Bonn saw him limp as he walked to the refrigerator. A large map taped to the refrigerator door allowed the appliance to serve double duty in the small office.

The major handed Bonn a cold canned drink and sat back down, somewhat awkwardly. "Bad leg," he explained, "mine took off part of my foot."

"I'm sorry, sir," Bonn said, and meant it.

"Chris," the stranger asked, "why did you volunteer to come to Recondo school?"

Bonn shrugged. "They offered it to me," he said.

"Are you that casual about being here?" asked the stranger.

"I'm an LRRP. This course is the best way I know of to learn more. You live longer that way."

"Why did you join the LRRPs?"

"It's safer. I know going out with a four-man team instead of a whole company doesn't sound safer, but it is."

"I think I understand," said the stranger. "You feel safer because out alone your fate is really in your own hands."

"Yes, sir. That's it. You can get killed in the infantry, and it won't even be your fault."

"So you want . . . control," said the stranger, cryptically not phrasing it as a question, and smiled again.

"Like a cigarette?" asked Allgood.

"No, sir. I don't smoke."

"Do you do drugs?" asked the stranger. "A little LSD at home? Some horse here? Thai stick? Maybe—"

"No. Never."

"Control again? A man on drugs is a vulnerable man, isn't he?"

"That's right," Bonn said, wary of the stranger.

"You're doing pretty well," Allgood told Bonn. "As a matter of fact, you'll be in the top ten percent of the class if you max your final patrol scores. I think you'll make it."

Bonn did not yet understand the purpose of the interview, but he kept his suspicions hidden. "Uh, thank you, sir," he said.

"There are opportunities for good men," the stranger said without elaboration.

"Have you ever worked with a Mike force?" Allgood asked, leaning forward just a bit toward Bonn.

"No, sir, I never worked with the dinks. We had sniper teams go out with the ARVNs before, but not me," Bonn answered.

"Do you think you could work with them?" the stranger asked.

Bonn mentally pictured himself out in the field with a Vietnamese unit. "I think so," he said, stalling, "if they were good. I don't want any dinks *di di mau*ing out on me," Bonn said.

Allgood and the stranger grinned at each other. The stranger faced Bonn and opened his file folder. "Chris," he began, "we have some . . . *operations* that are joint concerns of the South Vietnamese and the United States governments. We need experienced men to participate on these operations in a covert-action mode. Do you understand me?"

5

"Spying?" Bonn guessed.

"Not really," the stranger said. "These are raids and reconnaissance missions. They are conducted outside this country." Bonn's pulse quickened. He had heard rumors of such missions.

"How would you feel about going TDY to the Fifth Group for a while?" Allgood asked.

"T-TDY?" Bonn stammered. "My CO would have to approve—"

"We can handle it from here at the school," Allgood assured him.

"What will I be doing?" Bonn asked the stranger. "I don't speak any Vietnamese!"

The stranger smiled again. "That's no problem. Most of our indigenous personnel speak some English."

"Don't we get into trouble if we get caught doing something like this?" Bonn asked. "What happens if I get killed or captured over the border somewhere?"

"Bonn, this operation is secret," Allgood said. "It is *top secret*. We have to protect it as best we can. If you are killed, we rearrange the facts to place you somewhere else. If you are captured, you become missing in action."

"The NVA are in the same boat," the stranger added. "They're not supposed to be in Laos or Cambodia either, so we're all even."

Major Allgood laid both hands on the desktop. "How

about it, Bonn? I can get you a three-day R and R before
you ship out. You'll get the chance to go to jump school;
there will be TDY pay, jump pay, flight pay; it all adds up."

Bonn was ready. "Okay, sir," he said. "Can't be any more
dangerous than humping the hills in Kontum Province."

"Fine!" Allgood approved. "You'll finish Recondo school
here, get the leave, then go straight down to jump school at
Clark in the Philippines!"

The stranger pointed his finger at Bonn. "Let me explain
something. As of right now you are bound by the National
Security Act. You can't tell *anyone,* friend or family, what
you'll be doing."

"Don't worry, sir, I'm not going to say anything," Bonn
promised, feeling oddly pressed.

Allgood began to put his papers away. "Bonn, we have a
rather extensive network of covert operations going on. One
intelligence leak could get a lot of our people killed. You
understand the need for security," he said, to dull the edge
of the stranger's strict warning.

"That's all for tonight," the stranger said, standing.
"Thank you for volunteering, Bonn. I believe you'll do a
good job."

Bonn saluted and walked out. The brief but obviously
important meeting in the office weighed heavily on his mind.
So this is how you get into the big time, he thought. *No appeal
to cause or patriotism. Just a direct go–no-go option.*

Bonn knew little about communism and not a great deal
more about capitalism. The type of mission, not politics, had
swayed him. He believed he fought the good fight, if he
thought about it in those terms at all.

Operation/Intelligence Shop, Fifth Special Forces,
Nha Trang

"Get me the paperwork on those SOG volunteers," the
officer asked the clerk, sipping his coffee. The clerk unlocked
the safe and handed the files to the officer.

The request out from MACV practically begged for people, allowing provisions to accept non-Special Forces–qualified men who would never have been considered in better times. There were only a few records before him. He needed a stack a foot high just to satisfy requirements.

He read the files on each volunteer and consulted the Recondo school notes. It all looked good except for an Air Cav E-5 named Warner. He was behind most of the men in his tests, and one instructor had written that he should not be given any important responsibility.

The officer decided not to wash out Warner. He needed him too badly. If the C&C detachment wanted to send him back to his unit after it got the school report, fine.

There was also a priority demand for an unusual team. It was going to be operational from Command and Control North.

The staging point wasn't even one of the usual C&C detachment headquarters; it was a small "A" camp in II Corps. The officer raised his eyebrows. This was some kind of very important deal or some kind of big screwup. It was out of channels all the way.

Whatever it was, one man, a Ninth Division sniper named Pate was already assigned to the team and living at the "A" camp. There were no instructions on team skills except mandatory jump status if they didn't already have their wings. Nowhere did it say they had to be fully Special Forces–qualified. The officer decided the priority amounted to nothing more than attaching a LRRP team to an understrength "A" camp. He could fill those slots with anybody.

He assigned three of the available names he had before him to the special team, satisfying the priority. The names were Tan, Bonn, and Warner.

"Send these men on to HALO school for the quick course," he said, handing the files to his clerk, "and further assign them on to SF camp Five Tango."

Pate finished blackening his face and looked at the results in the shaving mirror. The whites of his eyes stood out like two lit windows in a dark house.

Sullivan stuck his head in the tent doorway. "You about ready? The sun's almost down."

Pate grabbed his Remington and followed him into the courtyard. A small group of men were waiting there, soft cap bills pulled low over their eyes. Each man's equipment was taped and tied down for silence.

"Now this is it," Sullivan said. "We take the trail out through the break in the wire and go until we hit the road. We'll set up on the hill facing south. Any questions?" When no one spoke, he led them into the wire without hesitation.

Nearly an hour of quiet walking passed before they reached the spot Sullivan wanted, and they spread out in the blackness. Pate took the highest point on the knoll, the rest of the patrol fanning out around him for security.

He pulled his Starlight scope out of its case and turned it on to check the adjustments, taking a look down the road. The road appeared in the viewer as light green, the trees and bushes beside it a darker green. The background was a green haze. He compared his riflescope with it for visibility.

The telescope did a good job of clarifying some of the detail, but it was poor compared with the Starlight. At least the telescope showed the colors right. He could have dismounted the telescope before the patrol and clamped the Starlight onto his rifle back in camp, rezeroing, but he would not. He had used his own telescope on the rifle both night and day, and he depended on it and his own eyes only. Besides, the bulky Starlight would upset the familiar balance of his rifle.

Pate listened hard. There were no telltale noises from any of the security people. *Fine,* Pate thought. *Now let the NVA come and try to mine* this *road tonight.* He stuck an unlit cigarette in the edge of his mouth and waited.

Command and Control North, Da Nang

"I think something's wrong," the lieutenant said. "We should have gotten something from Delta by now." It was late at night, and the ARVN howitzers were shattering the calm near the camp.

"The last thing we got placed them near Lac Sao. . . . When did we get our most recent report on Sugar?" the lieutenant asked, calling the native agent who lived there by his code name. "Maybe he can find out something for us."

One of the men went to the files to check, while the night crewmen sat at their desks and listened to the artillery.

"Here it is," the clerk said, flapping through the folder. "He was paid by the usual drop last month, but none of our people have contacted him for any assistance since last year, sir," he read.

The lieutenant was suspicious. "Call MACV and let's get another agent in there to look around. I don't like this."

The intelligence had been good! Pate spotted the NVA men with the Starlight scope not fifty meters from where he sat. They had crawled out from the bushes alongside the road.

Two men were digging a hole for a box-shaped mine, while others guarded for them. Pate knew there could be more of them in the woods, but he had his targets. He only wanted the sappers themselves.

He put the Starlight down, spit out the cigarette, and picked up his rifle, wrapping the leather sling around his forearm. He centered one digger in the luminous cross hairs and traversed to the other. The night shadows of the trees made the road even darker in places.

One of the sappers wore black, making him much harder to see than his partner, who was bare-chested. The motion of the black-clad sapper's forearms gave Pate all the sight picture he could get.

He aimed between the splotches of skin, hoping for a good chest shot. He steadied his breathing, controlled his posture, and squeezed the trigger.

The report was deafening. The figure in the scope vanished. Pate rapidly chambered another round and was locked on to the better bare-chest target before the man could drop his shovel and leap away. The muzzle blast from the Remington was a fireball that lasted for a microsecond in the night, illuminating the tips of the leaves and the grass.

Pate had a third round in and ready to go, but he was out of targets. The road was clear. He kept his rifle in his left hand and put the Starlight to his eye with his right. He could see one body lying beside the shallow hole.

He had thought he'd surely hit the first man squarely; but there was no evidence, and people shot with 180-grain soft-point hunting bullets don't usually run away. Even the mine was gone! *How in the hell did they do that?* Pate wondered.

Discipline was tight. None of the security men had opened up, just as Sullivan had instructed. The night passed slowly; everyone tensed; it became steadily obvious by dawn that the mining party had packed it in.

Sullivan radioed for a platoon of strikers from the camp, and it took them an hour to come ambling down the road, their point man walking with his carbine resting on his shoulder like a club. When Pate saw them, anger tightened his jaws. *Stupid gooks,* he thought, *don't they know there could be a counterambush waiting for them?*

Sullivan led the patrol off the hill and down toward the road. Pate could see the body of the sapper lying there. The strikers were looting it. Sullivan yelled at them to stop, but only a few even glanced at him in their haste to rob the dead.

By the time Pate got to his kill, all that was left on it was a pair of ragged shorts. Even the sandals were gone. He squatted and examined his handiwork up close, the first time he had ever had the opportunity to do so.

The bullet had struck the man in the abdomen and blown a big exit wound in his lower back. Bulging intestines clotted with black blood and fatty secretions protruded, lying in the dirt, where the ants were just beginning to find them. Pate felt a touch of nausea.

Sullivan took a photograph of the body. "Let's go get some sleep," he suggested.

6

As he listened to the briefing, the general, an old soldier, could understand the situation. The RF-4Bs had been ambushed in a most effective manner. The facts were chilling. The attack had to have been planned to the minute. The unarmed RF-4Bs were yet to meet their fighter escort and had been chopped exactly at the right time.

Only the EB-66, some ten thousand feet higher, had been witness to the loss of the four aircraft and eight men, and then only because it had been a little early. If it had been on time, the recon Phantoms would have been truly alone.

No parachutes were spotted by the EB-66, and no radio signals from the rescue transmitters of downed crewmen had been detected. The murky rain clouds over the Laotian jungles had swallowed everything.

"They've obviously emplaced some means of early warning to monitor one of our major air corridors," said the Air Force representative. "Apparently the enemy was fully prepared and likely knew he was jumping recon aircraft. Since we're flying mostly recon during this current bombing halt and covering them with EB-66s to provide anti-SAM detection and jamming, it was a safe bet."

"Was it surface-to-air missiles that got the Phantoms?" asked the general.

"No," said the Air Force rep. "They had a flight of MIGs, type twenty-three by the way, their hottest interceptor, not old seventeens."

"They had to pinpoint the Phantoms with radar at some point to carry off such a precise attack," said the general, "but you say that nobody, not even that know-all, see-all EB-sixty-six detected a radar scan."

"It is most likely some new type of radar band," an electronics technician speculated. "Everything we know so far points to it. It must still be experimental."

There was no comment from the staff. The CIA spokesman, a trim Ivy League college type, put his finger on the wall map beside the word *Hanoi*. "We think the site is located on a line from here," he said, drawing his finger slowly southwestward across Laos to the Thai border, "to NKP base here. . . . The majority of reports cluster in this region."

"Could there be more than one?" the general asked.

The CIA spokesman frowned. "We don't know that for sure, sir. Our strikes coming in over the Tonkin Gulf have had no unusual problems."

"Why do you think it's such a new type of radar?" the general asked the technician.

"Because *we're* working on low-signature radar. We believe it's possible. Soviet radar is, in general, inferior to our own, but they may have made a breakthrough. Our electronic countermeasures equipment can handle most of what they have now, but this new radar seems to be beyond our current ECM capability," the technician explained.

"Well, why can't we modify our gear to cover a broader band or something?" the general said persistently.

The technician appeared flustered. "Our ECM covers every known band they have right now! The detection equipment in question here needs study. It could be a different principle!"

"And that is?" the general asked.

The technician looked away. "I'm sorry, sir," he said, "that's classified." The general cursed and left the table, going to a painting of a young soldier that hung on the wall. The helmeted soldier, a first lieutenant, was fierce and confident, apparently leading his men into combat. It brought back memories.

"Okay," the CIA man said. "Here's what we plan to do." All heads turned toward him. *"We want to send in a team equipped with special instrumentation to find out more about the problem."*

"Then you know where the site is!" the general exclaimed.

"Yes and no," the intelligence agent said, a typical answer for him. "We think it may be one right on the border between North Vietnam and Laos, near Phu Chom Voi or in that area. We can't see the Russians risking one of their new, secret radar sets by planting it out in the Laotian panhandle. By locating it just inside the North Viet border, they can keep security."

"I thought you had a team in there not long ago," said the general. "We review these SOG missions on a case-by-case basis at my office, and I remember a recon near Phu Chom Voi."

"We did have a team there. They went in to take a look at a new concrete bunker complex we first thought was a communications center. That team was compromised, and all of them were killed. We now think that site is this radar unit. We have to move fast on this one."

"When will this new team place the instruments?" the general asked.

"Within a month," the CIA agent said. "The detectors are just being finished in the labs now."

"Are you positive there is such a radar set over there now?" the general asked.

The CIA man answered with a question of his own: "Can we take the chance?"

The general picked up his coat and walked to the door. "Whatever you're making up for those boys to carry, make it light. I used to be in the infantry myself," he said tiredly, and left.

The CIA man gathered his notes into a folder, nodded to the others in the room, and left a deliberate minute behind the general. He walked down the hall and entered an office, locking the door behind him. Two tense men waited inside, paper cups half filled with cold coffee on a desk between them. The younger was in a gray suit like his CIA partner. The suntanned white-haired elder was in Army dress greens, laden with ribbons and decorations.

"Well?" asked the waiting agent.

"I blew it right past him. We've got a go."

"I'm Colonel East," said the soldier. "I've met Ashton here. I presume you're Prescott."

"The colonel is our MACV and USARV liaison. He's on General Westmoreland's staff, intelligence and operations for SOG," said Ashton.

"I want to tell you for the record I don't want to have anything to do with this," East said.

"There's no record, Colonel," said Prescott as he sat down on a swivel chair beside the desk, "but feel free to say anything you want."

"SOG is a highly capable unit, Prescott, but you can't simply dream up a mission and expect us to get it done under the conditions you're imposing. A mission undertaken by us has to be planned and run by us."

"Colonel East," said Prescott, "it's not your decision. We'd like to have your goodwill, but we don't need it. We've gone to the secretary of defense on this. The mission is on with you or without you."

"You need our resources just to get started," East said.

"Colonel, that briefing I just conducted was only a formality. We've *already* started. We have a team forming up, we have the instrumentation being tested, and we're staging out of an 'A' camp, not one of your C and Cs."

"Why don't you just give us the op and let us do it?"

"Security. If we put the mission on your books, it might leak somewhere. Everybody's trying to find out what SOG is up to. The Russians know too much about your business now. Your usual recons, prisoner snatches, and raids aren't that sensitive in terms of national security. Radar is. It's like nuclear or chemical weapons or any other technology advance. We've got to write the op plan on this one."

"So you think you can keep a lid on it by organizing a mission and telling no one involved what he's doing? Not even the people who have to support it?"

"That's right."

"Then you people are goddamn fools."

"Can't your heroes do it, Colonel?" Prescott sneered.

"My *heroes*? You insolent bastard! I've got the best of the best, SEALs, LRRPs, Force Recon, Air Commandos, Special Forces! They deserve better than armchair quarterbacking from somebody in a Brooks Brothers suit!"

"SOG is actually *our* unit, Colonel. Don't forget that."

"You act as if it were your own personal war, too," East said.

"It's not much," Prescott said, "but it's all we have at the moment."

Bonn's class was graduated from Recondo school in high spirits, laughing, joking, and packing equipment. By noon of the last day most of the framed tents were empty, the newly christened Recondos returning to their units.

Tan sat on his bunk and read his orders. He was being sent to the parachute school in the Philippines. The news didn't surprise him. He was aware now that he had been sent away from his old unit not to come back.

As he packed his kit once more, he justified it to himself. *Perhaps,* he thought, *by learning to jump from airplanes, I will be able to kill more VC.*

Bonn picked up a copy of his orders from the headquarters clerk and read them slowly. It was official. The codes and abbreviations were mostly untranslatable for him, but he knew what it all meant. He was now on his way into Special Operations.

There was an E-5 sergeant's name on the orders Bonn recognized, a three-striper in his class. Bonn decided to find the man, right after he wrote to Linda. He would have to be careful what he said in his letter.

Sweetheart,

I'm changing units for a while. This new one is an all-volunteer outfit like the LRRPs and the job is about the same. We just stay out longer. I'm going to jump school next. It'll keep me out of combat for a while. Every day counts.

I'm not supposed to talk about this new unit, since it's classified, and they might read our mail like they do letters off the atomic subs, so if I don't give you a lot of detail, don't worry.

Sometimes it seems like I've been here forever. The States seem like a dream, a place I've only imagined. Reality is Vietnam. I really need to get home, hear some music, be able to talk to you, kiss you.

He sealed the letter, wrote "Free" on the envelope where the stamp should go, since a congressional favor allowed the soldiers in Vietnam to do that, and dropped the letter in the mailbag outside the orderly room as he went to find the E-5 on the orders. One of the school staff pointed out the row of faded GP medium tents where he thought the sergeant lived.

"Sergeant Warner?" Bonn asked, standing in the sunlight outside the tent, addressing a man asleep on one of the cots inside. "Sergeant Warner?"

The figure on the cot stirred. "Yeah, what?" came the reply. Bonn walked in.

Warner sat up from his nap, trying to survive the drinking bout with himself from the night before.

"My name's Bonn, Sarge, Chris Bonn. You and me are on orders together for HALO school. I thought I'd come and meet you. We're both going to Special Operations."

Warner lit a cigarette and looked at Bonn through aching eyes. "Oh, yeah . . . I've seen you in training. Yeah. Goddamn, my head hurts. What time is it?"

Bonn looked at his Accutron. "About chowtime. Everything has shut down around here. Everybody has shipped out except us."

Warner fumbled into his rucksack, produced a bottle of PX vodka, and took a long drink of it.

"We all have three-day R and Rs before we have to be at Clark," Bonn said cheerfully. "What are you gonna do with your time?"

Warner frowned and took another drink, as if to answer him.

"Looks like potent stuff," Bonn said.

"Want a drink?" Warner asked, hoping Bonn would. Maybe he would sit for a few minutes and talk. The guys at the Cav had avoided Warner. It had hurt sometimes when no one would sit with him at a mess table, when no one went with him as a friend to the nightly movies that were projected onto bed sheets at the mess hall.

"I'm not really much of a drinker," Bonn said, "but thanks anyway. I've got to catch the noon run to town."

Warner watched Bonn walk away. So he was just like the others, too goddamned stuck on himself just to have a drink and talk. *Well, fuck him,* Warner thought. Bonn was just a spec 4 anyway. A cut above nothing.

What *would* he do with his R&R? There was the NCO club and the PX. Both sold alcohol. Downtown there were drugs. Opium. Hashish. Marijuana. Maybe the spec 4 was going downtown after drugs. Everybody did it. The men just didn't admit to it. Warner knew that. They were no better than he was. They all were just goddamn liars.

Back at Camp Evans, Warner had been very careful not to be seen or get caught when he'd bring a little supply of hash back from town. Sometimes it was joints of grass. He knew the people and the schedules there. Here he didn't. If he got caught here, they'd take his rank for sure. But he could drink and forget the war.

Alone, Warner drank his vodka and endured the pain.

CCN, Da Nang

"I believe Sugar has turned on us. Look at this!" the officer said, handing the report to the NCO. It took him only a moment to read it.

"Let's get a team in there and kill the son of a bitch," the NCO growled, dropping the paper on the desk. The CIA report described, in brief terms, how Team Delta had been lured in and ambushed and even revealed the amount of money Sugar had collected for the job.

"Do you think he knows we have this intelligence on him?" the NCO asked.

"Probably not," the officer replied. "That was taken by one of our counterespionage people, a Japanese, who can travel freely in Laos and North Vietnam. He's rated class A reliable."

"Fine," the NCO said flatly. "We need to lure Sugar out and blow the bastard away."

The officer initialed the report. "Get a note out to MACV," he said. "Agent two-nine-nine, code name Sugar, should be eliminated as soon as possible. Get their approval, and let me know ASAP, okay?"

"Yes, sir," the NCO said, and went straight to the crypto machine.

Bonn hit the streets of Nha Trang ready for action. His rucksack and carbine were safely stowed back at camp, he was showered, his boots were clean, and his freshly laundered tiger fatigues displayed the inverted arrowhead of a new green and black Recondo patch on his left breast pocket.

He had three days and two hundred dollars to waste. He had been half a year back in the mountains along the Cambodian border, and on the street of wall-to-wall bars and women, he felt like a rocket leaving the tube.

The policy of the more aggressive bars was to take one of their best-looking girls, dress her in the sexiest fashion possible, and station her outside to lure in the GIs.

Bonn fell for the first come-on he saw.

The girl had an appearance that would have been comical under more normal circumstances, her face heavily covered with makeup that masked any real beauty. She wore a lurid pink dress that revealed enough cleavage to make a debutante sick with envy, which was her real asset in a land of basically unendowed women.

"How you, soldier?" she asked coyly.

"I—I'm fine!" Bonn gulped, surprised that he did not know what to say.

"You like to come in, see very pretty girls?" she asked. "Good prices, too! You come in, please!"

The door would have had to be bolted to keep Bonn out. "Thank you," he managed to say, and stepped into the room full of soldiers and bar girls. They were crowded so tightly he had to squeeze through, trying to find a seat.

The soldiers guffawed and cursed, tinny rock and roll played from a phonograph behind the bar, and the girls squealed, tittered and flirted, all in cigarette smoke so dense it was hard to see across the room. The tables were cluttered to the edges with beer bottles and drink glasses.

Bonn spotted a small couch against the back wall with a girl sitting on it and a vacancy beside her. A table surrounded by unattached girls was nearby, all of them seemingly in a contest of trying to outtalk one another.

Bonn sat down on the couch, and the girl turned to look him over. She smiled and moved closer to Bonn, who was suddenly running out of confidence.

"Wha' you name?" the girl asked, her voice obviously unaccustomed to the strange syllables, but to Bonn her broken English was a wave of sweetness. He had come to accept the gruff male pounding of the English language he heard every day as normal.

"It's Chris," he told her, enormously pleased with what he saw. She was demure and delicate in a way that made all the girls Bonn had known in school seem like lady wrestlers.

Her eyes were the shape of perfect almonds, with pupils large and dark, in an oval face surrounded by hair so black and silken that Bonn wondered why he had admired any other color.

"My name is Le Nha," she said. One of the girls at the table said something to her, and they all laughed.

"What was that about?" Bonn asked, feeling left out of the merriment.

Le Nha smiled. "She say you baby," she translated.

The pronouncement took Bonn back for an instant, but it did not anger him. He laughed with them, his tiger stripes contrasting strongly with the pastels the girls wore.

Le Nha was dressed in the traditional Vietnamese ao dai, but without the usual white silk trousers, the boldly side-slitted dress a floral print that seemed as rare and foreign to Bonn as she was. Her smooth legs were bare. "Wha' you do?" she asked, rubbing her tiny hand up and down Bonn's fatigue sleeve. "You Green Beret?"

"No, no," Bonn said, shaking his head. "I'm just a soldier." He wasn't about to discuss his new job with anybody after the warning from Major Allgood and the CIA agent.

A boy slipped through the crowd, set a thimble-size drink, complete with check, down on the low table in front of Bonn and stood there. "Tell boy what you want." Le Nha prompted Bonn.

"What do you have to drink?" Bonn asked the boy politely, and the girls laughed again.

"Got Coke, beer, whiskey-Coke," the boy said in surprisingly good English, a touch of impatience in his voice.

"Bring me a whiskey-Coke," Bonn said, and the boy darted off toward the bar.

Le Nha reached up and touched Bonn's short sun-bleached hair. "You hair is pretty," she said, and the simple compliment embarrassed Bonn, bringing on another round of laughter from the girls at the table.

The boy returned, bringing Bonn's glass and another tea glass for Le Nha. Bonn tasted the whiskey-Coke and decided it was more Coke than whiskey, without caring. Le Nha was sitting closer to him now, her hand on his leg.

She leaned against him, her weight insignificant. "You stay Vietnam long time?" she asked.

"I still have six months to go yet," Bonn said, feeling the warmth of her body through his fatigues. Bonn suddenly wanted the pretenses to be over, as his shyness was replaced with a desire for this butterfly of a woman.

He knew sex was why she was there, but he had no earthly idea of how to ask for what he wanted. The boy came again with another whiskey-Coke and a third tea for Le Nha. The pile of tissue-thin checks was mounting.

The prostitute smelled enticing. Bonn's sense of smell had been sharpened by his living in the forest, and the fragrance that hovered around her was like the fields of wildflowers he had sometimes seen in the jungle. He realized how effective perfume could be.

Le Nha knew from practice that Bonn had been conquered. He was in a state of willingness to part with any reasonable amount of money for her. "You like go and make love?" she whispered, but the words rang in Bonn's ears. He had never been asked anything so personal so directly.

He didn't trust himself to speak, so he nodded and set his drink down, trying to maintain as much nonchalance as he could under the circumstances. Le Nha stood and took him by the hand and led him toward a curtain-covered door at the rear of the bar.

Another GI and girl were just coming out, and Bonn was embarrassed again, in the face-to-face encounter. He let the couple pass him in silence.

There was a short hall that opened into a long back room. An old crone sat in the hall on a wooden stool, with a cigar box of money in her lap and a stack of clean linen beside her. "Give her one thousand piastres, please," Le Nha instructed. Bonn pulled out his wallet and peeled off a ten-dollar MPC note to the old woman, who handed Le Nha a clean, folded sheet.

A row of individual enclosures had been constructed in the room by hanging bed sheets to make semiprivate booths, each containing one cot. It was clear what was taking place in some of the enclosures, and the chilling, businesslike atmosphere of the place cooled Bonn's ardor.

Le Nha drew a striped curtain out of the way, and Bonn found himself looking in at a single army cot and a clothes rack. They entered, and she let the curtain drop behind them.

Le Nha indicated that he should sit down on the bed, and as he did, he noticed the curtains didn't drape all the way to the floor. The bedcovers hanging down from the cot next to their own were swaying in a vigorous rhythm. Bonn looked away immediately.

Le Nha undressed unselfconsciously, pulling the ao dai off in one smooth motion, and it stunned Bonn to discover her nude under the beautiful garment. He had never paused to consider what might be worn underneath.

The sight of her body arrested Bonn's concern about the surroundings, and his urges came stampeding back. She stood just over five feet tall, as sleek as a movie starlet, with skin the color of faded bronze and virtually no pubic hair.

She lay down, and Bonn undid the combat buckle on his fatigue pants, unbuttoning his fly. He had already decided not to undress under the circumstances.

The union between them was unsatisfying to Bonn. Le Nha lay back on the cot in an obligatory but detached way, allowing him to get what he had paid for, her head turned chastely to one side. The body he had admired so much turned out to be hard to the touch, virtually without breasts, and devoid of passion.

When he was finished with her, Le Nha called for the old woman, who took the bed sheet and left a towel and basin of water.

Le Nha moved the cot, then set down the washbowl and gave herself a short sponging bath, that ended with her squatting over the basin and washing between her legs thoroughly. Bonn watched the ritual in a state of mild mortification.

She took a bottle of perfume from under the bed and daubed some on her neck and shoulders, then re-dressed quickly. Bonn wanted to get out of the place as soon as he could. It had turned revolting on him.

Le Nha held her hand out, palm up. "You give something for Le?" she asked. Bonn handed her another ten. "Thank you," she said, "you like Le, you come back and see her, yes?"

"Sure," Bonn lied. He was having a hard time coping with what he felt. It had been too crass, too commercial. He did not know if it had been worth it. Revulsion from the girl and pity for her struggled within him.

They walked back out into the bar, and Bonn found the ice in his drink had melted. He picked up the stack of checks and gave Le Nha another five to pay for the drinks. "Good-bye, Le," he said, and she waved as Bonn left, making room for the next soldier.

The worst of it was knowing he hadn't been faithful to Linda. He had never had sex with another girl. Linda had been his first. For the moment he despised himself for substituting a whore for the girl he loved and wanted to marry.

Since arriving in Vietnam, he'd never been to a town for any length of time. The seduction of the moment had been too much. It was his first test of fidelity, and he'd failed.

The bitter dregs of conscience swirled around in Bonn until a stronger thought emerged through it all. How did he really know Linda was at home being faithful to him?

When he'd first gone into the army, all the way through the first months of his training, he'd feared at any time she would write him the devastating end-of-a-love letter he'd seen other guys get. But Linda stayed with him, and for a high school junior whose lover was expected to be gone for two years, that was remarkable. Linda had been steady, reliable, dedicated. He remembered her friends as flighty sorts, in and out of passions, constantly changing boyfriends in an endless drama of betrayals, arguments, tears, and new crushes.

He'd been going out with Linda almost a year before he'd first made love to her. There had been months building to it, of course. First the kissing, then feeling her through her clothes, then the time she'd taken off her bra, and the time after that she had let him slip his hand under her panties, her blue jeans pulled down almost to her knees.

Finally one night he had made love to her, both of them with most of their clothes on, in the backseat of his Monza, parked off on a deserted road. When it happened, it had been without hesitation. She had taken him as eagerly as he'd taken her. After that they did it on most of their dates, and he always told her he loved her, and meant it.

In an indefinable way after that he had been hers, as a given, and she showed it in the way she spoke, walked, and held his arm. From then on it was understood. They would be married.

That was all okay when I was home and safe, Bonn thought. *I'm in a situation now where any day or any hour I can have my ass kicked right off this earth. I can't put off my tomorrows. I don't have a future. Time won't let me wait that long.*

Back in the street, Bonn was glad to get out of the bar. In the space of an hour he had become twenty-five dollars poorer, was vaguely unhappy, and was worried about catching a venereal disease.

He looked around, wondering what he was going to do with the rest of his R&R.

7

Clark Air Force Base, the Philippines

The view out of the big hollow four-engine C-130 was too unreal to be terrifying. The Pacific stretched out into forever, as blue as a glossy postcard, and the islands below looked very small.

Bonn was first in the stick, a T-10 main parachute on his back and a reserve chute strapped to his chest. The chinpiece of his fiber glass jump helmet was adjusted tightly, and the dark nylon jump suit he wore over his fatigues at least helped cut some of the mile-high altitude's chill. None of the trainees carried weapons or field equipment. They were too inexperienced yet for that. His T-10 was hooked by static line to an overhead steel cable. If it failed to open, he was supposed to yank the reserve's D ring to deploy it. The reserve was a smaller, faster-dropping chute with little maneuverability, for genuine emergencies only.

Warner was in line behind Bonn, and Tan, who as yet was still just another trooper as far as Bonn or Warner knew, was at the rear with several other men from different units, who were there for their own reasons.

The small group of students moved to the rear door of the C-130 with fixed stares at the horizon the way they had been told, to keep from looking down.

Then, on signal from the jumpmaster, Bonn ran out the door into the void, relying on the static line as he had never relied on anything before.

It worked.

The big green parachute jerked him back from his plunge, and the wind carried him inland.

Above him the other volunteers floated down as well, tiny men suspended below their canopies, struggling to steer their chutes for the first time.

The school was geared to produce high altitude, low opening experts in the full course or passable free-fall parachutists in a few days. The small SOG group Bonn was with received the quicker course. No one involved with them at that point actually expected any of them to have to do any complicated jumps without more intense training.

After a morning of learning how to put on a parachute and practicing parachute landing falls from a low platform, they were given a brief hand in a training harness and instructed how to maneuver the chute on the way down. Following lunch they were fully equipped and went up to do the first jump.

Bonn guided his descent clumsily, spinning himself around more than once, trying to get somewhere close to the drop zone. Too far to the left became too far to the right as he tugged and pulled at the steering loops, gaining experience, but he kept his feet together as he'd been told, bracing for the ground that was racing up at him.

He performed a PLF as if he'd been doing it all his life, remembering to spill the air from his chute quickly and get out of the harness in combat fashion.

As he waited for the recovery truck, he realized he'd been thrilled rather than frightened, and he was more than ready for his next jump.

Bonn wondered what real HALO drops would be like. He knew the technique had been developed from the situations faced by pilots who were forced to bail out of incapacitated aircraft. The jets had reached altitudes no one had flown at before and altitudes no one had jumped from before. Pilots had passed out from lack of oxygen. They had spun uncontrollably as they fell. Their parachutes had failed to open properly. After much testing and study, solutions had been found. Volunteers had jumped out of balloons so high up the gondolas were covered with ice and out of bombers skimming the limits of outer space, right out of the bomb bay doors.

Reliable equipment and technique had been developed for aircrew safety. The HALO program had evolved as a classified side effect. It was seen as being useful for the secret insertion of intelligence agents or commandos. The parachuters wore helmets, goggles, oxygen gear, and insulated suits. They had automatic altimeter-activated drogue-stabilized main chute openings at suicidally low levels. They could fly down from the stratosphere in free-fall, steering to a preplanted radio beacon on the ground for pinpoint landings. Genuine HALO was an involved, complex course.

The class had one more static line jump to get the feel of it and then proceeded to free-fall technique. Bonn listened to the instructor and hung on every word, as falling and steering with arms and legs were demonstrated.

Warner was seriously scared and showed it. Often he had to be told things twice, so tense he looked as if he would vibrate like a bowstring if someone could pluck him. He would have gladly broken both legs to get out of the rest of the training.

Tan took the course without reservation, doing his best to understand the instructors, asking questions if he did not, and taking the usual ribbing small people do about not being able to bring a parachute down, as light as he was.

For free-fall, no static line would be used, the instructor said. The primary chute would be automatically opened by an altimeter-triggered device. If it failed, the backup could be deployed manually. Bonn's first thought was that it would be tough to fall and maneuver with one hand on the reserve chute D ring.

In his first free-fall Bonn left the aircraft and instantly missed the immediate, safe opening of his parachute. Instead, he fell. And fell. The island was getting closer. He experimented with his training by balling up to speed the descent and turning in the air at will by extending or retracting his arms and legs. By moving slowly and carefully, he could drift from side to side with a reasonable amount of control.

Wow! Bonn thought in midair. *I'm doing it!* He zeroed in on the drop zone target cross, finding the swimming motions quite natural. His main parachute opened right on time, and he steered easily toward the DZ and PLFed in, feeling for all the world like a master parachutist. *Damn,* he thought, *I ought to pay them sixty-five dollars a month to do this!*

The succeeding jumps were all higher, with lower openings. The standard combat simulation jump was an exit at ten thousand feet with the canopy fully open at a thousand feet. It was a minimum. The reserve chute would be worthless if the main failed to open at below that altitude.

They reviewed and critiqued, the classes free and informal. They studied hard in the morning, jumped in the afternoon, and found out the hard way about winds and other unfavorable conditions by experience.

At the end of the week they had a dozen jumps each and rudimentary knowledge about using a parachute without killing themselves.

Their final destination orders reached them their last night at Clark, and they discovered they were to become teammates.

Tan was living in the same barracks with Bonn and Warner, faces now familiar to him, and he'd read their nametags. With a copy of the orders in his hand, he walked to the end of the long building where the two Americans were sitting on their bunks.

"You are Sergeant Warner? Specialist Four Bonn?" Tan asked politely. "I am Phoc Tan, soldier of Army of Republic of Vietnam. I read your name on my orders. We go together to Special Forces camp in Military Region Two."

Bonn shook Tan's offered hand. Warner didn't. Warner's indifference didn't bother Tan. Many Americans were rude, but he didn't let them affect his social manner.

Warner didn't know Tan was an officer. The slim Viet wore no insignia of rank on his plain green fatigues. His personal instructions from a Vietnamese intelligence agent

at Recondo school had been to tell no one anything about
himself except his name while he was with the Americans.

"We're going to Camp Five Tango," Bonn said, reading
his copy aloud. "I know where that is."

Warner looked up. "Where?" he asked.

"Right by the border," Bonn said. "That's one of the little
SF 'A' camps. Everything out that way is named Plei something or other, Plei Me, Plei do Lim, Pleiku, you know. I
was with the Fourth Division up there."

"You have base camp near Pleiku, yes?" Tan asked.

"Yeah," Bonn said. "Our division base camp is just south
of town."

"We all be together, kill lots of VC," Tan said.

Warner opened the door to leave. "I'll be back later," he
said.

"Hey, Sarge," Bonn called, "that plane we have to be on
loads up at five in the morning. You sure you want to go
back to the bar?"

"Mind your own fucking business, Specialist," Warner
said as he walked out.

Bonn frowned. "What's wrong with him?" he asked no
one in particular.

"Hey, Pate," Sullivan said over morning chow. "We just
got the word. Your three other people are coming in from
jump school this afternoon, flying up from Saigon."

The news relieved him. He had been assigned to the camp
a month already, and outside of a few ambush and recon
patrols and the brief week he had spent at jump school himself, he had been idle.

He had seen to it the time had not been wasted, by becoming accustomed to the mountain country and the different
kind of warfare from what he had known in the south.

The delta was always hot and wet, booby traps abounded,
and most of the trouble came from Vietcong troops, who
liked to hit in small groups at odd places.

In the central highlands it wasn't the VC that was talked
about; it was the NVA, the North Vietnamese Army. It

came in much larger units, hitting harder, challenging company for company and battalion for battalion.

If you saw one man in the rice paddies in the delta, he might be alone. If you saw a single man in the mountains, he was probably the point man for a squad or platoon.

So far Captain Sullivan hadn't offered any information about the Special Operations Group, saying only that when the team was present and formed up, the orders and organization would come.

And that would be this afternoon.

Bonn, Tan, and Warner gathered their gear and weapons from the Huey, stooping to clear the rotor blades. Bonn had his carbine. Tan and Warner carried M-16s. The chopper took on a bag of outgoing mail, lifted off, and was gone.

Warner looked over his shoulder and watched the ship flying away. He would have given his left nut to have been on it rather than at this foul-smelling Special Forces camp.

The odor of cooking fish and garlic saturated the air. Native soldiers, with their camp livestock, a few pigs and chickens, watched them with mild curiosity. Five Tango looked a bit like a military slum

A tall gray-eyed trooper held out his hand to Bonn. "Hi," he said, "my name's Pate, Joe Pate. I'm on your team. I've been up here a month waiting for you guys!"

Bonn and Tan shook hands with Pate. Warner did not make the effort. "I am very happy to meet you, Mr. Pate," Tan said, bowing slightly at the waist.

The four men stood together for the first time. They were a team, a unit. For an instant they felt it, each one silently appraising the others. Bonn sensed suspicion among them, not trust, but he dismissed it. They just didn't know one another yet.

Captain Sullivan stepped in, and each man was introduced to him. When Warner warmly shook Sullivan's outstretched hand, Pate noticed, and an instant dislike was established.

"When you men get settled, we'll have a briefing tonight," Sullivan said.

"What you got there, an M-two?" Pate asked when he noticed the folding stock carbine slung on the side of Bonn's rucksack. Pate picked it up. "These things just shoot pistol ammo," he said. "That M-sixteen varmint round has more punch."

"I've zapped three NVA stone cold dead with it," Bonn said, "and they never complained."

"You can keep all them little toy guns. The M-fourteen is the least I'd carry. It fires a *real* cartridge, and they even put a full-auto switch on it so the infantry can hit the broad side of a barn with one."

"Carbine very reliable," Tan said, "but AK-forty-seven better. Dai Uy Sullivan, may I trade my M-sixteen for a carbine here? I prefer."

"No problem. We'll get you one," Sullivan said. "And don't worry about Pate. He likes to shoot the balls off gnats at a thousand yards with Mississippi handloads. Now you guys go settle in. I'll talk to you later."

It was a short walk to anywhere in the camp, and Pate quickly had them before a wooden framed GP medium tent that sat slowly rotting into the soil. It was bare inside except for grass growing through the floorboards and several scattered, sagging cots.

"Watch out for the rats in this place," Pate warned as he led them inside. "I've seen some big ones."

Warner dropped his gear on the floor and flopped down on a cot. "Wake me up at chowtime, Bonn," he said, and shut himself off from everyone by closing his eyes.

"You all just came out of HALO, right?" Pate asked as he helped Bonn align the cots in the tent.

"Yeah," Bonn said, "but we just had the free-fall course."

"Me, too," Pate said. "I was there while you guys were at Recondo school."

"Did you go to Recondo school?" Bonn asked.

"No. I was already sniper-qualified. I took the stateside

course and the in country school. I've been through all that good stalking and recon shit."

"We jump from very high," Tan said. "I see clouds from top. Fly down like bird!" He thrust his arms out and swayed right and left to make his point. Bonn grinned. It was an unusual display for the normally reserved Tan.

"I was a sniper down in the delta, Four Corps, before I got up here," Pate said. "What'd you do?"

Bonn was brushing dust off his cot. "I was with the LRRPs up here in the highlands," he said.

"The *LRRPs?*" Pate laughed. "No wonder you joined SOG! You were crazy already!"

"Can get one-oh-five boxes to make locker or wood for shelf?" Tan asked.

"We ain't got no one-oh-fives," Pate said, "but you can get some mortar crates out behind the big bunker." Tan hurried out the back door.

"What outfit'd you come from?" Bonn asked Pate.

"I was with the Ninth," Pate answered. "Where you from?"

Bonn reached in his pocket and pulled out the green and white patch of the Fourth Division, holding it up for Pate to see. "I'm not so far out of my territory," he said.

"They been getting the shit kicked out of them here lately," Pate said. "I heard a whole platoon nearly got wiped out 'bout a week ago."

Bonn stopped unpacking. "Did you find out what outfit it was?" he asked, family concern in his voice.

"No, man, I'm sorry," Pate said, understanding. "They probably got killed because they screwed up," Pate added, speaking as a sniper, one of the elite. The elite believed it was your own mistakes, not the enemy, that killed you. Total competence was the same as invulnerability. A man wasn't just killed. He indirectly killed himself and, in the opinion of the elite, probably deserved it.

Bonn was one of the elite, too, a veteran LRRP, and he believed as much as any of them in the immortality of doing everything right. The fact that a man could do everything right, absolutely everything, and still die was something the elite didn't usually admit. In order to do their jobs, they pretended that skill alone was enough. It was mental armor. Without it, no one who flew higher, drove faster, dived deeper, or fought alone could sustain. It was absolute, total belief in self.

Tan returned, two ammo boxes in tow. He set them up beside his bunk and began to stash his gear in them. "What'd you do before joining SOG, Tan?" Pate asked.

Tan smiled. "I belong to ranger battalion in Saigon," he said. "Ask question to VC, make talk! Kill *beaucoup* VC!" Tan held up his sheathed bayonet. "With this knife I kill twenty VC," he announced.

"Twenty?" Pate exclaimed. "With a blade?"

Tan looked very serious. "Yes," he said simply.

Pate looked at him respectfully. "We can use a dude like you!" he said proudly. "Hell, with me a sniper, Bonn a LRRP, and ol' Tan doing better than Jack the Ripper, we can't lose!"

"Have they told you anything yet?" Bonn asked.

Pate sat down on a cot and stretched out his long legs. "Nope, the captain said when you guys got here, we'd all get briefed. Some kind of orders are already here for us," he said.

"Mail call," said one of Sullivan's SF troopers, a hard-stomached man who wore fatigue trousers cut off at the knees and rubber-tire VC sandals on bare feet. He walked up to the side of the tent where the screening had rusted away. "Don't everybody jump at once. It's just one letter, off the last mail chopper. Who's Bonn?"

"Me," said Bonn, reaching for the offered envelope.

"Got to be from your old lady," said the trooper with a suggestive leer. "The perfume smells pretty good. Mine usually drags my letters between her legs a time or two before she mails 'em. I can pick them out of the mailbag blindfolded."

Bonn laughed, sat down, and opened the envelope. He'd written Linda from Recondo school, after the incident with the prostitute, but he hadn't told her about it. The trip to Clark and the delays getting back to Vietnam and then up to the central highlands meant this letter was the reply to his last ones. Just the sight of her handwriting was heartening.

Dearest Chris,

I received two of your letters at once, and you sounded so blue I thought I'd cheer you up. This senior year will be a breeze. I have classes only until lunch, and start a job at the sandwich shop. The school counselor got it for me.

I had my hair cut shorter, but it's still the way you like it, and my mom bought me a pair of new sneakers that are so cool. All the girls are wearing them.

Hazel has been going out with Mark, who graduated last year and is going to college at State. He's got long hair now, and a lot of the boys at school do, too, but not a Beatle cut, I mean, really long hair. Hazel asked me to sign a petition Mark had to get our troops out of Vietnam, and I did, because I want you back.

I ought to tell you Mark asked me out, and even Hazel doesn't know it. I didn't go. Everybody at school knows you and I are going steady, so the guys don't ask much, but you know I wouldn't go out with anybody. Mark is a jerk. He said anybody who went to Vietnam in the first place was stupid, and I should go out with him because you were going to get killed anyway. I about slapped him.

My father said you could get a house cheap on the GI Bill when you get home. They're building a really nice new subdivision near here. I'm stocking a hope chest now, and plan to save my job money to help us get started.

Jesus, I'm sorry about that . . . woman . . . in Nha Trang, Bonn thought, wishing Linda could feel his apology. *I'll make it up to her,* he promised. *I will.*

8

The night patrol had gone out, the listening posts were stationed, chow was over, and the moon had just begun to rise over the rim of the Chu Pong mountain range. The four SOG volunteers assembled in the main bunker for the briefing, expectations running high.

Captain Sullivan cleared the crates and tables that obscured the wall maps of Vietnam, Laos, and Cambodia. A pot of coffee bubbled gently on a hot plate in the corner, and the single dim electric light bulb hanging from the roof glowed with the variations of the generator.

"Make yourselves comfortable," Sullivan said. "We have a lot to go over tonight." Bonn and Tan sat on the floor, and Pate and Warner moved chairs around to face the captain.

"First, welcome to Special Operations," Sullivan announced, as if he were giving a rehearsed speech. "You will be part of Operation Thirty-five, specifically the deep penetration of Laos for intelligence-gathering purposes.

"I must instruct you at this time that everything you will do is top secret and that the release of information of any kind concerning Operation Thirty-five is a treasonable and court-martial offense."

Sullivan held up a stack of forms. "These are security forms. Sign all three copies. They bind you to silence and waive all your rights if you do talk, under the National Security Act." He handed them the paperwork.

Warner read the fine print and the prison penalties it specified for discloser. It raised the hair on the back of his neck, but he signed anyway. Tan signed without examining the sheets, caring little for governmental word work. Bonn signed without concern, and Pate did likewise, the legalese incomprehensible to him.

The forms were handed back to Sullivan. "Thank you," he said. "Now we can continue. I have the orders for the formation of your team from Command and Control North, the C and C that covers northern Laos.

"Your team is code-named Tango since you're staging out of my camp. Sergeant Warner, as ranking man you will be the team leader. Assignment of responsibilities within the team is up to you."

There was a lot the captain had to tell them, but there was a lot he couldn't tell. He was giving the prepared briefing MACV had sent, and he wasn't authorized to deviate from it.

The security on this team and mission was extra-tight. They were sanctioned right from Washington. He didn't even have any background information on them. He assumed the men were experts at something or they wouldn't be on such a mission. He'd seen more unlikely-seeming teams, but he couldn't remember when. "Any questions so far?" he asked.

Bonn raised his finger. "Is this the whole team? Will anybody else join us?"

Sullivan shook his head. "Probably not," he said.

"Any chance to make rank?" Warner asked.

Sullivan smiled. "Promotions have to come from your parent unit as long as you're with SOG on a temporary duty status."

Warner went cold inside. Rank was the only thing he wanted. It was the only reason he'd taken the insane risk of joining SOG. Rank guaranteed respect, something he didn't have. Enough rank even guaranteed safety. He was desperate for those things. Then he calmed. He had to play along, learn how to get what he wanted out of SOG.

"Yes, sir, I understand," Warner said, as he lit a cigarette with a match from an olive drab C ration paper matchbook.

Sullivan turned to the map. "Let me show you your target area," he said.

"MACV wants some black boxes planted in the area up here," he said, pointing to a spot high on the panhandle of Laos, on the border of North Vietnam. "They need some information about a classified site there. The instrumentation will give them constant electronic surveillance on the site.

"All you have to do is plant the boxes. That's the first part of the mission. The second part might be a little trickier. An agent of ours, now an agent of theirs, needs killing. You'll have to draw him out and do the job."

Pate nodded, knowing that would be his part of the operation. Sullivan stepped back from the map. "Get up here and take a close look at your area," he instructed. The team bunched around the map, all eyes on the narrow panhandle, where Sullivan held his finger.

Highway 8 ran down from North Vietnam a little more than thirty kilometers to Lac Sao. "The agent lives in Lac Sao," Sullivan told them. "His code name is Sugar. The reason we employed him was to provide assistance to our teams that might be operating in the region and to smuggle spies in and out of North Vietnam.

"He double-crossed a SOG team recently, and as far as we know, the entire team was killed. That's why we want him dead," Sullivan said.

"At the upper end of Highway Eight is Phu Chom Voi, just inside the border of North Vietnam. This is where you'll leave the instrumentation," he said.

Warner's stomach did a turn. *North Vietnam?* "Hey, Captain," he blurted, "isn't that a bit rough on a brand-new team? That's *North* Vietnam you're talking about!"

Warner had resigned himself into attempting at least one mission, as sickening as the prospect was to him, for appearances' sake. Then he could find a support slot somewhere. He knew it would even be possible to begin a mission and somehow abort it, end it quickly, and get back—but this was outside any scenario he'd imagined.

Sullivan looked at Warner as if he didn't quite understand. "Sergeant Warner," he said, "all of you are combat veterans, and you've trained for this. What's your objection?"

"What I mean, sir, is . . . ah . . ." Warner said haltingly, thinking quickly, "we don't know each other yet! We can't function as a team until we at least train together!"

Sullivan considered that, unaware it had come out of Warner's mouth only as a stalling tactic. "You have a point, Warner," Sullivan said. "There's still a week until the mission is due. I think I can arrange some combat patrols for your team in that time."

Warner felt relieved. He had won at least a short reprieve.

"Let's look over the operations order," Sullivan said. The team returned to their seats, quiet and attentive.

"The area around Lac Sao up to Phu Chom Voi is right in the mountains. It's high and rugged country. Highway Eight is nothing but a wide dirt road that's practically impassable in the monsoon. There are some steep sections in it that become mud slides.

"There are plenty of streams for water, and the concealment is excellent, being extremely thick. There are no friendly forces in your AO. You'll have it all to yourself, so you can shoot first and ask questions later if it comes down to it.

"You will be delivered by air, by free-fall from a C-one-thirty. It will be a dawn drop. The Air Force liaison officer will be here to brief you on visual landmarks and the weather prior to the mission. They're taking a new batch of aerial photos right now.

"After you get on the ground and group up, you'll proceed to Phu Chom Voi and accomplish your primary mission. Your daily situation reports will be made by air contact. Covey will be the bird we'll have up twice a day for the SITREPS."

Warner raised his hand to interrupt. "What about emergencies?" he asked.

Sullivan answered him, keeping a deadpan expression. "Emergencies are up to you to handle. That's what we pay you for. Once we put you in there, you're on your own."

Warner couldn't believe it but said nothing else.

"Extraction should take place ten days after insertion," Sullivan continued. "When we get the photos, we'll select a good LZ. A helicopter pickup covered by fighter-bombers will be used to get you out.

"You'll fire familiarization again on the AK-forty-seven. You'll be taking AKs with you on the mission, so you can use captured NVA ammo if necessary. You'll also wear unmarked foreign fatigues and use foreign web gear."

Sullivan consulted his notes. "I think that's about it for now. Any questions before we close?"

The team members looked at one another. "I've got one," Pate said. "How will we know this Sugar guy? How're we supposed to draw him out so I can get a shot at him?"

Sullivan stacked the security forms and briefing orders into a neat pile. "The CIA is sending us a file on him, with photos. It won't be that much of a problem," Sullivan said.

The team left Sullivan alone in the bunker, walking back to their hooch to sack out early, each man involved with his own thoughts. Captain Sullivan remained awake, drinking coffee and reading the day's reports.

Outside the dirt palisades of Five Tango, the jungles of Vietnam stretched westward and blended with the jungles of Cambodia. To the north Laos completed the triangle.

That night high-altitude photorecon planes flew over Lac Sao and Phu Chom Voi, while Sugar slept soundly under the cameras. His file was already in the morning mail pouch ready for the flight from Saigon to Pleiku, then to Five Tango.

Nocturnal animals played in the wreckage of the U.S. Phantom jets lost over northern Laos because their countermeasures instruments had apparently been worthless.

And under cover of night a large force of heavily armed

North Vietnamese regulars moved steadily on toward Five Tango, out of Cambodia, intent on attacking the isolated camp.

Everything was normal.

9

The excited voices woke Tan. The strikers had returned from their night patrol and were babbling in fear and pride about it. Their dialect was different; but Tan understood most of what was being said, and it meant trouble. He left his tent and joined the milling strikers as they boiled rice over their cookfires. Weapons and equipment were scattered by their feet.

"What happened on your patrol?" Tan asked one of the men. His aristocratic bearing caused the soldiers to respect him instantly.

"We have found the Communist soldiers, sir," the striker said. "Last night many of them walked by us!"

"Why didn't you kill them?" Tan demanded.

"Oh, sir, we could not! There were so many—"

Tan suddenly slapped him across his face; the man fell backward. "You cowards!" he shouted. "You see the enemy, and you don't even attack him!"

The strikers froze, and Tan stomped away. He found Captain Sullivan making his morning check of the machine guns on the camp perimeter. "Dai uy," Tan said, "what is patrol report from last night?"

Sullivan closed the feed cover on the M-60, wiping oil from his fingers with a rag. "They saw some NVA," he said.

"Yes, sir. But do they say how many?" Tan pressed.

"No, only thing the patrol leader told me was that they

had sighted an NVA patrol, but couldn't hit 'em because they were too far out," Sullivan said.

"Sir," Tan said, "I think we need to send out many patrol today. I talk to strikers, they say *beaucoup* VC, many, many! They hide like women so VC will not kill them."

Sullivan understood the danger Tan was warning of and jumped off the parapet, trotting for the operations bunker. "Go get your team out here on the double!" he shouted to Tan.

Tan ran back to the hooch, and woke everybody up at once. "VC close!" he said. "*Mau len,* report to captain!" His warning brought a flurry of motion as boots and weapons were grabbed by the team. The warped screen door slammed behind them as they raced to the main bunker.

Sullivan was outside the bunker, the other members of the SF team around him, listening intently as he gave instructions for preparation against possible attack.

"I want a basic load of ten boxes of ammo with each gun," he said, "and place crates of frags every five meters around the perimeter. Make sure every man cleans his weapon, and get the mortar crew registered on the road and the gully! Joe, you get Pleiku on the horn and arrange for the gunships and arty!"

Warner reached Sullivan through the crowd. "What's up, Captain?" he asked.

Sullivan gave him only a second of precious time. "Get your team ready for a patrol, draw all the rations and equipment you need from Snuffy, and get a carbine from one of my strikers for Tan!"

Warner ducked out of the group. "Pate, do you know where the supply shack is?" he asked, and proceeded to give orders before he received an answer. "Get us a PRC-twenty-five and a spare battery, some grenades, and some LRRP rations! Tan, you get a carbine from one of those people," he said, motioning toward a bunch of native soldiers.

Tan approached the men, looking at the weapons laid around their feet. He picked up a carbine that was less dusty than the others and snapped its bolt back several times.

Then he went straight to a soldier and reached into his ammunition pouches to pull out several rusty magazines. The man did not move. There was tangible hatred on Tan's face for the slovenly strikers. He turned smartly on his heels and walked back to the team. He placed the magazines in his own pouches.

As soon as food and ammunition had been distributed among them, the team reported to Sullivan. A worn map sheet was held on the hood of the camp jeep by stones. "Right out here," Sullivan said rapidly, "is where I sent those bastards last night. It was only two thousand meters. I want you people to get out there and see if you can find the spot where they stayed for their ambush. Get me some good intelligence!"

Bonn strapped on the radio, eager to get out and into action. Warner finished conferring with Sullivan and then turned to him. "Hurry up, Bonn!" Warner shouted. "Let's go *now*!"

Bonn took Warner's impatience to be genuine concern, but Pate didn't. "Hold it up, Sarge," Pate said. "Let him get the damn radio secured. We don't even have the freq yet."

Warner appeared to be on the verge of screaming at Pate but checked himself. He took a cigarette out of his pack, lit it, and, after a deep drag, said, "Okay, okay," and dashed into the commo bunker to get the frequency.

Pate sadly shook his head. "Son of a bitch," he muttered.

Warner jogged back to the team. "Forty-two-point-five!" he said, and Bonn dialed in the numbers, receiving instantly. "We're going to be Blinker One," Warner said. "Gimme a commo check." Bonn keyed the mike and contacted the radio operator inside the bunker with no problem.

The gate was opened, and the concertina wire dragged out of the way by strikers wearing tiger fatigues. The team walked out, weapons up and ready, going into combat as a unit for the first time. Bonn habitually took point, his usual position on a LRRP team, with Warner, Pate, and Tan strung out behind him down the road.

Bonn looked back over his shoulder and watched the

three men in mottled camouflage following him. Warner's eyes were almost fearful, scanning everything. Pate and Tan walked along calmly, not properly watching their zones of responsibility. None of them showed the cocky professionalism he had taken to be so universal in long-range recon. *I hope these guys straighten out quick,* Bonn thought, but there was little he could do about it alone.

Only a kilometer from the Special Forces camp the North Vietnamese regiment was halted in the hills and dug in solidly. With only two and three men to a hole, carefully emplaced under the trees and foliage, they were nearly invisible to the casual passerby, much less aerial recon.

Their advance scouts carefully probed the area around Five Tango, feeling out the situation. They watched the Special Forces patrols go out from the gates of the camp, comparing them with the activity of the day before.

Sullivan had anticipated that and dispatched only the same approximate number of men at the same times, presenting a facade no different from any other day. The NVA took the bait and sent runners back with reports of an unsuspecting camp.

The Special Forces patrols were allowed to complete their missions without incident, and by midafternoon all but Warner's patrol had returned within the walls.

Warner held up his hand for the team to stop, and they all sat, sweat pouring off them profusely. The sun was a killing thing. "Get a fix on us, Bonn," Warner gasped, taking off his hat and wringing it out. The cigarettes in his pocket were ruined, wet and disintegrating. Bonn dutifully took his compass and surveyed for a few moments, tracing the route they had taken on the map.

"We're here," he said with confidence, indicating a green spot among dozens of other green spots on the paper. "The map doesn't show the rice paddies over there, but both the hilltops coincide, see?"

Pate investigated the trees on the rise just above them.

"Here's where the zips stayed the night. Sure left a lot of shit here."

Bonn walked up and took a look at the empty ration cans and candy wrappers. "I can't understand these guys," Bonn said. "They don't seem to have any idea of how to act like soldiers."

Warner felt he had done enough. They had found the site; now he was ready to reverse azimuth and get back to the camp. He opened a fresh pack of cigarettes and lit one. "Everybody ready to go?" he asked just as Tan ducked.

Pate saw the interpreter's quick motion and dropped faster than Warner could respond. Bonn, still higher up the rise, simply crouched into the bushes.

"Look!" Tan said. "A man!" He was peering into the glare of the late-afternoon sun off the paddy water.

Warner strained his eyes. "I don't see nothing!" he said uncertainly.

Pate quickly pinpointed the movement. "I got 'im," he said, sighting on the figure through his scope. "Looks like some dude down there chopping rice or something."

Tan stood and clicked the safety off on his carbine. "We go get, make talk, say where VC stay," he said, and struck out down the hill.

"Hey, wait!" Warner blurted, running after him. It was nearly a hundred meters down the hill to the paddy. Tan fired a warning round that splashed the man with the stagnating water of the rice field, and the farmer's hands went up.

"Lai day!" Tan commanded. The man waded toward him, his loose black shirt and trousers hanging limply. Tan handed his carbine to Warner and frisked the man, finding nothing. The captive's face was leathery and well lined with woe. His hands were the hard, calloused tools of the dirt firmer.

"I want to know where the Front people are," Tan said to the man in his own language, his pronunciation as sharp as the knife he carried. "You have only one chance to tell me!"

10

Bonn stepped in to hold the prisoner by his arm, but the farmer panicked and pulled free to run away through the shallow water. It was a stupid move. The paddy stretched for an acre around them. *"Choi oi!"* Tan said in surprise, having expected no resistance.

"Hey," Bonn screamed. *"Halt!"* He swung his carbine to his shoulder but hesitated. The little man ran faster. Tan jerked his weapon from Warner's astonished fingers and cracked off a shot, the ejected brass flying past Bonn's nose.

Tan's aim was too low. The bullet sent up a geyser of water behind the man. The soles of the farmer's feet were pale, kicking up with each stride. Tan fired again and again, bracketing the man left and right.

Warner took aim, his M-16 thundering on full automatic. The spray from the bullet impacts totally hid the farmer from view, but he came running out of it, moving like a marathon champ. "I *know* I hit the son of a bitch!" Warner cursed, changing his magazine.

Bonn fired, spacing a fan of shots ahead of the man, trying to lead him. Tan resorted to automatic, as did Warner, and Bonn's single rounds were lost in the crescendo of gunfire.

The paddy around the dodging and weaving farmer exploded in a storm of water and silt. The man was hard to see for the mist, as he jumped, ran, and twisted through the dozens of violent waterspouts.

Suddenly Pate's rifle boomed, its authoritative report silencing the lesser weapons. The farmer fell, hitting the water facefirst. Bonn looked back at Pate, awed by the finality of the one shot. Pate recapped the lenses of his scope, no particular expression on his face.

Tan wasted no time. He began to push the rice around where the farmer had been standing, looking for the weapon he knew would be there. It was. An SKS carbine and a cloth bag of cartridges came dripping out of the water in Tan's white-knuckled hand. "He Communist!" Tan said.

"We better call Sullivan!" Warner said, reaching for the radio handset on Bonn's pack.

Pate turned and started walking out of the paddy. "You *better* get your ass out of the open," he said to them all, and Bonn felt mildly chastised by the obvious statement.

They withdrew up the hill to better cover, and Bonn contacted Blinker Six and described the incident, then listened briefly to the camp's instructions and shut down.

"They want us to stay out tonight and link up with some kind of friendly patrol," Bonn said to Warner, whose face dropped.

"Where?" Warner asked.

"Right here," Bonn answered. "We better get hidden before it gets dark." Busy in their duties, none of them paused long enough to mark the moment in their memories. Team Tango had drawn blood.

"Blinker One, this is Neptune Twenty-two," the radio crackled.

Bonn increased the squelch. "This is One, go ahead, Twenty-two," he whispered into the handset. The sun was almost gone, and soon there would be no light at all. Bonn was glad the patrol had reached them.

"We should be directly approaching your position, One, watch for us," the voice informed Bonn.

He lowered the mike and turned to the team. "They're coming in, real close, watch for 'em!" he said as loudly as he dared.

Vague noises disturbed the quiet of the forest. It was eerie for a moment, as they waited for those men who were making the muffled scrapings and rustlings to appear. *This is exactly what it'd sound like if there were nothing but NVA coming this way,* Bonn thought with dread.

An American carrying an ARVN backpack and wearing a narrow-brimmed flop hat appeared, and Bonn's breath returned. He waved to the man. The signal was observed, and the linkup was made. "How're you guys doing tonight?" the pleasant-faced olive drab fatigue-clad American asked, crawling in with them and sitting down, an AK-47 in his hands.

"How many men you got with you?" Warner asked, in no mood for conversation.

"Thirty of us," the soldier replied, "all Cambodes."

"Well, let's get into a perimeter," Warner urged. "The NVA are all over the place out here!"

The American grinned. "Take it easy, Sergeant," he said. "I know all that! We just passed a company of them getting in to you." Warner's cheeks paled.

Pate and Bonn glanced at each other. Tan was sitting too far away to be in the circle, guarding his edge of the perimeter. "We've been trailing a big unit of NVA out of the Chu Pongs for days," the man explained. "We were just sure tonight that they were going down to the Ia Drang and not up toward Kontum."

"What'd you do? Just follow 'em?" Bonn asked. The nonchalance of the man astounded him.

"Better than tangling with them!" the American replied. "I've got to get my people into an ambush," he said, excusing himself, and moved out to organize the large, silent group of Asian mercenaries who waited for him.

An L-shaped ambush was arranged, with the Americans at the junction. Once the Cambodes were in place, they made no further motion or sound. Tan knew they were dangerous troops. He personally had no use for the Cambodians, the animosity between his people and theirs centuries old, but he was glad for their presence tonight.

Claymores were strung front and back of the L by the last

few mercenaries up and moving. When they pulled in, the forest was as still and quiet as if no one were there at all.

Guard was arranged among the recon team by sign, Warner giving himself the last shift. Bonn tried to sleep, but the threat of the nearby enemy thwarted him. Insects chirped and sang in the darkness, and there was no wind.

Bonn heard the scratch of a match and realized Warner, who was on the other side of Pate from himself, had lit a cigarette. The sniper roused and looked at Warner.

"What the *fuck* are you doing?" Pate whispered.

Warner cupped the cigarette in his hands and didn't answer.

"They can see that," Pate said.

"I got it covered," Warner said.

"We're in ambush. Put it *out*," Pate said flatly.

Warner took another puff and stubbed out the cigarette. He sourly considered telling Pate who had the authority on the team, but with the woods full of NVA troops all around them, it wasn't worth it at the moment.

The moon was up later. Its light psychologically helped matters for Bonn somewhat, relaxing him. He finally dozed, but he dreamed of the running man in the paddy and bullets gouging torrents of muddy water. In the strange context of dreams, he became the running man, racing across the paddy, death and horror chasing him.

When Pate woke him for his guard, Bonn felt weak and edgy. He lifted himself up on his elbows and rubbed his eyes, remembering where he was. It all came back. The death threat was real, just different.

A half hour of Bonn's shift had passed when Warner loudly rolled over. Pate came instantly awake, saw who had moved, and touched Warner's arm. Bonn looked at them.

"Be still," Pate hissed.

"I think it was blue," Warner said.

"What?"

"Down at the bottom," Warner said.

Pate realized Warner was talking in his sleep. He shook his head in disgust and waited to see what was going to happen next. Warner lay still. *Thank God he at least doesn't snore, too,* Pate thought, and went back to sleep. Bonn watched the minute hand of his Accutron almost imperceptibly rotate around the dial.

A distinct change in the drone of the insects made Bonn raise his head. He held his breath, feeling more than listening. Something was wrong. He looked out into the moonlit grasses beside the thicket, not really knowing what to expect.

He saw the small shadow shape of a man. For the first time in Bonn's life, a chill truly ran the length of his spine. The man was deadly grace, moving through the underbrush like a creeping spider, without a false step or a broken twig. He carried no rifle, using both hands to clear branches and vines from his path.

Not far behind him came a squad of pith-helmeted infantry, with weapons. They were slowly working their way directly toward the ambush. It all seemed unreal. Bonn reached and shook Tan and Pate, and was stretching to touch Warner when the first Claymore exploded.

Warner jumped as if he'd been electrocuted, and the night was involved in a flashing hellfire blitz of Claymores and automatic rifles.

It was over before a second breath could be drawn. Bonn's carbine was still on safe.

The stunning crashes of the antipersonnel mines left everyone's ears ringing. Leaves loosened by concussion filtered down on the ambushers from the trees, and a pall of bitter smoke hung in the night air, stinging their noses.

11

Bonn heard the telltale clicks of magazines being changed down the line and the chambering of new ammunition, but nothing else, not even a voice. No wounded cried out. No orders were shouted. The stillness was frightening.

When Bonn looked down at his Accutron to note the time of the ambush, he couldn't see the luminous dots on the dial face. His night vision had been ruined by the glare of the explosions. He put the watch to his ear. The tiny tuning fork within it was still humming. Bonn hugged the ground and wondered why Warner didn't ask for the radio to report the enemy contact, but he didn't question his team leader about it. The silence was too threatening for that. If the mercs wanted it quiet, Bonn was going to stay quiet. There was no sign of the infantry squad they'd hit. It was so easy to die if you were in the wrong place at the wrong time. Bonn didn't go back to sleep.

The dawn came one eternity later, infiltrating cold light onto the scene of the massacre. The American leader of the Cambodian mercs waved some of his men out as security.

"Warner, you awake?" Pate asked. Warner peered out of the bushes.

"Goddamned right I'm awake!" he said, frantically lighting a cigarette. "What was all that shit about last night?"

The mercenary leader overheard him. "About as good an ambush as you could want," he said happily.

The Cambodes not on security went out to examine the

kill, looting money and personal belongings from the corpses, being careful to avoid the blood and gore as they searched pockets and equipment.

"Were you *expecting* those guys last night? We were set up just perfect for their approach," Bonn said to the merc leader.

"I figured they'd show up," said the affable man with a half-smile. "We were tailing their main body, but I knew we had a recon team tailing us. They were pretty good, too. Damn near stepping in our own footprints! I pulled us up short and waylaid 'em. They assumed we were still ahead someplace."

"Why didn't you tell us what was going on?" Bonn asked.

"Sorry about that. I thought you knew. You gotta always figure on a tail out here."

Tired from the long night and feeling a little stupid, Bonn turned and heard Warner finishing his radio report, telling the camp to expect them back as soon as possible.

"Good work, Kuy," the American said to his executive officer. "Tell the men we will eat here, but we must have half on guard at all times." The stocky Cambodian, a red bandanna around his neck and dressed in baggy fatigues, ran off to implement the order.

"You're gonna eat breakfast here?" Warner exclaimed. "After last night?"

The American smiled. "It's good for morale," he explained.

Warner turned to his team. "Get your shit together," he said, "we're getting out of here!"

"The right thing to do, Sergeant," the American said, "is for all of us to go back together to Five Tango."

Warner was tightening his rucksack straps. "Fuck you, buddy!" he said haughtily.

"Fuck you, Captain, sir!" The man laughed, holding out a set of silver bars he pulled from his pocket.

Warner saw them, and his mouth fell open. "I'm—I'm sorry, *sir!*" he said.

The captain only grinned and put the bars back into his

pocket. "Don't worry about it," he said, and left to see how his men were doing.

The smell of fish, rice, and garlic drifted into the trees from the common cookfire. The team sat apart, watching the perimeter, and ate their own freeze-dried LRRP rations, reconstituted with hot water. They moved closer to the fire after they finished and were replaced by Cambodian guards.

The Asian mercenaries sat cross-legged on the ground, eating with their fingers from small bowls. A glass jar was being passed around. Bonn was offered a drink. The liquid was weakly green and smelled rotten. He politely refused, and the jar went to the next man.

"What in the world is that?" Bonn asked Kuy, the blocky little chief.

The Cambodian thought hard to phrase the answer. "Drink Vietnamese liver, make strong, not afraid of enemies," he said. "I don't know what is called, bitter part."

"What kind of liver? What do you mean?" Bonn asked slowly.

Kuy laughed, realizing Bonn's apprehension. "No animal," he said. "Liver from Vietnamese man!"

Bonn gaped at him. He walked out to the corpses, to see for himself, still not sure of what Kuy had said. Flies and insects had found the squad's wound-riddled bodies already, but one was teeming with them. His shirt was stripped off, and there was a massive, hollow gash across his side almost black with milling ants.

Boon thought he had been around long enough to take such surprises, but he was wrong. He gagged like a student doctor at his first autopsy and lost his chicken and rice LRRP ration on the spot.

It was noon before the mercenaries and the recon team arrived at the Special Forces camp. They had lost no time getting back after breakfast, obeying Sullivan's orders to get out of the hills quickly.

Sullivan met them all in the compound, slapping the merc leader on the back and congratulating everyone on a job well done. The team trudged to their hooch and fell onto their cots, allowing their equipment to lie where it hit the floor. That afternoon they slept.

By 1600 hours the last patrol was inside the gate, and the usual night ambush was not sent out. Sullivan wiped his mouth and flipped his empty C ration can into the burlap garbage sack. "What's the situation?" he asked his XO. The lieutenant had just finished marking the wall map.

"Well, TAC Air from Pleiku is on alert, the One Seventy-five's out, and the Fourth of the Forty-second are standing by, and all local patrol reports from our strikers are zip," the officer said.

Sullivan nodded. "They're out there, Joe. I can feel it." Then, to ease the tension of the night, he remembered an old military joke. "They can't get away from us this time, by God. They've got us surrounded!"

From out in the compound the strikers heard them laughing and wondered why.

The North Vietnamese recon pulled back and gave the okay to come up with the mortars. By 1800 hours the mortar crews had dug in and were ready for action. All the ammunition that had been carried so far was stacked beside the tubes, charges cut, and the fuses primed.

The three infantry assault companies deployed at 1900, staying five hundred meters from the perimeter of the camp. A platoon of demolition and mine-clearing troops spearheaded each unit.

The role of each man, squad, platoon, and company was planned and memorized. They had to act with timing and precision, hitting hard and quickly, to take the camp.

Their job was cut out for them. Five Tango's three sides were walls of death. A defoliated kill zone two hundred meters wide had been sown around it, and fences of rusty razor and concertina wire ran wickedly everywhere.

Thousands of bamboo punji stakes bristled against the embanked walls, and rows of deadly Claymores threatened to make the field of wire and mines a vast potential slaughterhouse for anyone caught in it.

Each corner of the fort mounted a machine gun, placed in elevated sandbag-reinforced bunkers. Five Tango was as prepared as Sullivan's "A" team could make it.

So quietly, so carefully the first teams of sappers crawled forward and began to cut through the wire, many hands supporting the strands so that not one tin can of empty rifle cartridges suspended in the wire clanged. They dragged heavy satchel types of demolition charges with them, accurate plots of the camp in their heads.

The road to Five Tango was blockaded, ready for any relief column that might try to make it in to help the camp. The conditions were right for a great deal of killing on both sides.

12

Bonn was asleep in his hooch with the team when it happened. A satchel charge on the north wall disintegrated the machine-gun bunker there, killing both the gun crew and the unlucky sappers who had placed it but couldn't get away in time. The blast threw Bonn out of bed onto the wooden floor of the tent.

"*What the fuck?* Over." he said, a slang parody of radio procedure he sometimes used, but in the shock of the moment it was a sincere question.

"Incoming!" Pate yelled, thinking it was mortars. "We're gettin' hit!"

The camp perimeter opened fire, and an incoming volley of shoulder-fired B-40 RPG rockets hit the kitchen beside the main bunker. The cooking gas propane tanks ruptured and spewed flame brilliantly within the compound.

Bonn found his carbine, collided with Tan in the dark, and dashed out the back door of the hooch for the nearest bunker.

In those first few moments of confusion a shock platoon of desperate NVA troopers made a try to rush the hole left by the satchel charge. They came screaming through the wire, throwing down logs to flatten it, and ran straight into a massacre.

Panic fire and grenades from the strikers on the wall savagely raked them, and none of the dodging commandos made it through the breach alive. The North Vietnamese behind them continued to pour out an aimed fusillade of automatic fire and RPG rockets, tracers ripping sandbags right off the parapets and direct hits from the RPGs collapsing sections of the palisade.

The Special Forces people tried to be everywhere at once, getting the mortar into operation, urging and directing fire from the strikers, and pulling cowards from hiding.

A Green Beret stuck his head into the opening of the bunker where Bonn and Tan had found to burrow. "Anybody in here?" the man yelled.

"Yeah!" Bonn said. "Two of us!"

"I want you two on the roof of the supply shack! Get those SOBs over there to cover the goddamn west wall! Go!"

Bonn responded, leading Tan to the ladder up the side of the main bunker, onto a half-roofed strongpoint that commanded a good view of the chaos. The machine-gun crew were on their stomachs, not firing. Tan shouted at them, swinging his carbine, and they leaped to the gun, putting out suppressive fire like a man with a water hose trying to wash a swarm of hornets from the air.

The first rush hadn't worked. The NVA commander did not see the flare that would have meant his men were inside. He sent the runner to have his mortars add more weight to the attack.

The NVA crews on the four Chinese 82 mm tubes were terribly fast at their job. They had a dozen shells in the air before the first one hit the ground. Their aim was only approximate, but experience and the nearness of the target helped.

The camp was smothered in a barrage of explosions that completely disrupted the defense. Warner, who had been attempting to make it from the hooch to a bunker, was tumbled into a ditch, his weapon lying in the dirt overhead. He made no effort to retrieve it.

Pate had tunneled into a mound of sandbags from a fallen wall, and there he balled up, covering his riflescope with his body, senses stunned by the ferocity of the mortar fire.

As the firepower coming from the camp slackened, the

NVA rushed a squad armed with Bangalore torpedoes in close to the wall and blew the wire away near the breach. Then they came storming over the wall, even with their own mortar fire falling into the camp.

A green flare shot up and burst in the sky, the signal that they were inside. The mortar barrage lifted almost instantly, and the struggle for the compound itself began.

The first North Vietnamese soldiers through swiftly overran two bunkers inside the walls, killing the disorganized strikers in them. That made a hole for more of their people to fill.

Bonn saw disaster and turned Tan so he would know, too. The M-60 was worked around to fire inside the camp, throwing lead toward the captured bunkers, trying to slow the invasion.

Pate knew what was going on. He had seen the sweep of enemy soldiers coming over the crest of the palisades, and he thought the camp would be lost. He found an M-16 in the dirt beside its dead owner and quickly robbed the corpse's ammo. He fed magazine after magazine through the weapon, not even trying to aim, just spraying the part of the camp he knew was in enemy hands. He had just run out of ammo when the mercs counterattacked.

The American captain at their front, the mercenaries came out of their trench with primitive battle cries, moving together like a tidal wave. They hit the NVA troops fiercely, swarming among them, shooting everyone in sight—including a few strikers—and chased the surviving enemy back over the wall.

Star shells exploded in the sky as the artillery support rallied to the call from Five Tango, Captain Sullivan himself on the radio giving the direction. The NVA had lost, and it knew it. The air power and artillery would be on it shortly, and it had no plans to stay around just to soak up punishment. The North Vietnamese mortars fired their last rounds, and the crews hurriedly dismantled them for the retreat back into the jungle.

The camp kitchen was still burning, its tin-roofed veranda

missing, and choking dust and smoke obscured the wreckage within the walls. Bonn realized the incoming fire had ceased and slumped to the sandbags, exhausted.

Tan climbed down off the roof of the main bunker to the ground and began to check the bodies of the NVA troops by the breach, where they lay tangled in the barbed wire and torn sandbags. He found two wounded Communist soldiers who were not yet dead. He shot them.

Warner peered out of his hole, reached for his abandoned weapon, and jerked it in with himself, looking cautiously all around, hoping it was over.

Pate dropped the overheated M-16 and stood up, brushing the dirt from his uniform. The Cambodian mercenaries were taking the weapons from the slain enemy, going so far as to sortie outside the wall to steal more.

The Sky Raiders came a few minutes later and blindly dropped their napalm canisters into the jungle, the billowing clouds of reddish orange flame burning among the trees like erupting volcanoes. The NVA knew better than to shoot back at the aircraft because muzzle flashes would only give it away, so the near-miss bombing was more morale than tactical support to Five Tango.

The camp executive officer climbed up into one of the gun towers, relieving Sullivan, and took over direction of the heavy artillery fire, the 175 mm shells striking indiscriminately out into the night-shrouded forest like vengeful lightning.

Bonn watched the defenders working to put out the fires down in the compound and gather the dead and wounded. His ears hurt deep inside from the thunder of the battle. The native machine gunners left the M-60 beside him and climbed down to the compound to help. Strikers were calling *bac si* for medics.

Bonn's leg began to shake, and he stilled it, but soon it was trembling again. The delayed reaction of fear was catching up with him. Nerves, he thought, just goddamned nerves.

As the dead were being laid out, he could see at least a

dozen of the strikers and several of the merc force in the lines of bodies beside the walls.

The NVA corpses were dragged unceremoniously away from the camp fatalities, and Sullivan stood there, supervising the gathering of the dead, keeping a careful count.

The stiffening bodies lay in awkward positions, chunks of their flesh shot away, most of their blood gone, having soaked into the soil around Five Tango.

For some reason Bonn thought about all the toy soldiers he'd had as a boy, a dislocated memory only just in the margin of sanity. He remembered battles he'd waged with those mute little plastic warriors with their indistinct faces and feet molded to square bases.

They were so small. Skirmishes could be fought on tabletops. His soldiers barracked in a shoebox. They were never hungry or tired or scared. They never screamed or bled or prayed. They were just little figures that you knocked over with a godly hand when you wanted them dead and set up next time when you wanted them alive again.

The bodies before him seemed so small. They were knocked down forever, toy soldiers for politicians.

Bonn recognized Kuy, the jaunty Cambodian mercenary, in the row of camp dead, and a sorrow for the man whom he did not know rose in his heart. All at once the reality of lying cold and broken for the foreign fight of another people became clear. *The sun will rise, and so many of us will meet it dead,* Bonn realized, *and will anyone really care?* His leg was shaking again.

13

The helicopters came with the first rays of dawn, to airlift the wounded to the big field hospital near Pleiku city. Twenty wounded strikers were loaded aboard the Dustoff ships and sent in. The wounded mercenaries stayed. No Vietnamese hospital would take them, and they did not want to be separated from their own kind anyway.

Captain Sullivan was with his strikers, going to their posts around the wall, thanking and praising them for their bravery. He promised awards and promotions to the survivors and cash payments to the widows.

A Huey came in low and fast, circled tightly, and landed in the center of the clearing outside the compound, shutting down its engine. Sullivan jumped off the embankment and walked to the helicopter, hoping his plasma had arrived. An American, dressed in new jungle fatigues, with an over-stuffed briefcase and taped map tube under his arm, stepped off the Huey, ducking under the still-spinning rotor blades. He was sweating, unaccustomed to the heat, and his haircut and paunch were civilian.

"Any blood on this ship?" Sullivan asked. The pilot shook his head as he pulled off his gloves and helmet. Sullivan looked into the cargo bay of the chopper. A wooden crate lay securely strapped to the deck.

"Is Team Tango all right?" the man with the briefcase asked.

"Yeah," Sullivan said, obviously disappointed at the cargo.

"Would you call them together, *please*? I need to brief them on this equipment," the civilian requested.

"We've just had a bit of a hard time," Sullivan said, "and the operations bunker is full of wounded right now."

The civilian was frowning. "Isn't there anywhere else I can hold my briefing? This is very important, Captain."

Sullivan pointed to an old prefab frame covered with a tattered roof. The screened-in sides were perforated with shrapnel. "That's their billet. Do it there," he said.

The crate was unloaded from the chopper and carried by Vietnamese strikers to the bunkhouse, and the team roused from their sleep. The civilian watched as the four tired volunteers, sore and smelling of smoke, gathered themselves together and sat quietly.

"I'm glad to see you boys didn't get hurt last night!" the man said to seem friendly, but he didn't get a smile. "I'm Don Jones from Saigon, assigned to the Studies and Observations Group. I've brought your special equipment and some photorecon material from the Air Force."

Pate stared at the visitor. "You a spy?" he asked in a monotone.

Jones laughed nervously. "No! I'm an electronics specialist! I'm here with my company on contract to the Army," he said.

Bonn took a bayonet and pried the lid off the crate, finding two shoebox-size black crackle-painted metal boxes packed inside, with a plastic bag of wires and fittings.

Jones set the two boxes on a cot and went through a short class on connecting the wires to the boxes, switching them on, and arranging the antennas properly. It had all been designed to be as simple as possible to operate.

The class was ended with Jones's warning to the team that once the devices were activated, they were armed, and any attempt to move or disturb them would result in the destruction of the sets and possible injury to anyone near them.

"You mean those things are almost bombs, right?" Warner asked, chain-smoking.

"Not actually," Jones said. "They just have an explosive antitamper system built into them."

Warner considered that. "I hope they're at least shock- and waterproof! If they don't work, our whole mission is a washout."

"I suppose they are," Jones speculated. "They really didn't tell me much about them either."

The AK-47 in Tan's hands shook his whole magazine pouch-strapped torso as he ran through a magazine on full automatic. The old paper target silhouetted downrange jerked with the impacts, shredded by dozens of previous hits.

Sullivan took the weapon from Tan and dropped the empty magazine out, taking an extra second to check the chamber. "Ever used an AK?" he asked Bonn, handing it to him.

The weapon was heavier than the M-16, being made of wood and steel, not plastic and aluminum. "We fired them in Recondo school," Bonn replied.

Sullivan began to reload the magazine. "Our M-sixteen is five-point-five-six millimeter, exactly twenty-two caliber. The AK uses a special short rifle round, in seven-six-two millimeter. It's a heavier, slower bullet, and the wounding effects are different from our round," he said, clipping in the last cartridge.

Bonn noticed the Soviet cartridge cases were steel, not brass. In Recondo school he'd been told a lot of Eastern bloc bullets were steel core, not lead, like U.S. issue, and would go through a tree as if it were cardboard. The Soviets used steel because it was cheap, jacketing their bullets with brass or copper to protect their weapons' rifling and to conform to the Geneva Convention.

"The boattail design of the M-sixteen bullet makes it un- stable when it hits something. That's what gives it the spin- ning or tumbling effect entering a body," Sullivan said. "The

AK round is more conventional. It doesn't make the nasty, unpredictable wound that the sixteen does. It just blows a big hole every time."

Bonn grimaced at the reminder.

Sullivan took the AK-47 back and locked the magazine into it. "We use a twenty-round magazine; they use a thirty. Both weapons will fire full auto. The trick feature on the AK is that the *first* position coming off safe is full automatic!"

Sullivan tucked the weapon into his shoulder and squeezed off a shot at the target. "The AK will kick a little bit, so it takes some practice to stay on target with it. Thank God the average Vietnamese doesn't have the ass to hold one down too well on full auto!" he said, clapping Tan on the back and smiling. Then he pointed to the khaki ammunition pouches Tan wore around his waist. It was Chinese Communist issue, with three big flap-top pockets for magazines across the stomach, the flaps secured by wooden peg fasteners rather than buttons or snaps, and smaller pouches for grenades on the sides. "The ammo for the AK is heavier, naturally. The basic load for the NVA is usually only three or four magazines," he said.

Bonn lifted one of the extra weapons off the parapet. "What about jams?" he asked.

Sullivan shook his head. "It's more reliable than our M-sixteen," he said, shaking the one he held to make the parts rattle. "It's built loose like the forty-five."

The weapon Bonn held was different from Sullivan's in that it had a folding stock. "What kind of AK is this?" he asked, swinging the stock out to the extended position.

"That is a paratrooper model of a new type of AK that's been showing up for a year or so now. I think the Russians call them AKMs," Sullivan explained. "They're lighter. Got a stamped receiver, plastic pistol grip, and a kind of muzzle brake to improve control on full auto."

"I sure would rather have one of these than the full-stocked one," Bonn said. "It feels a lot handier."

Sullivan nodded. "We have at least four of those in good

shape here, they take the same magazine as the AK-47, so I don't see why not," he said.

Bonn noticed there were detail changes between the AKM and the AK-47, but no important functional differences. The markings on the weapon showed it was truly Russian-made, not Czech or Chinese or Romanian. There would be some satisfaction in using it against the enemy.

The team burned up a few hundred rounds each, using AKMs like Bonn's from the stockpile. They practiced how to field-strip and reassemble the Soviet weapons until they felt they were thoroughly familiar with them.

"Not a bad trigger," Pate said as they cleaned the AKMs after the shoot, "but I'm not carrying one. My Remington's all I need."

"How come we don't get something really tricky with a silencer on it?" Warner asked, cleaning rod in hand, swabbing out the muzzle of his AKM.

Sullivan held up a Soviet 7.62 mm round. "You'll be using the same ammo as Charlie does, your weapons will sound the same, and magazines will be no trouble."

Bonn polished the blue steel of his newly adopted weapon, thinking Sullivan's reasons indicated they could be using the weapon a lot. *We'll be in a world of shit if that's the case,* he told himself.

14

Sullivan pinned the first photo to the easel. "We can't tell too much about the area from this one, except to mark a few trails and streams. Notice this heavily forested area, though," he said.

"This infrared gets the heat emissions. Those light spots are campfires; the other clutter is probably generators or whatnot. That, gentlemen, is the target."

The heat picture showed a ghosting of blurs and smudges. The team studied the photo with the seriousness that only risking one's life can give to an undertaking.

"Ought to bomb the shit out of it and not waste no time," Pate said. "Why risk our asses when we have pictures like this?"

Sullivan had been expecting just that question. "We want to learn about it, not destroy it. That's why we have the snoopers to plant," he said.

"That place has got to be guarded with a damn division!" Bonn exclaimed, but Sullivan was prepared for that as well.

"Not a division, just a light regiment," the captain said, "three companies." He was sure of his facts.

Warner felt the bottom drop out of his stomach. *"Jesus Christ!* They're just waiting for somebody to come in there!" he said, unable to conceal his astonishment.

Sullivan sat down at his field desk. "That's right." He agreed with Warner. "But that ought to help you get Sugar." Warner didn't care as yet about Sugar; he was presently stunned with the idea of walking into a regiment of the NVA.

"How will that *help* us get Sugar?" Bonn asked out of morbid curiosity.

Sullivan looked confident. "When you make contact with Sugar, he'll go straight to the NVA, right?" he asked.

"Right." Bonn agreed. There was no doubt about that.

"And they'll come after you ASAP, right? And Sugar will be right there with them, up front, to point you out, and you can get a good bead on his brown ass!" Sullivan said, as if it made sense.

"Yeah," Pate said, "and the minute I plug the SOB they'll be on us like stink on shit!"

Sullivan grinned. "Hold on," he said. "That's not all. Shooting Sugar is the diversion while you actually plant the snoopers! They won't be looking for you in two places at one time!"

"What?" Warner nearly shouted. "We could have *two* teams in the fucking area for all they know! This is suicide!"

Sullivan still grinned. "Take it easy! We've got that covered, too! *The NVA will know that you're coming* and that there are only four of you, but not what your actual mission is. We have a cover for that."

The team was in a collective state of shock. Sullivan had apparently lost his mind.

"How will they know?" Warner asked, afraid of the answer.

"We leaked the intelligence to Sugar already. He's expecting you," Sullivan said, now straight-faced. It crossed Warner's and Pate's minds to resign right there. Bonn was digesting the impact of what he heard. Tan simply stared at Sullivan in disbelief. Telling the enemy your intentions was not in his comprehension.

"The idea," Sullivan said, "is that the NVA will wait to bag you all at one jump, when you contact Sugar. They think you're coming in to find out what happened to the last team. It's perfect cover. This way we keep Sugar from getting suspicious, and you get in."

"I suppose we have to split up to do this," Bonn asked, sensing a near mutiny among his team.

Sullivan nodded affirmatively. "That's your only real risk," he said, having finally fully covered the CIA-ordered operations plan. It was a wild one, but weren't they all?

The next day an Air Force colonel arrived and briefed the team on how the flight in would be made. "It'll be a dawn drop from fifteen thousand feet," he announced. "The time will be ten minutes after BMNT day after tomorrow morning. That'll put you on the ground early, so you'll have plenty of time to get your objective."

Warner was getting sick at the thought of another jump. He felt his forehead becoming sweaty and hoped he could make it through the rest of the briefing.

"Our C-one-thirties usually don't have escorts, so your plane won't either, but there will be a flight of Phantoms nearby making a harassment strike. We want Charlie to be focusing them on his radar and not you."

The team listened to the extended weather forecast—hot and dry—and learned how their extraction was planned. Primary and secondary pickup zones that looked good on the air recon photos had been chosen, both near Lac Sao. Bonn hoped they were not the same ones as the prior team was supposed to have used. If the NVA had its map, those PZs would be marked and watched. The actual extraction would be by a SOG helicopter unit, with air cover if the getaway was a hot one. The air liaison mentioned that planes would be on call at any time during the mission.

Bonn remembered a question he'd had in mind. "Exactly what kind of air support can we get if we need it?" he asked, wondering about the types of planes.

The colonel grinned. "Son, I can put up anything we have in an emergency," he said. "Any of you men trained in the Fulton Recovery?" he asked. No one had been. "Well, I know you've seen it. A plane hooks a balloon you're rigged to and pulls you up."

"I understand," Tan said, who knew something about it.

"Airplane grab man fast, make fly." Warner closed his eyes, wishing he were somewhere else.

"We can get you out with the Fulton rig virtually anywhere," the colonel said. "It's been used on rescue operations many times with great success. You boys can count on us."

The team drew rations and equipment from Five Tango's supply room right after breakfast. They signed for the AKMs and the codebooks and packed the snoopers very carefully in a padded drop bag.

Tan carried the team aid bag, with two serum albumin blood expander kits that could be given intravenously to keep a dying man alive in the absence of whole blood or plasma transfusions. As team leader Warner took the drug kit, containing morphine Syrettes and "green bomb" dextroamphetamine pills that could jolt an exhausted soldier into a wide-awake condition. In street jargon the green bombs were known as speed.

Bonn and Warner both carried radios. Bonn took the main URC-68 long-range set, Warner the infantry model PRC-25, to use as a backup to talk with Army aircraft or rescue units. Warner had also been given a small URC-10 walkie-talkie that was normally part of a pilot's survival kit for ground-to-air commo with Air Force planes. An odd fact of the war was that the Army and Air Force did not share common radio equipment that allowed ground troops to talk directly to the air support.

Their ammunition, pyrotechnics, and signal equipment were basic to any patrol. A box of Claymore mines, smoke and fragmentation grenades, and parachute flares, fabric marker panels, and signal mirrors was set out and divided among them.

Chinese-type canvas chest pouches full of loaded AK magazines and canteens, rucksacks, and sling bags captured from NVA troops were their load-carrying equipment. They were not given the snap link–equipped STABO body harnesses to aid helicopter-winch extraction usually worn on SOG missions.

For the three Americans, Sullivan had LRRP rations. For Tan, he'd picked indigenous rations from his strikers' supplies. These were plastic-bagged meals of rice and dehydrated meat, fish, and vegetables made for Asian tastes.

Pate took an extra box of military match grade ammunition to supplement his home-loaded supply. They left all their personal identification locked in Sullivan's command bunker.

Each man carried a bundle of nondescript uniforms resembling North Viet issue. There were faded khaki shirts, brown and black trousers, olive drab fatigue jackets and shapeless flop hats in washed-out green. Rubber-soled canvas shoes replaced their jungle boots so no lugged sole marks would give them away.

Bonn wrote a last letter to Linda, not knowing when he would next get the chance. It was a letter fueled by desperation, the sort of letter soldiers have written on the eve of battles since there have been soldiers and letters. His words were chosen to conceal, not reveal. They were promise and bravado, and they came from his heart. He wrote them knowing how easily death could make a mockery of his few wishes.

Sweetheart,

I don't want to wait until you're out of school. It'll only be a short time until your graduation when I get home. I want us to get married, very quietly by a justice of the peace, and not let anybody know until you graduate.

I love you and miss you. I'm sorry I haven't been writing as much as I should. We've been moving around a lot, and mail is very erratic. I can't even guess right now when I can write again.

We'll honeymoon at the beach. I dream about that, and you. Sometimes dreams are all I have to keep me going.

We're having a bad time now, lots of action, but I know how to take care of myself.

When Bonn dropped the letter in the bag inside the command bunker, Sullivan was issuing Pate an AN-PVS-2 Starlight scope in a rigid carry tube with a sling. "Can you use a camera?" Sullivan asked Bonn, who nodded. The captain gave him a 35 mm SLR and extra film. It was a good civilian model with a short telephoto lens.

Sullivan wished them luck as they boarded the Huey taking them to New Pleiku Air Force Base. A jet transport there flew them to Nakhon Phanom in Thailand, where they arrived before dark.

They met the aircrew that would be flying them over the Laotian panhandle the next morning, attended a mission briefing with them, and drew their parachutes and jump gear. The Air Force lent them cots and an empty concrete-block building near the hangars to sleep in, and after a full equipment check they went to bed early, the call to arise set at 0230 to begin the mission.

Warner had been speaking to everyone in grunts since they'd flown out of Vietnam. He seemed distracted, as if he were deeply occupied with the details of the mission. Actually he was walking and talking only by reflex. Time and reality had stopped for him before the team boarded the plane. His mind had shut down, suspended in a protective, denying anesthesia, like a prisoner being dumbly led to the executioner.

At first, waking up that morning to a sendoff breakfast he couldn't eat at the Special Forces camp, he'd been ready to quit, just go to Sullivan and flatly quit. And be ruined, be finished. It'd be in his records. He'd never get rank. No outfit promoted a known coward. He'd run from college because he was afraid. He'd run from the Cav because he was afraid. There was nowhere to go now. Everybody always made him do things he couldn't do. People wouldn't let him alone. No one was on his side. He had to take care of himself.

He'd decided to go on the mission. Not all the way, of course, but to make it look as if he'd tried. He would abort the mission as soon as he could. He was team leader. He could do that. There were ways. He'd keep the team on the ground for only a day or less, and even that was unbelievably, horribly, terrifyingly dangerous. In his besieged mind, where there was no one and no reasons but himself, he believed he had no choice.

Bonn couldn't have slept that night if he'd been awake the previous week. He lay on his cot and listened to the jets take off and land through the night, wondering where they were bound, their roaring making the building shake at times.

He had a weak feeling inside that he was about to be irrevocably involved in something for which he was not ready and it was going to cost him. He tried to quell the feeling; but it stuck, and his attempt to drive it out and replace it with the confidence he used on long-range patrols wouldn't work.

There were indistinct, frightening premonitions lurking in his mind, but he dared not let them out for examination. *Feeding doubt only makes it stronger, until it conquers and paralyzes you,* he thought. *I'll go on their damn mission and give it everything I've got.*

15

The C-130's paratrooper warning light was broken, so there was no equipment to alert the team to action. Instead, the loadmaster walked back to them, a paper cup of hot coffee in his hands, and looked at his watch. "About time, gents," he said over the noise of the engines.

At fifteen thousand feet, almost three miles up, oxygen equipment wasn't essential, even though the plane was pushing at the limits. Real HALO drops were made at thirty thousand feet and higher, sometimes much higher, up where the stars were visible and the curve of the earth apparent.

Fifteen thousand feet had been chosen for the team's jump altitude as a compromise they hoped would fool the enemy. It was too high for normal combat parachutists and too low for genuine HALO.

Almost no team insertions were ever made by HALO, and even lower-level jumps to get men into a target area were usually impractical. The instructors had said so at Recondo school and at Clark. This long fall into Laos was, in Bonn's opinion, some mission planner's idea of a John Wayne stunt. In his fiber glass helmet, goggles, and zippered jump suit pulled on over his clothing and equipment, Bonn felt more like an astronaut than a soldier, making his watch appropriate for once, and he couldn't even see it because it was under his sleeves.

The interior of the big four-engine plane was poorly lit, cold, and loud. The whole airframe vibrated with the power of the turboprop engines, making loose straps and clamps rattle on the deck.

Bonn sat hunched over forward in his nylon net seat, making room for his parachute. The altimeter dials mounted to his reserve parachute were right under his chin. He heard the loadmaster and tried to smile, but couldn't. He was really scared this time.

His only consolation was that none of the other team members looked any better. Warner had his face covered with his arms, slumped onto the equipment pack containing the snoopers, and both Pate and Tan wore expressions they might have thought stoic but in truth looked more like nervous paralysis.

The whine of the cargo ramp door servo, almost lost in the roar of wind and engines, raised Warner's eyes. The eastern horizon became visible as the door lowered, a bar of light in the pitch-darkness.

The team stood and shuffled to the door, clumsy in full gear. The loadmaster plugged in his headset to consult with the pilot and held up his hand, all fingers extended, meaning five minutes to wait.

Bonn adjusted his helmet and checked his straps and snap links. His AKM, stock folded, but with a magazine in it, was tied tightly under his left arm. He looked down at the blackness. Nothing was apparent in it. Not even a dot of light shone.

Training was the primary thing in Bonn's mind now. He remembered the instructor's words: "Jump as a group! If you get strung out at high altitude, you'll be landing in different countries!"

The loadmaster yelled, *"Now!"* and they ran out the door and off the ramp together. Behind his goggles Bonn's eyes closed involuntarily as his feet left the aircraft, then popped open to view the world.

The sky was lighter than he expected. In the sunrise the sparse clouds glowed brightly, and the blue of a new day was starting to fill the void through which he plummeted. It was an incredible sight.

He looked to the left and right and saw the other team members falling with him, faces down, arms and legs outstretched. *We've got to stay together,* he thought, moving his legs a bit to drift toward the closest man.

Swimming in the air, they maneuvered inward, forming a rough circle. The jungles of Indochina hid in the night that still covered the land beneath them. Bonn watched his altimeter needle swing around the dial face toward the red zone.

He held his breath when fifteen hundred feet registered on the instrument, trying to remain relaxed, so the shock of the opening would not hurt him, The drogue left the pack first, slowing down his descent; then the main chute billowed out, and his weight hit the harness. *Thank God,* Bonn thought, grabbing at his steering loops.

He saw treetops and assumed the protective position, crossing his legs and covering his face; then he was violently crashing into limbs and vines, all impacts but no immediate pain, his velocity taking him deep into them.

Somehow he stopped before his feet touched solid ground. Then he felt the pain. It was too dark around him to see. He was tangled in his own parachute lines, amazed to be alive, hanging out of a tree in Laos.

Bonn's training prevailed. Nothing seemed to be broken, but God, did he hurt now. He hung there, catching his breath, and felt for his knife. It was still attached.

I don't know how high I am, he realized. *I can't cut loose before I find out!* As he tried to see into the darkness, he heard noises. Someone was moving nearby.

He went limp in the harness, holding absolutely still. The noises came closer. He lifted his goggles and stared into the dark, but it was like being blind.

The idea that it was probably one of the team looking for him calmed his heart for a second, and he thought about calling out. He was drawing in his breath to speak when the man on the ground beat him to it.

The voice hissed a plaintive sentence in Lao, answered rapidly by another. The words were short and clipped; the speakers, anxious. Bonn went rigid.

The two searchers never slowed down. They hurried under him and pushed off into the jungle, Bonn could not breathe. His worst fears about the mission were coming true, and he was not even out of his parachute harness yet.

The sun took its own good time to rise, caring little for the matters of men. *Oh, Jesus Christ!* Bonn thought, feeling his bruises, hanging alone. *We're crossed up for real! Probably scattered for half a mile!*

Then the distinctive sounds of a man moving in heavy jungle reached him again. It was just getting light enough under the trees to make out shapes. Bonn dangled like a fish on a line, caught out of water. His equipment was twisted, the AKM knocked around to his back; his rucksack, which was worn in front for the jump, under the reserve chute, was jammed where the weapon had been. All his gear had protected him from being seriously injured by the branches.

A figure stepped out from behind a nearby tree.

Bonn, knife out, prepared to cut the harness and tumble to the ground, to attack the man hand to hand, when a familiar voice stopped him.

"What in the hell are you doing still in a tree?" Pate asked. Tan stood beside him. "Cut the damn lines and let's go! There's gooks all over the place!"

Bonn sliced his lines and fell the last few feet of the long drop he'd begun into Laos. "What about the parachute?" he protested as Pate led him away.

"Fuck it! Go!" Pate gasped, and Bonn said nothing more, taking a minute to shed his helmet and jump suit, rearranging his equipment, weaving along behind Pate, knocking branches out of the way, and shouldering his rucksack.

Bonn was quickly straightening his faded olive drab fatigues and equipment. Tan wore an actual North Viet field green uniform, and Pate's lanky frame was covered by a spotted brown and green camouflaged shirt and a pair of black trousers. All of them had on their canvas NVA rucksacks and Chinese ammo pouches and droopy, short-brimmed hats.

Bonn fed a round into his AKM, pulling the bolt back

and sliding it slowly forward by hand. "Where's Warner?" he asked Pate, who already had his Remington assembled and loaded.

"He went down somewhere north of us, about a hundred meters away," Pate said. "I was the last one to land. I saw where everybody hit."

"*Beaucoup* Communist soldier," Tan said, "maybe get sergeant and kill him!"

Bonn had already considered that but had heard no shots. "I'm set, let's do it!" he said, with more bravado than he felt.

They had not moved more than fifty meters when a flurry of gunfire split the dawn ahead. The fire was wild and disorganized, the reactions of men totally surprised. Bonn could tell only one thing from it. All the weapons involved were AK-47s. They made the unmistakable booming reports he had learned so well in the central highlands.

"He's in trouble!" Bonn said, crouching.

Pate cautioned everybody to stay down with a hand signal. "Wait . . ." he mouthed to Bonn, almost soundlessly. The firing subsided briefly, and people began to run recklessly about, crashing through the woods. "Sounds like just two or three of 'em," Pate said. "Let's go scare 'em off!"

He stood, and the grim little band followed him toward the fight. Pate caught close motion on his right flank and fired the sniper rifle from the hip at it, the blast echoing in the hills. Bonn and Tan fired short bursts for effect.

"Warner!" Pate shouted. "Where are you?" Bonn winced, sure that everyone in Laos could hear him.

"Over here!" Warner yelled, a violent burst from his AKM drowning out his voice. Pate dashed straight for Warner's voice, bulldozing through the ferns and vines. He found Warner flat on his stomach, behind a tree. His helmet was missing, but he was still in his jump gear.

The team drove in beside him. "You hurt?" Pate asked.

"No!" Warner said through clenched teeth. "I just dropped right on top of those motherfuckers, that's all!" Bonn and Tan covered the rear. Bonn listened. There was no more noise. That was a bad sign.

"Musta seen us land!" Warner said bitterly as he fought out of his jump suit. *"We're not gonna make it!"* Bonn could not believe what he had heard Warner say. An unspoken rule in the LRRPs was never even suggest such a possibility out loud. You maintained your composure, your buddies maintained theirs, and you drew strength from each other.

"I think they're coming back this way," Bonn whispered to Pate. The sun was almost above the trees now, with few dark hiding places left.

Bonn's hands were trembling, and he gripped his weapon tighter to steady himself. A bush moved ten meters out. Warner pointed his AKM at it. High grass rustled on the left. They were getting closer. Tan moved his fire selector to semiautomatic. Dry leaves crackled. Pate pulled his rifle butt into his shoulder.

Bonn saw a flicker of motion through the hanging curtains of vines and bit his tongue. The form of a man became visible.

The man wore pants with the legs rolled up to his knees and a green T-shirt. His hair was long, black, tied into a tail, and his skin was very dark. He was looking from side to side as he slowly advanced, using the barrel of his AK-47 to push away the vines.

Four weapons swung to meet him. He planted his feet deliberately, high-stepping over the clumps of leaves and thorns. Warner could stand it no longer. He opened up with a thunderous burst that ate half a magazine and disintegrated the Oriental's head and shoulder, blood spray fouling the vegetation around the falling man.

Bonn chopped a blizzard of suppressive fire left, while Tan did the same on the right. Empty gray steel shell cases that had ejected from their smoking weapons lay scattered beside them. Warner emptied his AKM across the front as Bonn and Tan reloaded, putting out a fresh salvo in the direction of the dead man.

Bonn was ramming another magazine into the smiling receiver of his AKM, heart racing, when Pate grabbed his shoulder. "Hold it! They're unassing the area!" he said. Tan paused and cocked an ear. It was true. People were running away.

"They must be Pathet Lao!" Bonn exclaimed.

Warner slipped his arms into his rucksack straps. "We're getting the hell out of here!" he said breathlessly. "Let's go!"

16

The team held its position. It took Warner an instant to realize the men were waiting for orders. "Bonn, take point!" he said. "Get us to somewhere safe! On top of a hill, yeah, uphill!"

Bonn moved out, looking for a high ground. He was fast, splashing the team through a morass of swampy lowland to the first rise. They climbed up the gullies and slopes of the hillcrest, scrambling in the foliage, pulling from tree to tree, sacrificing noise for speed.

Bonn made the top and collapsed, gasping for breath, aware if there had been any Pathet Lao nearby, the whole team would have been dead. *God, what luck,* he thought, *we're alone up here.*

"Perimeter," Warner croaked, pointing his finger around the hilltop. He shredded a pack of cigarettes, trying to open them. Tan crawled off to one side, Pate to another. Bonn stayed where he was, and Warner lay next to him. "Get your map out and find where the hell we are," Warner said to Bonn, finally getting a bent cigarette lit.

Bonn pulled the map sheet from his pocket, took it out of its plastic bag, laid his compass on it, and oriented them both north. He could see only a handful of hilltops from where he lay, and they all looked alike.

He compared the drop zone on his map in every possible way to the hilltops in his limited field of vision. "No use, Sarge. I can't see enough. We'll have to get a radio beacon from Covey," he said to Warner, unfastening his poncho and liner bedroll from the top flap of his rucksack to get to the radio, which was on a support frame under it.

Warner's face turned from ashen white to angry red. "Goddamn it, you're supposed to know this shit! Don't waste time with that! *Locate* us!" he spit, shaking his fist at Bonn, who tried the map again, this time assuming positions, but in the end it was no better.

Warner sat with his back to him, veins flaring from his temples, smoking furiously, breath drawn in ragged whispers. Bonn mounted the antenna and switched on his radio, disgusted with Warner. "I'm making contact with Covey," he said.

He set the frequency and began to transmit in coded phrases, repeating the team call sign and asking for a direction-finding fix. The team had been promised the plane would be up for two hours after the insertion, to assist however it could.

After a minute the receiver responded. Bonn keyed his set, so the aircraft could ride the transmission beam in toward them. He released the button, instantly receiving another command to transmit.

In ever-shortening replies, Bonn and the plane communicated, until the aircraft located them. *"Shackle message coming,"* radioed Covey. *"Prepare to copy, I shackle—"* Bonn had his pen ready and copied the coded groups of letters as the radio message specified them. He keyed back his acknowledgment and switched off.

"Give me the codebook, the Black Horse shackles, I've got our coordinates!" Bonn said, and Warner tossed the pad to him. Bonn quickly converted the letters to numbers on the code pad and plotted their position on his map.

"We're miles from the right DZ!" he said in a mixture of anger and disbelief. "We're way too far west!"

"I'm calling the mission off," Warner told the team as they huddled around him at the end of the first day. "We're too far from the DZ, we've already been compromised, and the snoopers are lost."

Pate's jaw dropped. He hadn't noticed the bag wasn't tied to Warner's gear. *"Lost?"* he blurted. *"You're* supposed to have that bag, team leader!"

"It was lost in the firefight when we landed," Warner said, feeling he had the perfect excuse. "I couldn't help it." While still in Thailand, he'd made up his mind to "lose" the snoopers during the drop. The Pathet Lao just made it easier. No snoopers, no mission.

Bonn blinked, speechless. Tan was too puzzled to arrange sentences, so he said nothing.

Pate reached out and grabbed Warner by the collar. "You must've threw the snoopers away right after you hit the ground, you son of a bitch! I'll bet you planned on aborting this damn mission before we got on the airplane!" he said with murder in his voice, not knowing how right he was. Warner pushed at Pate's hand, twisting his way free.

"I ought to kill you," Pate said, swinging the muzzle of the Remington directly into Warner's face.

"No, no!" Warner choked. "I dropped the snoopers when the gooks surprised me!"

Warner was only a finger touch of pressure away from 7.62 mm retribution. "You're not going to fuck up this team!" Pate growled, and Tan braced for the shot.

"Put the gun down, man!" Bonn said.

Pate glared at him. "Shut up, you gung ho asshole" he told Bonn. "This idiot'll get us all killed!"

Warner was standing frozen with fear. "It was an *accident*!" Warner begged, just the right tone of honesty in his pleading

Slowly, doubt in his eyes, Pate lowered his weapon, recovering his temper. "Okay, all right, but no more shit, Warner!" he said. "I had you pegged since I met you."

Tan stayed out of the confrontation, hands on his AKM, noticing something neither Bonn nor Pate saw, because they were too involved with each other.

He had recognized the selfish cunning in Warner and

sensed the lie he had invoked to save his life. He understood Warner to be a terrible hazard to them all, but he wasn't sure what to do about it.

The first night they hid like animals evading hunters. Pathet Lao patrols were probably out looking for them, but the jungle did not tell. It engulfed everything and kept secrets.

Pate found it difficult to rest. He was sure Warner would start talking out loud to some dream character in the middle of the night, and the enemy would be ten feet away and hear it and the already doomed mission would end in a wild pre-dawn firefight.

Chris Bonn worked his way down from the tight level of anxiety of the day to a condition where he could at least sleep. He had to rest, and he knew it, or soon his responses would erode, and he could die from the result.

He had learned a lot so far. He was with the wrong people. They were not at all like the well-knit recon teams of his LRRP company. It was a disaster. Warner was crazy. Pate was crazy. Tan seemed to be the only stable one, but he might dump them all and take off on his own anytime, to save himself.

Warner's open display of cowardice was demoralizing to Bonn. How could they not have seen through him at Recondo school? Warner was hollow behind those three stripes!

And Pate! At first he'd seemed like a reasonable enough guy, but when he'd lost his cool and stuck his rifle right against Warner's nose, Bonn realized the sniper could have killed Warner right there with no thought about the consequences to the team.

But we're not a team, Bonn figured, not as he understood the term. *We're individuals, with no business being together. Were they so short of men it has come to this?*

His attitude collapsed, dropping from the one-for-all spirit that prevailed in his long-range patrol company to strictly watch-out-for-number-one.

The best I can do is get back alive, Bonn resolved.

He felt let down on all counts. No one had checked; no one had cared. *They threw us together and sent us off, and not one person in authority had taken the time to see if it might not work,* he realized despondently.

He had never thought a great deal about the competence of the higher command that moved men about in war like chess pieces, but that night it was the main thing on his mind. He felt like the lowliest pawn.

17

They stayed out of sight until the sun was up. Freeze-dried rations were opened, and mushy meals made, their warren becoming an impromptu camp, the vines and roots cut back and flattened, making a hollow in the thicket.

All discussion was done in lowered voices, just an octave above a whisper, and often a facial expression or a hand sign sufficed for an answer.

"We should go back and try to find the snoopers," Bonn suggested.

Warner scowled. "You're crazy!" he said. "We got dinks all over us! They've found the snoopers and the parachutes by now."

"Well, we ain't getting any closer to Lac Sao by sitting here," Pate said. "The sooner we get this motherfucker over with, the sooner we can get back."

Warner held up his hand. "Wait a minute. I'm in charge here, and we'll do what I say," he said firmly. Bonn glanced at Pate, to catch his reaction. "Forget about what happened yesterday," Warner continued. "We're going to act like a military unit, not a pack of renegades."

Pate's eyes were dark with doubt, but he listened. Tan also gave his rapt but suspicious attention. "We all were confused yesterday," Warner said, a different person from the groveling coward who had been under Pate's gun. "We dropped straight in onto those sons of bitches. The loss of the special equipment was unavoidable."

Tan suspected what Warner was doing, but by the faces of the other team members listening to him, they did not. Warner was lying, as the monkey lies to the tiger so the tiger will not eat him.

"We'll continue the most important part of our mission, to recon the site. We'll scrub shooting Sugar," Warner said, warming to his role, "and there will be no more incidents like yesterday. I'm the leader of this team! If anybody fails to follow orders, I'll have him court-martialed when we get back. This is a combat zone. I have that authority."

Warner spoke to the team slowly and clearly, bringing out all the essence of command he could muster, knowing the training a soldier receives affects him deeply, and the defiance of authority is not something he can do easily. Warner was using his shield of authority for all it was worth, but it was not his sanity that prompted him; it was his insanity.

Warner's fears had crested the day before, with the parachute jump and the firefight, and finally, after he had had Pate's rifle thrust in his face, the last vestiges of reason had left him. He had spent the night awake, incubating an idea, a solution.

It would cover his loss of the all-important snoopers, which would surely ruin him if SOG ever found out. It would avenge his humiliation from the team that he knew now hated and mistrusted him and possibly gain him the promotion to E-6.

The solution was simple: *No one but he himself could return from the mission.* He didn't actually have to kill anyone. He just had to create the right situations, and the killing would take care of itself. He just needed the nerve to do it. Nerve was the key.

When he returned, his story would be undisputed. He had found peace in the solution, and he knew perfectly well how to accomplish his goal.

Bonn took the bait, finding relief in being guided again, and Pate decided that he had scared some guts into Warner. Tan alone sensed the truth, but not the worst part.

Warner's plan justified itself to him beautifully. It was

simply self-protection. He pictured the rocker across the bottom of his buck sergeant stripes. He deserved it. He needed it.

The dextroamphetamine pills he'd taken earlier gave him strength. They calmed him, even reduced his need for cigarettes. The green bombs were at least some help, and he needed them. They were just stay-awake pills. They were okay. Army issue. And he had them, as team leader. Nobody else could have them. He needed them. They gave him nerve.

"What are we gonna do at the site without snoopers?" Bonn asked, adjusting the ride of the NVA rucksack against his back.

Warner smiled, rolling a ready answer off his tongue. "Try and locate the place, at least," he said. "Get a look at it, get some photographs; we'll do what we can." There was a ring of resolution in his voice.

"It's oh-eight-hundred hours now," Warner said. "We have about twelve clicks to go to reach the objective. We'll do six today, moving slow and careful, and set up somewhere tonight. Watch your rations; we could be a day or two longer than we planned. Let's go."

AKM in hand, Bonn took the point and led the team from the encampment, referring to his compass frequently to keep the proper azimuth. To end up anywhere near the site, he could not vary in his direction more than a degree.

Bonn didn't fight the jungle; he flowed through it. His shoulders twisted to bypass entanglements; his head bobbed to duck vines; his feet stepped over the tripping mass of roots and saplings. Warner mimicked his actions but found it difficult to penetrate the foliage the way Bonn did without disturbing it.

Pate had to hold his rifle close to keep it from catching in the bushes and limbs. The scope caps protected its lenses from scratches, but he paid extra attention to keeping anything from striking the scope itself and knocking it out of alignment.

The team had more than seven miles to go to their objective. On a country road or in an open pasture, a man can walk a mile about every fifteen minutes if he is not hurrying. The distance could have been driven in two minutes in a jeep or flown in thirty seconds in a helicopter.

But in the jungle, with the man trying to be quiet, it can easily take all day to travel only a mile. To go three miles is really to push. Even though Bonn's pace was excellent, his progress orderly, and his security good, he knew he would not make the distance by sundown.

The full heat of the day couldn't get to them below the double canopies of treetops, and it was no small favor. Even so, the sweltering air near the ground was oppressive, and the jungle stank in its own compost.

Even boosted by the green bombs, Warner could take no more by midafternoon and whistled for Bonn to stop. He was red-faced and drawing his breath heavily. "Rest," he wheezed, and sank to his knees, shedding his rucksack. Then he actually blacked out for a few minutes, body and mind crashing together.

Bonn was glad to rest. He took two salt tablets and drank the last of the water from his canteen. He had three more full ones, which were not to be touched until he'd refilled the first one.

"We gotta find water," Bonn whispered to Warner, who had quickly gone to sleep. Pate saw Bonn holding up his canteen and waved back that he understood.

Tan had his back to the team, covering the rear. He glanced around at Pate when he heard him get up to move to Bonn. "How much water you got?" Pate asked Bonn.

Bonn fastened the empty canteen back into its cover. "I've finished two canteens so far. I need to get some more for cooking," Bonn said.

"What's your pace count?" Pate asked.

Bonn thought for a second, fatigue hazing his memory. "Twenty-eight hundred meters," he said.

"That's close enough to mine," Pate decided. "What do you say we stay here the rest of the day?"

Bonn pointed to Warner. "That's up to him," he told Pate, who made a sour face.

"That jerkoff don't know shit," Pate said. "The only reason he's talking so big is he knows I'll blow his ass off if he screws up."

Bonn grimaced. "Goddamn, man, we've got enough trouble without fighting among ourselves. I wish you hadn't pulled your gun on him like you did last night."

Pate lowered his voice a bit more. "Look . . . I didn't come out here to get killed. I'll let him play sergeant right up to the point that it affects my ass, understand?"

"Yeah," Bonn said, "I do. But let's try to work together, okay?"

Pate didn't respond to Bonn's plea. He crawled back to his own position, brushing by Warner.

The mosquitoes and leeches soon found the team in its attempt to rest, making reason to move on for better ground a necessary thing. Bonn resumed the point again, with Warner behind, partially recovered from the heat. It seemed like hours to him before they finally found a stream. Bonn knelt and raised his hand; the team paused. Bonn signaled there was water ahead by pointing to his canteens. The others kept watch, while Bonn dropped only one iodine water purification tablet into each canteen since the stream appeared to be swift and clean.

"How far have we gone?" Warner whispered to Bonn.

"Over three clicks," Bonn said, "almost three and a half."

The distance pleased Warner. "We'll set up here tonight. Let's get the radio going and make the SITREP." Bonn nodded and lay down beside the water. Warner popped another green bomb when no one was watching.

Their second night was different from the first in many ways. After the commo was complete, no one spoke at all. Meals were made using heated stream water to reconstitute the food packages, and equipment was shed, but laid close, so sleep could be more comfortable.

A guard shift was established, with each man doing three hours of duty, Warner giving his instructions for the night by written note. The procedures seemed normal. They were functioning as a team. Bonn was assigned first guard and sat up while the others reclined, all of them grouped in a close huddle, so reaching and touching to warn or awaken could be accomplished without unnecessary noise.

Warner actually slept very little. He was tired but felt clearheaded and lucid. There was a certain sense of power in being awake when others thought you were asleep, he mused. The power was of life and death. He throve on the confidence and alertness the pills gave him. They made it so easy to concentrate. He was becoming used to them.

Tan covered himself with his leaf-pattern camouflage poncho liner, the sweat evaporating from his fatigues chilling him. Pate had done the same. Bonn kept his gear packed but put on a dark blue NVA sweatshirt as a light jungle sweater.

It's really quiet up here in Laos, Bonn thought as he leaned against a tree, his weapon across his knees. Night covered the hills rapidly as the sun went down. There wasn't even a good sunset. One moment it was daylight; the next the light was fading and stars began to shine overhead, distant and bright.

Bonn was especially thankful for their unbelievable luck. *We made over three clicks and didn't see one dink.* He congratulated himself. *We must've lost those guys yesterday for good.*

He had noticed Tan's withdrawal since Pate had threatened Warner's life but considered it natural. *Poor guy,* he sympathized, *he must think he's out with a bunch of loonies.*

When the hour came for guard change, Bonn woke Tan and lay down to sleep. He felt he could afford to now. Tan took his place silently, his poncho liner around his shoulders, protecting the team in its most vulnerable time.

Once the war had been for others, not for him. Hue had been so majestic and peaceful, built like the Imperial City at Peking, and he had studied there, removed from the vulgarities of soldiers and their intrusions into the academic and social functions of his life. Even the suburbs of Saigon, where the affluent lived, walled, gated, treelined, were immune from the war then.

But the rockets came. Huge 122 mm cylinders with solid-fuel motors and blunt nose cones. Spin-stabilized, unguided. Rockets that shrieked in from ten or more kilometers away, loaded with chance and death.

A rocket had hit his house. He wasn't home that one night, of all nights. The rocket had come down a little short of the city. It was only pointed, it couldn't really be aimed. It had no tactical targets. No ammunition dumps. No airfields. No fuel storage sites. Just the city. Just people. It was fired to terrorize.

What could a sleeping bride know of such things? How is it possible to match such delicate flesh against high explosives? What could a rocket gunner in the jungle know of the true target of the big missile he mounted on a slanted stand, wired, and shot away?

It would have left the launcher in a boom and scream, tail afire, accelerating, the earth blurred below.

She would have been so unknowing, so small.

It would reach an apogee, then nose down from its shallow arc, all of Saigon ahead. It would go straight to *his* house. Go straight to *her*.

In the dark no one could see his tears.

18

Day blossomed in a manner unknown to most civilized people, who live with walls between themselves and the world. It was still and cool as golden light touched the tree-tops, making the dew glitter on the leaves and moss, the jungle morning perfectly calm and serene.

Pate held last guard. He gently poked Bonn and Tan with a stick to wake them. Warner was already awake, eyes open. Tan roused at the poke, feeling rested. Water for coffee was boiled with small lumps of C-4 plastic explosive stuck to the bottom of their canteen cups, but no words were exchanged as they drank the morning coffee.

To speak would have been to begin the day officially, and no one seemed to be in the mood to do that. It was the kind of morning that raises the spirits, when people look forward to the day. In another context, the team could have been four sportsmen enjoying a pleasant, slow awakening before a hunt.

The fear and hate of the previous day seemed an absurdity. Pate even passed Warner a canteen out of courtesy when he saw that to get his own, Warner would have had to move from a comfortable slump.

"Damn, I hate to put on all that shit and go looking for the site," Bonn said, his web gear at his feet.

"I know what you mean," Warner muttered, his second cup of coffee in his hands and a cigarette in his mouth.

Bonn reached toward his rucksack for a candy bar, and a

hint of motion in the jungle caught his eye. He turned away
from the group and looked out into the forest.

"This is the way it used to be in Mississippi on a summer
morning when I was in the Scouts," Pate said, and Warner's
eyebrows arched slightly.

"You were a Scout?" he asked.

"Sure was," Pate said. "I would've made it to Eagle, but
we didn't have the money for all the projects I needed to
do." Bonn was listening to the nearly whispered conversation with one ear, but the other was tuned outside camp. He
was still looking at the place where he thought he had seen
something move.

"I was an Eagle," Warner said. "Only six of us in my
troop made it."

Pate grinned and shook his head. "Shit, I would have
never—"

Bonn suddenly clasped one hand over Pate's mouth and
lifted his AKM with the other. Tan and Warner quickly
grabbed their weapons, concern contorting their features.
Pate's rifle was behind him, out of quick reach.

A volley of shots cracked in the morning reverie, unrea-
sonably loud, as rude as a slap in the face. Fresh earth flew
up in spurts through the camp as the bullets hit.

Bonn fired off an instant return burst, the clatter of his
AKM bolt like a worn-out jackhammer, giving the team the
opportunity to scatter. More incoming rifle fire raked their
rucksacks, tossing fabric shreds in the air.

Bonn scampered out of the line of fire, heart almost bursting, trigger finger down, his AKM blasting into the bushes.
Tan backrolled out of the way, unable to locate the enemy
but smacking off single shots in all directions.

"Squad to our rear," Bonn yelled, changing magazines, as
Pate tore the lens caps off his scope, huddling against a tree
trunk for protection. He held his fire, wanting a target but
unable to see one as nervous sweat popped off his forehead.

Warner dived into a nest of roots, going for their very
bottom. Several bullets slashed through the tangle, past his
face, stinging his cheek with wood splinters that brought

blood. He could hear six to eight weapons banging away at one another.

Bonn fired and moved, breathing like a sprinter, then fired and moved again, so the NVA would keep hitting where he had been. Bonn saw two of the attack party, hunched men, running low as they advanced, taking cover in the high grass, and Tan stitched it with a full magazine, watching his fire beat the grass the way hail pelts wheat. A body bounced up out of the dancing grass, arms swinging like the vanes of a windmill.

Twenty-five meters away from Bonn, men shouted and cursed in a language he could not understand, trying to find him, shooting into bits the areas where they thought he was.

Teeth bared, face flushed with exertion, Bonn was jumping and diving from tree to tree, never letting his weapon cool. He hit someone out there who screamed, and then another man, who tried to run away.

The firefight ended abruptly, as the single survivor of the ambush patrol crashed madly back into the jungle, away from the morning's encounter with death.

"I go get!" Tan yammered, flying into the forest after the escaping soldier. Bonn saw him, but Tan was gone before he could yell. Pate rose slowly from behind his tree, his rifle yet unfired. He wasn't accustomed to close firefights with no definite targets. He sickly examined a bullet hole in the trunk of his tree, very near to where his head had been.

Warner waited, coiled in the banyan roots, not willing to trust the cease-fire. He was choking down his own terror, biting his fist.

Tan caught sight of the running man, who was still moving at top speed. "Help me, I'm hurt!" Tan called out to him in Vietnamese, acting as if he were injured, by covering his face with his hands and running erratically. The man stopped, staring back at Tan, and saw too late that it was not one of his own men. The pause was fatal.

Tan shot him off his feet with a fast burst, then walked up and kicked the corpse to make sure.

Bonn and Pate checked the four bodies. One of them was

still alive, but only barely. Pate collected the weapons, stripped the bolts out of them, and threw them away. Bonn checked their bloody pouches for ammunition, to replenish what the team had lost. All of the men in the attacking patrol wore NVA fatigues and carried full ammo belts. Their pockets were filled with personal items and papers, bullet holes in their photos and letters, blood gluing the pages together.

The septic smell of bowel was sickening. One of the soldiers had been shot several times across the lower stomach and the combined force of the bullets had perforated and exploded his gut, like a rubber sack of greasy offal hit with a nail-spiked club. Bonn held his breath as he took the dead man's magazines, listening to the distinct hisses and bubbles of intestinal gas escaping from the shredded belly.

The wounded man had his eyes open but did not seem to know what was happening around him. His torso was distended with multiple hits, his back possibly broken. He could live only a few minutes longer.

Tan returned to the camp, where Bonn and Pate were watching the soldier die. He knelt beside the man, speaking to him in his own language. The Asian tried to reply, but the effort was more than he could manage. Tan frowned and removed his bayonet from its scabbard, placing the point of it over the soldier's heart. Calmly using both hands, he drove the blade into him with one forceful motion.

Pate and Bonn grimaced but said nothing. The man twisted for an instant, then stopped moving for eternity. Tan withdrew the blade and cleaned it on the dead man's uniform.

"He can no talk to us, no good for him," Tan declared.

Warner walked out of the camp, his cheek swelling from the splinters, holding his AKM up at the ready. Pate looked at him, almost spoke, but changed his mind and stalked away.

"We killed all of them," Bonn said. Warner lowered his weapon and fumbled out a cigarette, trying to hold the rifle and light a match all at the same time.

They gathered their gear. Bonn started to sling his rucksack onto his shoulders when he saw the rips in it. *"Oh, no,"* he said aloud as he untied the flap and pulled out the radio. Four direct hits had junked it, even ripping open the battery. "At least we still have your radio," Bonn said in disgust to Warner, who was watching.

"My—my radio was in the bag with the snoopers!" Warner said. "The walkie talkie too!"

Pate hit him with a roundhouse punch squarely on his swollen jaw, knocking Warner to his knees. Bonn grabbed at Pate but stopped himself when Pate drew his fist back at him. "Don't move!" Pate threatened.

Warner was doubled over and cowering on the ground, his weapon lying untouched beside him. "I'm sorry!" Warner choked out. *"Stop, please!"* Pate had not expected the fight to be over so quickly. He hovered over Warner, ready to kick him, chest heaving with his temper.

"You bastard!" Pate cursed, spit flying from the edge of his lips. "You may have killed us all!"

Bonn saw Tan lift his AKM. "No one moves, I shoot," Tan said evenly. They all froze in their tableau of discord. Bonn and Pate raised their hands as if they were prisoners.

"We fight Communist soldier, not fight friends," Tan said.

The shock of Tan's action and Warner's surrender took the hostility from Pate. He let his hands drop to his sides. "Right, right . . ." Pate muttered. "I'm sorry, Warner."

Warner had no intention of reaching for his gun or making hostile moves. He stood up weakly, a spreading bruise blackening his eye and cheek. He worked his jaw experimentally. "Okay, sure," he said to Pate. "I understand, we'll make out the best way we can." He reached down and picked up his AKM in an inoffensive way, pretending to ignore Tan.

"Let's get the hell out of here!" Bonn said, hurrying them. "Everybody knows where we are by now!" The team packed up quickly, and Bonn checked the compass azimuth as they rushed from the camp, moving as fast as the terrain would allow.

The dead men behind them were North Vietnamese, not Pathet Lao troops, Bonn knew. They were probably part of the defense force around Phu Chom Voi. Three kilometers would certainly be within the patrol radius of the guarding troops at the site. North Vietnam was getting closer by the footstep.

Warner's face hurt, but not as badly as his pride. *It will be good to kill them,* he promised himself, and Pate would be the first. Then the gook. But what about Bonn? Uncertainty clouded his plotting. Bonn had tried to stop Pate, hadn't he? Warner wavered in his murderous thoughts, but he found an excuse soon enough.

Bonn knew about the snoopers, too. He would have to die for that, if for no other reason. Satisfied with his decision, Warner congratulated himself on handling the situation with Pate, knowing that being weaker than Pate would work better than being stronger. He took a fresh green bomb and washed it down with a swallow from his canteen.

Bonn counted the pace, knowing that behind him the team was doing the same thing, perhaps each man considering every meter passed one less left to live. Irritation had set in on Bonn, and he wanted out. *I've got to live through this,* he thought with conviction. *I can't die because of this fucked-up team!*

Two hours later, reinforced by the speed, Warner halted the advance, calling everyone in close for a meeting. "This is it," he whispered. "This is Charlie's territory for real. We can't go in there screwed up. I've got to have the best from all of you, understand?"

Three deadly serious faces stared back at him. Pate raised a finger. "What happens if we get in the shit?" he asked.

"We won't try to stand and fight; they'll outnumber us a hundred to one. We'll have to run for it," Warner said, making the wiser choice.

"I think we're five hundred meters from the site now, if we find it at all," Bonn said, "if we're on a straight course."

"Okay, keep it tight," Warner said, and motioned for Bonn to move out. Bonn crouched and began to pick a path through the foliage. Warner let him get ten meters ahead before he followed, turning to indicate to Pate to maintain the interval.

The team, members well spread out, chose each step as if they were in a known minefield. The late-afternoon sun threw long shadows in the trees, and the birds and animals went about their business as usual, undisturbed by the careful movements of the team.

Bonn wondered just when his foot touched down last in Laos and stepped into North Vietnam. The pink border line he had looked at so many times on maps became a sore reality. There was just no way of knowing. The jungle was all the same.

Bonn paid close attention to the sounds of the wildlife, figuring that the closer they came to the site, the fewer animals he would hear. He listened for voices, or the sounds of motors or generators, and strained his eyes looking for anything that might be man-made, an orderly disruption in the randomness of the jungle.

He stopped to rest every few moments, shifting his gaze from side to side, unable to see in every direction at once and regretting it.

The AKM in his hands seemed heavier and bulkier than at any time before, catching on more branches and vines, slowing him down considerably, as he removed each delaying obstruction with desperate patience.

The soles of his canvas shoes, much more pliable and thinner than jungle boots, became too clumsy. He wished he were barefoot.

Bonn willed his heartbeat to be regular and controlled his breath. He steadied his nerves, trying to be slow, deliberate, methodical, and a survivor.

He scanned the area before him fully every few moments, from left to right and up and down. He was looking up when he saw the first sign of human habitation. It was a platform built in a tree, partially camouflaged. He could see the bottom clearly from where he stood.

Was this how the deer felt, discovering the hunter? Bonn

halted, his sweat icing on his forehead. He made no sudden
moves. He was taking no chances. He inched down into the
bushes to study the lookout post.

Warner saw Bonn sink from sight and did the same, not
knowing what was happening. Bonn was making a decision
based on the condition of the platform. It was in good condition, not rotten the way unattended and unrepaired wood
becomes in the jungle.

They're here, Bonn decided. *We've found them!* He reasoned the NVA was not likely to have the same type of
security around its bases as the Americans, so he ruled out
trip flares and barbed wire. *They'll have people out here instead,* he told himself.

Bonn looked at the sky. It would be dark soon. He
crawled back to where Warner waited, never exposing himself above the ferns and bushes.

"There's a sentry platform in the trees about fifty meters
from here," he said to Warner, whose eyes narrowed at the
news. "Since it'll be dark before long, we ought to sit right
here to watch, see if they put anybody on it." Warner nodded, pleasing Bonn with how well he took the news, and
rose up enough to wave in Pate and Tan. "We stay here
tonight," Warner instructed them, "and keep down! There's
a goddamned guard platform just out front of us!"

Tan pulled the Starlight out of its carrying tube and
checked its adjustments in preparation for the night. Pate
inspected his rifle and scope. The team formed a well-hidden
space under the surface of the natural growth, cutting the
lower plants away with their knives and pressing them
down, but making sure to leave the higher ones undisturbed.

Tan found a place in the foliage where he could observe
the platform, after Bonn showed him exactly where it was.
No one removed his equipment for the night. The sleeping
arrangement was two up and two down, Warner and Pate
taking first guard, sighting up at the platform every fifteen
minutes throughout their shift with the Starlight until mid-
night. Pate slept. Warner throve on his dextroamphet-
amines, tense and alert.

Bonn and Tan took on the watch until dawn, keeping the schedule, the Starlight's electronic eye dissipating the darkness like a nocturnal Cyclops with supernatural powers.

The vigil was rewarded only shortly before sunrise. Tan heard the man approach before he saw him and focused the tree in the viewer. A lone soldier began to climb the tree, his image shimmering in the greenish scope, using the thick vines that wrapped around the trunk for handholds. A portable field phone was slung from his shoulder, probably to be attached to wires already run up to the platform.

The man went up in the tree in a manner that suggested he was familiar with the duty, pulled himself onto the platform, then sat, busying himself with the field phone and his grocery sack.

Tan handed the Starlight to Bonn, who took a long look. *They must think they're secure,* he mused, *to post their guards only by ones instead of twos. That's all the better for us,* he knew. It seemed the guard tower was occupied only during the daylight hours, so it might be part of the very outermost ring of security.

We must have only just missed the guy leaving yesterday, Bonn realized with a shudder. He tapped Warner, who woke from a seminap and sat up swiftly. "There's a dude up there in the tree," Bonn said in Warner's ear, through cupped hands.

The first dim light of dawn was outlining the jungle. "Let's get him down to talk," Warner said under his breath, feeling aggressive and confident. Bonn wondered briefly if Warner was serious, coming on so strongly, but nodded yes.

Bonn slowly took off his equipment, drew his knife, and motion for Tan to do the same, showing him in hand signals they wanted the man in the platform alive. Tan understood perfectly.

Warner aroused Pate, whispering to him what was going to take place, and Pate calmly sighted the guard through his scope so nothing could go wrong enough to get Tan or Bonn killed. Warner lifted the Starlight to watch the capture.

Bonn went first, crawling under the dense growth, showing Tan the best way to go without creating a revealing wave at the tops of the bushes. Tan was proving good at the art of stealth, weaseling along behind Bonn, making no errors.

Bonn veered slightly to the side of the target tree, discovering the trail the guard had used. Once in the open, he stood up and silently walked the short distance to the base of the tree.

A good twenty feet above them, the guard sat directly in the center of the platform, right beside the access hole. The cracks between the boards showed the sky, and it was turning lighter by the minute.

Bonn ran his fingers all around the tree and found the commo wire. He cut it with a deft pull of the knife and knew the commitment was made to follow through.

Tan touched his shoulder, pointing with his bayonet first to himself, then up at the guard. Bonn stepped back so Tan could climb. It all seemed almost unreal in the half-light of dawn to Bonn. He went through the motions, feeling strangely detached.

Tan slipped off his shoes and shirt and laid them on the ground. He clamped the bayonet in his teeth, then went up the tree, monkeylike in his sureness.

Tan was quickly under the platform. The guard was still unaware of the threat, placidly looking hundreds of meters to his front while the enemy was only inches from him.

Bonn picked up a small piece of wood and tossed it out into the bushes. It hit with a deceptive rustle. The guard leaned over to see what had happened, and Tan catapulted himself through the hole in the platform, swinging at the surprised man with an open palm.

The soldier dodged Tan's slap, backing away, but Tan had the ferocity of a tiger. He slashed the man with his bayonet, opening a gash across his arm and shoulder, then rammed the heel of his free hand savagely into the stunned guard's nose, blinding him with pain.

The soldier was beaten before he understood what was happening. Tan was sitting on him, blade pressed hard against his throat. "Cry out, dog, and I will kill you!" Tan hissed.

Bonn popped through the platform hole, seeing the blood spattered on the two men. "Everything all right?" he asked.

"Yes, very good," Tan uttered savagely, killer hate in his voice. Bonn crowded onto the platform, waving to Warner that everything was okay. Tan tied the guard hand and foot in commo wire and gagged him with a bloody rag. Bonn was ready to ask how they were going to get their prisoner below when Tan simply pushed the man off the edge.

Climbing down the tree, Bonn began to appreciate what Tan was all about. It scared him. Tan waded into the bushes and jerked the dazed man to his feet. The fall had been cushioned somewhat by the heavy foliage.

After gathering his shoes and shirt, Tan pushed the bleeding prisoner back to the overnight camp. He kicked the man's feet out from under him when they arrived.

Pate and Warner moved to give Tan room. Bonn put his own ammunition pouches and equipment back on as the interrogation began. It took ten long, agonizing minutes for the soldier to die, but he answered all of Tan's questions. Tan killed him a step at a time, smothering the screams with the gag, as the three Americans watched in unbelieving silence.

Tan followed his ritual of cleaning his bayonet blade on the victim's uniform and turned to face the team. "He say base camp near here, maybe two hundred meter. Many soldier there all the time. They have radar machine to see airplane. Trail go to base. They know we come, have patrol busy to find us everywhere."

Warner wiped his lips, starting to lose the green bomb's edge. "Goddamn, Tan, why'd you have to slice that son of a bitch up like that?" he said.

Tan silenced Warner with a glance of undisguised hate. "He *Communist* soldier, Sergeant," Tan said, as if talking to a child.

"I cut the commo wire," Bonn reminded Tan. "How often was he to report in?"

Tan was clearing a small spot in the dirt to draw a simple diagram. "He call every hour. We hurry now, have almost one hour. This is VC camp, look."

Tan's marks in the earth were very revealing. They depicted three square buildings in a rough triangle. "Number one hooch, where radar machine stay," Tan informed the team, "is most north place. Then is hooch for radio sets, here, west, and last is where soldier sleep. They are not Vietnam soldier; they like American, maybe Russian."

"Russians!" Pate exclaimed. "I've got to nail one of those bastards! I've got to!"

"Where are the NVA that are protecting the camp?" Bonn asked.

Tan buttoned his shirt. "All around. One platoon stay in camp, two more patrol all time. Communist stay camouflaged, move all time, not like American soldier," he said to Bonn, who thought he detected a note of hostility in the statement.

Warner made some decisions. "Bonn, you go point. When we get to the site, take out your camera and get as many pictures as possible. Tan, you back him up. Pate, you and I will cover them. Don't fire unless you absolutely have to, understand?"

They made a complete equipment check, making sure that everything was in place and secured so it would not rattle or snag and that their weapons and magazines were in perfect order. With no further discussion, they moved out to do the job. The objective was just ahead.

Warner's personal objective was also at hand. He palmed another pill down, then another. Capsule courage. He held his weapon tightly because his hands trembled.

The morning situation reports by the CCN communications officer seemed normal enough, because half the patrols had not yet reported. Team Tango was one of them. The officer initialed the paper and went back to his other duties. A second report would be out that afternoon, so no action was required unless the same team still had not responded.

It was not unusual for a situation report to be twenty-four or even forty-eight hours late. The conditions in which the teams operated did not always allow the opportunity of setting up long enough to make a call just when the relay aircraft was on station.

Bonn had moved only fifty meters when he saw the first enemy patrol. It was several men walking casually through the woods, weapons slung except for the point man, who carried his AK-47 in the crook of his arm. None of them appeared cautious. Bonn stayed low as they passed, the sickness of fear in his throat, the boost of adrenaline in his body.

He had to make himself go on. *This is like mice trying to bell the cat,* he told himself in a silly thought provoked by the intense pressure. He had to draw each breath consciously, starting and stopping his lungs each time he wanted to listen.

One hundred meters from the team's starting point it happened again. Three Vietnamese, all in camouflaged uniforms and further concealed by fresh green foliage tied to their caps and equipment, had stopped to rest. Bonn did not see them in time.

The sitting soldiers heard Bonn and the team pass only a few meters away, concealed in the trees. One of the Vietnamese spoke out loud to them, under the impression he was hearing one of their own patrols. The other two men with him laughed, and Tan laughed back, still walking, but motioning frantically at Bonn to hurry.

Drugged and awake too long, Warner had started to hallucinate. Everything seemed unreal and distant, his walking body separated from his hot, speeding brain. The NVA troops were pop-up targets, flat photos of men.

Warner had pointed his weapon, almost ready to fire on the NVA patrol, but Pate thumped him in the ribs with his rifle barrel, and startled, Warner moved out at a double time to catch Tan.

Oh, Christ! Bonn screeched inwardly. *We just missed it by a hair,* so he put enough distance between the enemy patrol and his team to where he could stop and settle his heart.

He turned back and looked at Tan, rolling his eyes in relief. Bonn could not believe that it was happening the way it was. His stomach was souring, and he could taste bile in his mouth. *I was crazy to do this.* He condemned himself. *I just didn't know!* He moved his hand nervously from his weapon to his rucksack to check again for the camera, realizing it was the third time he'd done it.

He closed his eyes and relaxed, replacing his hand on his AKM. He knew his condition wasn't caused so much by the enemy, since he had been in close contact with them before, as by his own team. He did not know what any of them was going to do at any time, and it was worrisome as hell.

He came to his feet again, ears tuned to the crash a leaf makes when it falls, the roar of the breeze in the treetops, and the pecking and chirping of birds a kilometer away. The torrent of blood circulating in his veins was too loud, underscoring everything with a dull thunder. When he allowed himself to breathe, it was such a rasping sound that he wondered why it did not draw fire.

Drying vegetation under his canvas shoes shattered in a deafening manner, blending with the amplified rustling of the bushes he pushed out of his way. Each footfall was an earthquake, and the sweat oozing from his brow stung his eyes, since he was afraid to blink and miss something.

Then he found the site.

Bonn dropped to his knees and rubbed his eyes. It had been concealed so well he had almost walked into it. An elaborate roof of netting and artificial treetops covered it all. Spread out in the compound were the three buildings Tan had described, but they were concrete bunkers, not huts.

The roofs of the bunkers had been sodded and planted, a trick Bonn recognized as brilliant, since the infrared photography detected the false camouflage by the condition of the foliage, the living plants registering differently in the infrared spectrum from the cut ones.

Vietnamese guards were posted at the door of the largest

bunker, the sunlight casting the shadow of the netting above on them, their well-oiled AK-47s gleaming dully. An oddly shaped dome, painted flat black, covered the roof of the bunker.

Bonn laid his weapon down, fumbled the 35 mm camera from his rucksack pocket, and set the basic adjustments with numb fingers. He began his photography with the dome.

Tan could not see into the compound well but knew Bonn was getting it all on film. He had his weapon on full auto, ready to engage anything that interrupted the precious moment. He felt at last he was helping to hurt the enemy in a big way.

Warner and Pate had gone down into concealment when Bonn did, and Pate shouldered his rifle, to take a better look forward with his sniperscope. *

Warner seemed too nervous to sit still. Pate noticed and laid a steadying hand on his arm. Warner's head snapped around at the touch, and Pate was shocked by the expression he saw on his team leader's face. Warner's eyes were bulging, and his nostrils flared. His lips were partly open, and rapid, shallow breathing wheezed through them.

"Get up, go and cover Bonn!" Warner said to Pate, his voice cracking. Pate hesitated. "Go!" Warner said, and Pate was glad to do it, to give him as much room as he wanted.

Warner was at the moment of truth. There was no more control. No more time. He wanted to scream, but he didn't. He waited, watching Pate vanish into the bush. *I've got to kill them,* he thought. *Now! Now!*

He thumbed the AKM fire selector down off safe and, pointing it in the direction of the team, pulled the trigger. The thirty rounds in the magazine flamed out of the muzzle as fast as the pistoning bolt could feed and fire them, Warner's emotion finding release with the bullets, a demonic leer twisting his features.

Bonn was pressing the shutter for the eighth time when the shooting started. It took only two seconds for the clatter of fire to begin and cease, but he was down before the last round had left the chamber. The trees smacked with hits all around him, leaves falling from the limbs.

Tan flattened, thinking they had been hit from the rear, wondering why he didn't hear return fire from Warner or Pate. He saw Pate scamper in, trying to get out of the way of the bullets.

A silence, the lull before the storm, followed. The guards in the compound were on their bellies, and each security patrol halted in its tracks. All heads turned in the direction of the gunfire.

"Oh, shit!" Bonn cursed, believing the team ambushed, and opened up on the Vietnamese he could see in the compound, instantly bringing down one who was racing out of the radar bunker, the stray rounds gouging concrete around the doorway.

Pate looked back for Warner. He wasn't there. "Let's go!" Pate shouted, thinking, like Bonn, an ambush was in progress. Bonn crawled backward and bumped into Tan, and their eyes met, in realization that everything had gone wrong.

"Where's Warner?" Bonn blurted, reaching Pate.

"I don't know. Let's get the hell out!" Pate said, automatic fire breaking out from the compound.

"Tan, come on!" Bonn cried as Tan threw a devastating sweep of fire that scattered the running soldiers in the compound.

"Come on!" Bonn yelled again.

Tan glanced over his shoulder. "Go back!" he said. "I cover!" At that moment a counterattack rushed from the compound, firing madly, homing in on Bonn's shouts.

"Crazy motherfucker!" Pate snarled, assuming a kneeling position and squinting into his scope. The big rifle boomed, its recoil slamming Pate's shoulder, and a running soldier coming out of the bunker area dropped instantly.

Bonn expended a full magazine, trying to give Tan the chance to get up and escape, but it was becoming horribly clear he could not. Pate grabbed Bonn by the pack straps, almost jerked him off his feet, and ran for safety with Bonn in tow.

Tan did not even look back. He was living the last few moments of his life, and he had more Communist soldiers around him than he had ever seen. He didn't care that he was going to die. It only mattered to him how many he killed.

A score of them were lying dead in the bushes, before the North Vietnamese got close to him. It was only after all his magazines were empty. Tan dropped his overheated AKM and did the unexpected as they rushed. He drew his bayonet and attacked, screaming, *"Sat cong, sat cong!"*

A burst caught him in mid-leap, but he fell on the nearest man, wildly stabbing and slashing. Another blast staggered him in the act, and he collapsed, committing one last vengeful murder as he did so.

It was his final retribution for his beloved wife the Vietcong had so accidentally, so deliberately killed with their rockets. They had taken everything away from him the night she died. He died willingly, nothing else to lose.

19

Bonn and Pate ran for their lives. Bark flew from the trees as shots ripped by them and into the forest.

Pate's longer legs hurdled fallen trees and bushes more easily than Bonn, but Bonn, knowing when to dodge and duck before obstacles hit him, had superior field experience that made up for that.

The gunfire spurred them on like whips cracking across their backs. Such was their speed and haste that they ran right over a perimeter patrol that was down and taking cover, both sides too involved in their own situations to exchange fire.

Bonn recognized the trail ahead near where they had stayed the night. "C'mon!" he puffed to Pate, tacking to the left.

Bonn took the lead, legs pumping, racing through lighter foliage on the edge of the trail. Pate held his rifle chest high and stayed right with him, his mighty strides eating up the distance.

The firing had ceased, but that was nothing to Bonn. The NVA could be right on their tails. He tried to think, to plan something, as he plunged toward Laos.

Fifteen minutes and a thousand meters from the radar site, Bonn flopped into a gully, and Pate fell in beside him. Both of them had to recover from the run, and they lay and gasped like fish out of water. Their hands and forearms were bloody from grass and thorn wounds, the sweat stinging into the cuts, diluting the blood and making it run freely. Their web gear was full of twigs and bits of vines that had caught and broken in their flight.

Buttons were missing off their uniforms, some grenades were gone, and their gear was in a general state of disorder. Pate had lost his hat and two canteens. Bonn reached inside his shirt and extracted his camera, thankful it had not been lost as well.

"I guess we're all fucked up," Pate wheezed. "They killed Tan and Warner, we ain't got no goddamned radio, and they're coming after us right now."

Bonn wouldn't hear it. "No!" he retorted. "We'll get away, we have to, we've got to get this film back."

Pate swallowed and nodded, understanding.

"Okay," he asked Bonn, "what do we do now?"

Bonn was counting his AK magazines but answered at once, no doubt in his mind about what needed to be done. "We'll E and E out of here, make visual contact with one of our aircraft, and arrange for a pickup."

"What about that son of a bitch in Lac Sao? Do you wanna go in there and get him?" Pate asked, feeling his strength returning.

Bonn had forgotten Sugar. "This film is more important," he argued. "Since Warner dumped the snoopers, we don't have shit to show for this mission."

Pate stood guard, watching through his riflescope at the area they had just come from, while Bonn took out his map and compass and tried to figure approximately where they were. He looked on the map for a spot that might make a suitable place where they could hide and signal a plane.

"Hey," Pate said in a low voice, "there's somebody out there!"

Bonn folded the map and tucked it securely into his shirt pocket. "What does it look like?" he asked, taking a last compass reading.

Pate was holding very still. "Gooks," he said, "in the grass. There they come, must be twenty of 'em!"

Bonn peeked over the rim of the gully. A well-organized

unit of the NVA was spreading out across the broad green clearing. "They must think we're waiting for a chopper."

"We should be so goddamned lucky," Pate replied, ranging on the man he thought was the patrol leader. "I could really fuck those people up from here," he hinted to Bonn.

"Don't shoot!" Bonn warned. "Save your ammo for when we really need it! We've got to stay out of sight and not pick any fights!"

Pate reluctantly capped the sights on the rifle. "Okay, no sweat, man," he assured Bonn.

"Tan had the damn Starlight," Bonn said, checking his pockets for his all-important map and compass. "What have you got left?"

"A bad attitude and a high-powered rifle," Pate said.

After all their equipment was repacked, they left the protection of the gully, traveling southwest. They crept along the remainder of the day, no thought of stopping to rest or eat, only hoping to stay ahead of their pursuers.

By sundown the physical demands of the day had taken full toll. Bonn managed to find a good spot to sleep overnight, deep into a heavy concentration of bamboo.

Packs and weapons were shed, and at first they just lay and tried to find the strength to eat. Bonn realized that all day he had not really felt the heat, hunger, or thirst, in his ambition to get away.

The lack of attention to his body was hitting him hard. His muscles were tightening, intestines knotting, and his tongue was swelling. He took a swallow of water from his belt canteen, and the pain of it made him choke.

The second sip came more easily, and the third opened the track all the way to his stomach. He was overcome by a ravenous hunger, and he dug into his supply for a LRRP ration, tempted to eat it dry. It was only by stiff self-control that he made himself pour the stream water from his canteen into the packet and give it a few minutes to soak.

Pate had done the same, and together they ate the cold mush with their plastic spoons, scraping out the corners of the packets to get all the food that was trapped in the folds.

They ate the candy bars the rations contained and felt good enough to make coffee afterward.

With a meal under their belts, and hot coffee in their canteen cups, morale improved considerable. The sun was going down, and twilight settled comfortably into the encampment.

"Damn shame we lost Tan and Warner," Pate said with as much feeling as Bonn had ever heard him put into words. "I didn't like either of 'em, but I hate to see the gooks get anybody."

The statement puzzled Bonn. "I thought you were going to kill Warner yourself," he said.

Pate frowned. "I got a temper," he said, not telling Bonn anything new, "he needed killin', but I don't really think I would have done it."

"You could have fooled me," Bonn said truthfully. "I could understand Warner, but what did you have against Tan?" he asked, curious to hear Pate's point or view.

"He was a gook," Pate said. "My business is shooting gooks. I ain't got no use for them little bastards."

Bonn decided not to press the issue. "Where are you from, Pate?" he asked, wanting to know something about the man he had been shackled to by the Army.

Pate flipped a bug off his leg. "Mississippi. Down around Jackson, little place you probably never heard of," he said, watching the bug land and crawl away.

"I'm from Florida," Bonn volunteered.

Pate grunted but didn't ask for details. There was a long silence. "How old are you?" Pate suddenly asked, a note of interest in his question.

Bonn hesitated, Pate having found a soft spot. "I'm almost twenty," he said defensively.

"They musta got you young," Pate gibed. "You RA or U.S.?"

"U.S.," Bonn said. "They drafted me right out of high school."

Pate sighed. "I joined this motherfucker," he said. "I figured I'd never get out of my hometown if I didn't."

"You married or anything like that?" Bonn asked.

"Naw," Pate said. "I had me a girlfriend or two, but one of 'em came up pregnant, so I took the bus to Jackson and enlisted. I send her money every month for the baby."

"Boy or girl?" Bonn asked.

"I don't know," Pate said with resignation. "She won't write me back. You got a girl?"

"A good one. I'm planning on getting married when I get home."

"*If* you get home," Pate said.

"What kind of work did you used to do?" Bonn asked, to change the subject.

"Anything I could. Hauled produce. Plowed. What'd you do?"

"Warehouse. It paid pretty good, too. I bought my own car, a Corvair Monza that needed engine work. I fixed it myself. Have you got a car?"

"Hell, no. All I could afford was an old pickup. Had to use that to haul. When I get my car, it'll be a four-twenty-seven."

"My Monza is a twin-carb six. What I want one day is a Porsche, a four-cam roller crank Carrera. They'll go a hundred and thirty, and they're only four cylinders."

"I ain't got no use for them foreign cars. Buncha junk. Anyway, nothing's faster than a big block Ford."

Bonn started to tell Pate differently but thought better of it. Instead, he thought about the Carrera he wanted. One just like the rounded, hunched-down silver gray coupe that had once raced past him on a rural road, a metallic blur with a sharp snarl of exhaust. Its dual vented engine lid and taillights were all he could see until it vanished around a curve far ahead. There was no way his Monza could even stay with the Porsche, two extra cylinders or not.

"What are you going to do when you get back?" Bonn asked.

"I don't know. Not much back there for me. My granny's dead now. She kinda raised me. My momma's always drinkin', hangin' out in the bars. My real daddy got killed in Korea in 1952. He was a ranger."

"I'm sorry," Bonn said.

"Yeah. You know I always wondered how things would have been if he'd come home. Momma wouldn't have gotten married again. She wouldn't have been messin' around with them drunks. My stepdad used to get drunk and beat the hell out of me. I finally hit him in the head with a fence post. That was the day I left home."

Pate picked up his rifle, contemplating it. "My real old man got the Silver Star. Momma showed it to me a long time ago. She ended up pawning it. He got killed gettin' it, and she *pawned* it to buy a goddamn *drink*. You know, when I was really little, I used to watch movies about World War Two. I thought it was the Japanese that had killed my dad. They got slant eyes like the Chinese. Like these gooks here. That's why I hate these bastards."

Bonn allowed that bit of information about Pate's past to sink in, leaving a decent interval between questions. "You know," Bonn recalled, "I never did hear Warner say anything about where he came from."

The badge of an Eagle Scout flashed across Pate's memory. "Forget it," he told Bonn, "you'll never find out now," and he settled down to sleep, finished with the conversation.

Bonn reclined on his rucksack, holding his AKM across his knees. He watched Pate go quickly to sleep, knowing he would have to take first guard. He hoped his choice of thicket would keep the enemy off them.

Thailand had been the first place he'd ever heard of in the region. It was beside what was still referred to in his old geography book as French Indochina. Thailand had been the subject of a *Weekly Reader* issue while he'd been in grade school, about how the country was once old Siam, and featured a photo of Yul Brynner in *The King and I*.

The first he'd ever heard of Laos had been in a newspaper article he'd read as a student in 1959, about an obscure battle there and places called the Plain of Reeds and the Plain of Jars.

Vietnam had popped up for him in newsmagazines in 1962. There were color photos of suntanned American advisers against lush green backgrounds. It was a place President Kennedy was becoming associated with at the time, and the 1963 magazine and TV news was about a dragon lady named Madame Nhu and a coup that assassinated South Vietnam's president, Diem. Three weeks later Kennedy himself was dead.

Thailand, Vietnam, Cambodia, and Laos were far away, even small on a world globe if you took the trouble to find them. He'd paid scant attention to news from Vietnam before he was in the Army, and not even a great deal afterward. Vietnam was too distant, and the Army too big, for it to involve him. He'd just come out of school, just got his car, his girl, and for Christ's sake, it had still been *summer* when the draft notice came.

Now he was in the middle of it all, propelled over the years from a safe grade-school desk and the *Weekly Reader* to the reality of Laos, where he could die or be maimed at any moment, maybe blown apart like the gut-shot soldier at the camp ambush. It made every minute a separate worry, made hours weigh like ages. It was better not even to think about whole days and nights.

Exhaustion had precedence over fear, and in a while Bonn's head slowly rolled back, his eyes closed, and the two survivors of the team slept soundly.

20

Covey stayed on station for an extra hour, flying and waiting for the report from Team Tango, but it never came. CCN was alerted, and Tango was put on the priority list in the commo shack.

"This is over forty-eight hours with no contact," the radio operator said. "I think those guys are in trouble."

The officer regretfully agreed mentally with him but did not say so aloud. "Would you get me the mission folder on Tango?" he asked the operator. "I don't remember ever meeting any of those boys."

When the slim file arrived, the officer sat and read through it from beginning to end, letting a fresh cup of coffee go cold beside him.

"Who was responsible for this team?" he asked the clerk, a wave of anger in his voice. The young specialist shrugged. "Okay," the officer said, "get me MACV on the horn."

It took only a moment for the priority call to be patched through on the VHF net. "This is Charlie Charlie November," the officer identified. "Get me your Two section."

There was a pause, which helped the officer better formulate his questions. *"Two shop here,"* the unscrambled voice said from MACV.

"We have an overdue team attached to CCN, and I thought you'd better know about it," the officer said. "It's Tango."

"Wait. Let me take a look at my operations list," the

MACV intelligence officer said. *"When was your last SITREP from them?"* he asked CCN.

"Eighteen hundred hours two nights ago, nothing since," the CCN officer said.

"Damn," MACV cursed, *"we need to reestablish contact with them! Can you send a rescue team in?"*

"We're fully deployed, but I'll have aircraft up looking for them," the CCN officer assured the MACV voice, "but I do have a question myself," he said, "about the formation of the team."

"A question?" the voice replied.

"Who put that team together, who briefed them? Why didn't they come here before they were sent out?"

"I, er . . . I don't know," the voice stammered.

"That's what I thought," the officer said. "I'll notify you if anything comes up."

"Okay!" the MACV voice said. *"As soon as possible. I have a Pentagon notification to make!"* The officer allowed MACV to break the circuit and end the call.

"We've got some shit now," the Command and Control North officer said to the noncom seated at the next desk.

"How's that?" the noncom asked, turning slightly in the swivel chair.

"Tango was made up of all green troops. The Recondo school report recommends washing out the team leader, and the Vietnamese interpreter's security check is bogus," the officer said, his temper throbbing.

The noncom grinned. "Getting harder to find good help all the time, ain't it?" he joked, but the officer didn't laugh.

"They were *airdropped* into Lac Sao," the officer said, "to try to recon a target over the border in North Vietnam. It's the goddamned CIA again. They took one of our teams without asking! I wondered why they had a Delta code and not one of ours. This is a first-class screwup!" The noncom's smile faded.

"The Pentagon had another hard-on to do something!" the officer continued. "They wanted that mission out ASAP, and nobody stopped long enough to check on shit!"

* * *

Bonn woke up with the warm sun on his face. He checked his watch. It was almost noon. He reached over and touched Pate, whispering loudly, "Wake up, wake up!"

Pate blinked his eyes a few times. "What's wrong?" he asked, reaching for his rifle.

"We've been asleep too long," Bonn said.

Pate looked at him with disdain. "Don't get shook," he said, "they ain't found us yet."

Bonn realized he was still nervous, and Pate's nonchalance had a calming effect on him. "Yeah, yeah, you're right," Bonn said.

Pate sat up, feeling more human than the night before. He cleared a spot to prepare breakfast, tossing the dead leaves away. "What are you doing?" Bonn asked.

"I'm gonna eat," Pate informed him. "It might be awhile before I can again."

Bonn took stock of his remaining rations. He had a dozen meals left. He opened one and heated the water for it with a pinch of C-4. As the meal reconstituted, he left the camp to take care of his bowels and kidneys.

When Bonn returned, his food was ready, and he felt physically better prepared to continue the mission. "That's the first time I've stopped to take a crap on this whole patrol," he told Pate. "Couldn't do it till now."

"It's the being scared," Pate said. "It makes you pucker up tighter than a cow's asshole in fly time." Bonn smiled, amused at the sniper's deadpan humor, and he ate breakfast with a brighter outlook on their chances.

"You said we ain't done much on this mission," Pate mentioned, scooping the stew into his mouth. "I got an idea. Old Charlie will be looking for us to get the hell out, right? So we go back *in* and kill Sugar."

"Hey," Bonn protested, "remember Captain Sullivan telling us in the briefing that they'd be *alerted* we were coming in. That's crazy!"

"Come on, think for a second," Pate argued. "We ain't done nothing right yet. We were supposed to use shooting

Sugar as a trick to draw troops off Phu Chom Voi, but that
was a crock of shit. They had enough men to cover both
places and still have a fuckin' company left over!"

"So what?" Bonn asked.

"So," Pate explained, "they won't be looking for us to go
in and get Sugar now. They'll think we're hotfootin' it out!"

Bonn was still not convinced. "How in the hell do you
plan on finding Sugar?" he asked. "I don't even know what
he looks like."

"Easy." Pate smirked. "He'll find us. You can bet your ass
the NVA got him humping up and down that trail twice a
day, every day. And I know what he looks like. He's got a
gold tooth right here," Pate said, his finger on one of his
front teeth. "It was on his CIA identity photo."

Bonn almost laughed. "How are you gonna get him to
smile?"

"You don't understand," Pate said sharply. "We get in
there and watch the trail and see who travels it every day at
the same time!"

Bonn thought it over. The way Pate put it, they could
accomplish at least half of their mission. "What about my
photographs?" Bonn asked.

"What the hell are they going to do with a few snapshots
of a goddamned gook bunker?" Pate chided him. "Those
snoopers would've told 'em something useful, if Warner
hadn't shitcanned them!"

For the first time Bonn considered that the film might not
be such a big help. "You have a point," he admitted to Pate,
"but we're going over thirty clicks from Lac Sao, and that's
about eighteen or twenty miles! It'll take us four days to
walk down there, if we're lucky."

"What about the road?" Pate pointed out. "We could do
it in no time if we got a ride!"

Bonn raised his eyebrows. "We can't take a chance like
that!" he said. "If we get out on the road, they'll catch us for
sure."

Pate balled up his empty ration packet. "Me and this rifle
can get us any kind of ride we want," he said, slapping the

stock as if the weapon were a friend in good standing. "Let's go," he said.

They buried the bags left from their meals and carefully arranged the bamboo and leaves so it looked as if they had not been there.

Bonn headed south, aiming for Highway 8. He was worried even though he was willing to go along with Pate. Without Warner there, he felt free, as if a weight had been lifted from his back. It seemed reasonable to continue the mission and go after Sugar, and being with someone who desired action and knew how to do it right only baited the hook.

The dog teams converged on the camp not two hours later, and the North Vietnamese searched the area well. The ration packets were dug up, and the dogs barked and pawed at the human feces they found. The radioman reported the position, and the dogs regained the trail again easily. The Americans had gone south.

The commander of the chase team pushed his men hard to catch them, knowing the enemy had to be disorganized and on the run.

Bonn knelt behind a tree on the hill and observed the road. It had been paved at one time, but that had been years ago. The weather and traffic had rutted and broken the surface so badly that bits of rock lay in the dirt only as a reminder that things had once been different.

Carts with big wooden wheels trundled by, pulled laboriously by water buffalo. Impassive farmers sat atop their cargoes of cane and rice, with soldiers in shorts and sun helmets riding beside them.

"What are we supposed to do?" Bonn asked. "Nab a fast wagon?"

Pate lay on the other side of the tree, being patient. "Just take it easy," he answered, "and wait for something with a motor on it."

Highway 8 did not have a lot of traffic. Most of it went west, back to North Vietnam, and the majority of that seemed to be military. Worse, the traffic moved only by hoof or foot, increasing Bonn's anxiety about being immobile.

The day had almost ended when the unmistakable cough and rattle of an aging Lambretta filled the air. It sounded great to Bonn, who had watched the traffic diminish steadily as the hours passed. His spirits had sunk with the sun, but now the deserted road held promise.

Pate slipped off the hill down into the bushes, to get a better look at the approaching vehicle. He was just in time to see it approaching. It was a dirty white three-wheel motorscooter with an open passenger cabin built on behind. A soldier drove it, his uniform covered with the dust of the road. Two of the driver's comrades hung on in the cabin. Pate waved to Bonn, holding up three fingers, and Bonn flicked the safety off on his AKM, reminding himself not to hit anything vital on the machine.

Pate let the Lambretta get directly abreast of them and fired once, his bullet tearing through both passengers, who fell sprawling into the road. Bonn also squeezed off a single round, ending the driver's career at once, the body tumbling from the seat of the vehicle into the ditch, and the unguided Lambretta lurched to a stop, its tiny engine idling stubbornly.

Bonn jumped down from the hill and followed Pate, checking the dead soldiers and dragging their bodies off the road, keeping their sun helmets as camouflage.

"Good shooting!" Bonn said, putting on a helmet and straddling the driver's seat as he looked over the controls.

Pate had no time to bow. "Let's get the fuck outa here," he said, taking Bonn's weapon and sitting on the floor of the cabin to conceal his height.

Bonn twisted the throttle, the worn centrifugal clutch almost stalling the engine, and they bounced off into the gathering darkness, chugging over the potholes on the road. The dim headlamp on the handlebars Bonn left switched on for a more normal appearance, its beam dancing before them with the gyrations of the Lambretta.

They drove for a long time without meeting anyone, and

Bonn prayed for a clear road all the way into Lac Sao, but he knew the luck couldn't last.

It didn't.

A truck and group of civilians was stopped on the side of the road, apparently broken down. They yelled and waved at the Lambretta as it approached.

"Keep going!" Pate said, punching Bonn in the back, holding the AKM ready. Bonn pogoed past the crowd, lowering his head to the brim of the helmet to cover his face, the exhaust of the one-cylinder engine stuttering spasmodically.

The chase team found the bodies of the Lambretta crew, the dogs going straight to them, and flashlights were shone into the faces of the dead. The dogs became confused, smelling up and down the road, but the patrol leader understood. He radioed his headquarters that Lac Sao should be alerted and began the long march into Laos, not waiting for the trucks that were on the way.

Bonn opened and closed the throttle a few times, hoping the engine's bucking and missing resulted from dirt in the carburetor, but the real situation became apparent when the engine finally quit.

"What's wrong now?" Pate asked as Bonn coasted the vehicle to the side of the road.

"We're out of fucking gas!" Bonn said, sliding off the seat. "Let's see if there's a reserve tap on this thing anywhere."

Pate sat under the metal roof of the cabin, watching the road while Bonn examined the engine. "I can't find anything," Bonn said. "We might as well walk. We can't be too far from Lac Sao anyway." Pate ducked out of the cabin and handed Bonn his AKM.

"You want to hide this thing?" Bonn asked about the scooter. They tried to push it over the berm along the side of the road, but the hump was too high.

"Goddamn, this thing's heavy," Pate grunted, trying to lift the rear wheels as Bonn pushed on the handlebars. They succeeded only in getting the vehicle tilted up onto the embankment before they quit. "Fuck it," Pate decided, "let 'em find the damn thing. We'll be gone by morning anyway."

Bonn checked his compass. Its luminous dial was the only light besides the stars. The azimuth he wanted took him north and off the road. "I think we'll hit the trail if we go this way," Bonn said. "We might even get there in time to catch Sugar on his morning run."

They left the Lambretta in its awkward position and stepped out into the fields that lined the road. The walking was easy, scrub grass only a foot tall covering the rolling fields. Scattered trees made darker clumps in the night, each one a possible ambush, like so many traps set for the unwary, the perfect example of the valley of the shadow of death.

Bonn carried his AKM across his stomach, one hand on the pistol grip and the other on the forestock, a round in the chamber and the fire selector on full auto. He took frequent compass readings to check his direction, since there was no daylight for visual references.

He was walking along that way, attention on his compass, when he stepped off into space. He landed with a tremendous splash, mired into thick, cloying mud.

Pate stopped and knelt, leaning forward on one hand. Bonn surfaced, spitting and choking. *"Quiet!"* Pate warned.

"Watch it," Bonn whispered, water pouring off him. "I just fell into a damn stream or something."

Pate walked around the bank and avoided the knee-deep water. "This is a rice paddy," he told Bonn. "There were some on the photos. Don't swallow any water. They fertilize these things with pure shit."

Bonn began a fresh round of hacking and coughing. "Fuck"—he gagged—"and I got a mouthful!" He splashed around and spit vigorously. "Lost my hat, too," he added.

The trail proved to be where Bonn expected. He first saw the wall of trees ahead and pushed on into them, having to feel every step of the way because of the darkness, making distance only by sheer persistence.

Bonn kept the soft green glow of the compass dial under

his nose, reaching the trail by refusing to move from the correct course regardless of the difficulty of the terrain. He reached an open space, knelt, and ran his hand over the dirt. He could see night sky above in a gap between the trees, marking the trail from above.

"We're here," he whispered to Pate, and they backtracked for a short distance and sat down.

In the darkness they could not even see each other. "Think this is the right trail?" Pate asked quietly.

Bonn slipped the wet packstraps off his shoulders. "Yeah," he murmured. "It's the only big one in this area. Runs right out of Lac Sao to the north."

Pate lay back, stretching out his legs. "Let's get some sleep," he said. "It'll be light in a few hours, and I want to find a good place to watch the trail from at dawn."

Bonn was chilled. He opened his rucksack and took out his poncho liner, which he draped over his shoulders. It was wet, too, but it was better than nothing. He listened to Pate's breathing, relaxed and regular as he slept, but Bonn did not feel like sleeping. He sat wrapped in his blanket, cold and miserable, trying to dry out.

He wished he were back in his tent at base camp in the central highlands of Vietnam, dry and safe. The night animals moved about in the forest, scuttling and scratching loudly, paying the two intruders no mind.

Bonn shivered and pulled the poncho liner up around his cheeks. *I shouldn't be so cold,* he thought. *Maybe I'm getting sick.* He cursed mentally, knowing that would be all he'd need at that point.

He became aware of an itch on the calf of his leg, absently reached down to scratch, and felt the fat bulk of the leeches through his trousers. He exhaled sadly and fished around in his rucksack for his insect repellent bottle, all of which he poured onto his trousers and boots.

He supposed he'd gotten the leeches in the water. He rolled up his trouser legs and scraped the leeches off with his knife. They popped, bloated with blood. *That's what's wrong,* Bonn realized. *They've been on me for half the night, and I've lost too much blood.*

He inspected his crotch and waist and found more, feeling sicker by the minute, killing the fat, tough leeches one at a time. He stuck his knife into the ground as nausea swirled in his system. *I am sick,* he admitted. *Those damn leeches have given me an infection or something.*

His fingers gripped the poncho liner more tightly with each wave of illness, his resolve eroding away as his health broke down. He tried to think about being home again, back in the United States, but it seemed like a dream, not a possibility. He thought with anger that he would never get home, that he would never make it out of the war.

The seriousness of the situation weighed heavily on him, without the bravado of youth or the camaraderie of a well-knit team to conceal it. He was sick and almost alone in a hostile country, and a good part of the North Vietnamese Army was out beating the bushes, trying to find him.

He had been worried on missions before; but the hard-edged truth of the night wedged into the depths of his heart, and he felt his weakness keenly.

He wondered how long they had been in Laos and counted back five days, not believing it had been so short a time. It seemed so long ago, so many nights and so many days, and he wondered if he would see the run rise and set again.

I'm probably going to die, he pondered. He wanted to pray; but the words were not there, and he grieved because he felt God had forsaken him as well.

He thought about sin, and it was confusing. Surely he was too far gone to face judgment. He tried to count his kills, but he could not remember them clearly. He felt he was a damned soul before reaching twenty-one years of age, so he reached out and drew the rifle under the blanket with him, holding it between his knees, to try to draw some security from the weapon. The AKM was a friend in a friendless night. He ran his fingers up and down the receiver, feeling all the rivets and indents in the steel.

This is all I have, he thought despondently. *This goddamn gun is all I really have.*

His coming death confronted him, and he remembered the men who had died under his own gun, seeing again the shock, surprise, and agony of the end of their lives.

The animals don't worry about dying, he thought, and wondered why men did. He had read somewhere that the original sin of mankind in the Garden of Eden was to discover the truth of death and that the loss of innocence was the loss of paradise.

In his sickness, not even tears would come.

21

Pate knew by his natural clock when the first rays of the sun were ready to illuminate the jungle. He opened his eyes and yawned, still lying in the same position in which he had gone to sleep. The sun was just breaking over the hills. Bonn was rolled up in his poncho liner, leaning against a tree.

Pate tapped the sole of Bonn's shoe with the toe of his own. Bonn stirred and poked his head out of the liner, hair matted and eyes crusted with sleep. "Wake up, good-lookin'," Pate growled, and stood up to take a piss.

Bonn hurt all over. He made his way to his feet, staggered a few steps, and vomited a thin bile. Pate watched with concern. "You okay?" he asked, helping Bonn sit back down. There was no answer. "Take it easy," Pate said. "I'll make you some coffee."

Bonn rubbed his eyes and shook his head. "God . . . I really had a bad night," he muttered weakly.

Pate had a hot canteen cup pressed into his hands before he realized any time had passed. "Drink it, you'll feel better," Pate said.

Bonn took a sip and rinsed his mouth with it, spitting out the coffee to rid himself of the bitter taste on his teeth. "I got into leeches in that rice paddy last night," Bonn said, drinking larger and larger swallows of coffee.

He finished the cup and handed it back to Pate. "Thanks, man," he said, "that helped, no kidding. Give me some time to get ready to go." Bonn mustered all his strength and stood up, slowly taking off his fatigues. His legs were white and covered with ugly black and blue sores that resembled rotten spots on fruit.

"Jesus Christ," Pate exclaimed, grimacing, "I never saw anybody ate up that bad. Must be some different kind of leeches than we got down in the delta."

Bonn sat on his poncho liner while Pate daubed antiseptic from his survival kit on the wounds. "You must have lost a lot of blood," Pate said, pointing to the fatigue trousers Bonn had hung on a branch. They were stained from the belt down with overlapping reddish brown splotches.

Bonn checked all his canteens. "I'm out of water," he said. "We haven't stopped to refill since we found the radar site, you know."

Pate pulled one of his own canteens, a two-quart collapsible, out of his rucksack and handed it to Bonn. "This is the last one I got left," Pate said. "Go ahead and fix you something to eat. We'll get water today."

Bonn prepared a ration and ate it, the warm bulk of the food filling out his stomach, and he could feel his strength returning. Pate had a meal himself, using the last of the water for the LRRP ration cocoa. Bonn had no second set of clothing to change into, so he stripped off everything he had and laid the filthy pieces beside the bloody trousers to sun.

Pate picked up his rifle and wiped the dew off it with a handkerchief. "I'm going to recon a bit," he said. "You stay put till I get back."

Bonn lay down to recuperate as Pate crept off toward the trail. The wet uniform had chafed and cut him where his web gear made it bind, and the sun bathed his welts with healing heat. Bonn fell asleep on the poncho liner.

Pate found an excellent spot on a small rise. He had a commanding view of the trail, and that meant a deadly field of fire for his sniper's rifle.

In the awakening town of Lac Sao, and in the host of smaller villages around it, the people had begun their daily routines, so the trail was already busy with travelers going to market and to visit.

Pate studied faces in the rifle telescope, looking at the men, women, and children of the Laotian panhandle. He wanted to see a golden smile. Communist soldiers mixed freely with the people.

The cross hairs of the sight swept over dozens of them, tough brown little men with lean faces and drab clothing, Chinese and Soviet weapons slung over their shoulders.

How many of them could I get before they got me? Pate wondered, his trigger finger caressing the safety on his rifle. Three, four, maybe even six? The thought intrigued him, much as some people who look down off tall buildings are nearly hypnotized at the prospect of falling.

The mood passed, and he continued his search for the betraying agent in the human traffic below him.

Bonn woke later, thirsty, but remembered that Pate was gone and that there was no water. He did feel better and re-dressed in his stiff fatigues, tying a scrap of cloth around his head to replace his lost hat, pulling on his dry socks and lacing up the rubber-soled canvas shoes. After packing all his equipment, he sat down to wait for Pate to return, taking his AKM apart and cleaning it thoroughly with a rag.

When Pate came back, he was glad to find Bonn alert. "That old GI chow fixed your ass right up, didn't it?" he joked.

Bonn managed a feeble grin. "Yeah, I'm okay now," he said. "What'd you see?"

Pate squatted beside him. "More gooks than you would believe, just over that rise," he said, indicating the direction with his thumb.

"See Sugar?" Bonn asked.

Pate shook his head. "Naw, not yet. I guess we better get out of here and find some water, then get set up on the trail. We are exactly at the assembly point. You know your map and compass, I'll say that."

Bonn stood up and shouldered his pack to show his vital-ity. "Lead on," he invited. Pate took point, heading away from the trail. They walked a long, slow hour before finding a stream. The water was shallow and sluggish.

They dipped the water from the stream with their canteen cups, filtered it into the canteen necks through a piece of cloth, and dropped two iodine tablets into each water bottle before sealing them.

When the tablets had dissolved, Bonn tasted the water. The familiar tang of the purifying iodine and the taste of canteen plastic soured his tongue, but the water quenched his thirst.

Pate found their way back to the trail and his chosen roost. He noticed that the traffic had thinned out a bit since the morning, but there were still people moving along the wide footpath.

Bonn lay where he could peer through a bush and see, covering Pate, who moved up to where he could aim his rifle in either direction with nothing in the way to interfere. He casually put an unlit cigarette in the corner of his mouth.

As the noon hour came and the heat of the day increased, the trail users became fewer. By early afternoon there was no one to be seen. The absence of humanity was disturbing to Bonn. A dozen good reasons for the lack of travelers crossed his mind, but one continued to plague him. What if it were deliberate? After a while in the hot silence, it seemed as if he and Pate were the only living things in the panhandle.

A pebble bounced off Bonn's back, and he looked around at Pate, who was pointing up the trail. Bonn could not see what Pate was indicating. He crawled out of his bush a bit farther, and what he saw made his jaw drop.

Sergeant Warner was being led along the trail by an NVA soldier. Warner's hands were tied behind him, and there was a leash around his neck held by the soldier. His shoes were missing.

A large number of combat soldiers followed, almost a full platoon, their attention on the trees to each side of them, weapons up. A man in the front carried a megaphone, and Bonn realized that the enemy was specifically looking for

Pate and himself. *They caught Warner and he brought them right to where he knew we'd be,* Bonn thought in anger.

Pate centered Warner in the telescope. The unlit cigarette drooped from the sniper's lips. He saw they had badly beaten the team leader. Warner walked with his eyes downward, jerked along by the strand of rope if he faltered. Pate swung the scope to the man beside him, a short Asian carrying an AK-47 and wearing a bleached-out khaki shirt and trousers. Then he sighted on the man with the megaphone, who was clearly an officer. He had a leather Tokorev pistol holster on his belt and an intelligent appearance about him.

As Pate watched the officer, he noticed the man walking behind him. The depth of field of the scope made it hard to distinguish much about the man, walking as closely behind the officer as he was, but he did not seem to be wearing a uniform.

"*Step back . . .*" Pate urged, using the mental telepathy of the sniper to move his target into place. The group stopped, only a hundred meters away.

The megaphone was held to Warner's lips. "P-Pate! Bonn!" Warner called, his voice strained with terror. "You've got t-to give up! They won't kill you!"

Pate ground his teeth together, listening to the words echo from the megaphone. The good point was that Warner was talking to the other side of the trail. *They don't know if we're in here or not,* Pate realized. He damned Warner for bringing the NVA in on them, blaming him for not being dead.

After a short wait the party of soldiers began walking again, toward the spot where Bonn and Pate lay. Pate still had his eye to the scope, the sight reticle solidly on the officer, when the man behind stepped into full view.

He was a civilian, his black mop of hair cut in soup-bowl style, and he sore a green print sport shirt and dark blue shorts. Pate judged the man to be in his middle thirties, and he prosperously displayed a gold ring on one hand. The man spoke, saying something to the officer, and Pate smiled as a second gleam of gold struck his eye. It was the gold tooth!

"I see Sugar. I'm going to open up when they're twenty-five meters off," Pate said through clenched teeth. "Hit 'em with all the firepower you got when I nail him; then we'll run for it."

"What about Warner?" Bonn whispered.

"As soon as I plug Sugar, yell for Warner to get his ass over here." He'd wanted to say just *fuck* Warner, but he couldn't let the gooks have anybody. He'd give Warner his chance.

"He'll never make it," Bonn said.

"Tough shit," Pate snarled.

Bonn unfolded the stock on his AKM, placing the butt of it tightly against his shoulder, his pulse gathering momentum. He didn't argue Pate's decision. The men came closer. Time slowed down for Bonn, his perception narrowing to the feet of the NVA troops, pacing off the distance to the ambush.

Warner's feet were pale, the mark of those who wore shoes. It was not so with the NVA's feet; they were the same shade as the soil. Pate let the cigarette drop from his lips.

He can't miss at this range, Bonn knew, his heart thudding in his ears, and he tensed his finger on the trigger.

Pate let Sugar walk right into it. The thunderous crack of the rifle was like a bomb exploding. Sugar fell into two men behind him as the soft-tip hunting bullet spun him off his feet.

"Warner! Warner!" Bonn shouted before the men on the road fully realized what was happening. The team leader's eyes lifted to look like a doomed prisoner suddenly given one last unbelievable chance.

Then Bonn pressed the trigger down on his AKM holding the weapon tightly, pouring fire into the tightly grouped NVA men. He could not tell in the blur of humanity who was falling and who was fleeing. He tore the empty magazine out and locked a fresh one in faster than he could blink and had the AKM rolling again, catching the stumbling, leaping men in a whirlwind of plunging automatic fire.

Pate rammed his rifle bolt back and forth without ever taking his eye from the scope. The officer was framed within the ranging reticle, mouth open, dropping the megaphone, and the high-velocity round smashed him down and out of the sight picture. The third special load Pate fired was for Warner's keeper, the impact turning him a crude twirl into the bushes. Warner reacted with amazing speed, running straight for the source of the gunfire.

Bonn blasted the retreating NVA, laying down a torrent of sweeping fire, expended magazines piling up around him. He was shouting and not realizing it, killing men rapidly, seeing their bodies roll in the dirt.

Warner ran straight into Pate, uprooting saplings in his way, and Pate kicked Bonn, screaming, *"Go! Go!"*

Bonn had to tear himself away from the ambush, the dozen or so bodies lying tangled on the trail holding him for a moment like a spell.

The three Americans sprinted back into the forest, dodging trees, and the shouting, shooting horde of NVA piled over the rise after them.

The chase through the forest was enough to incapacitate ordinary men, but the threats and the incentives in operation took the participants out of the ordinary class. They were men insanely trying to kill and men desperately trying to survive.

The North Vietnamese fired as they ran, pointing their weapons instead of aiming, with no targets except split-second glimpses of the Americans' backs or the crashing and thrashing of the foliage.

The NVA shot two of its own leading men, the wounded Asians falling under the feet of the others, and the pursuit continued.

The team returned no fire at all, bullets cracking by them at every jump, tearing down fern and thornbushes and snapping vines in their escape.

"Stay together!" Pate roared, Bonn running just behind him, Warner off slightly to his left. He knew they could not keep up the race long. He looked madly for an out.

"Got a Claymore?" Pate yelled at Bonn.

"Back rucksack pocket!" Bonn shouted, fighting his way

over so he could run in front of Pate, who jerked the mine from Bonn's pack.

Bonn had the Claymore ready for use. The blasting cap and wire were neatly coiled, and the detonating clacker was taped to the side of the mine. Pate stuck the cap into one of the arming wells, no easy feat while he was trying to run at top speed through the jungle.

"Wait," Pate said, stopping to balance the mine head high in the fork of a tree. Bonn turned and covered the rear, breath coming to him in gulps, but Warner kept going.

Pate unwound the wire, backpedaling through the bushes, hearing the enemy closing in on him. "Goddamn it, they're right out there!" Bonn wheezed, but Pate said, "Hold your fire! I'm gonna blow 'em all away!"

Chattering bursts of fire made Bonn and Pate hide as the NVA spotted them. They hugged the ground, and Pate held his breath and laid his thumb on the clacker lever. The Communists came running at the last place they had seen the Americans, and Pate blew the Claymore.

The jungle rocked with the explosion, thousands of leaves filling the air, followed by cries from the mortally stricken Asians. Bonn and Pate stayed on their stomachs, ears ringing in the wake of the blast.

Nothing moved. Bonn raised his head and saw that the tree where he had placed the mine had been splintered to the roots. A clearing had been created by the swath of the Claymore, arcing out from where the tree had once stood.

Lesser trees leaned away from ground zero, tattered and split, nearly barkless, the trunks pierced by countless tiny steel balls. Human garbage lay in shapeless sacks of bloody clothing in the ruins of the trees.

"Now run!" Pate said sharply, and the two of them dashed off into the forest, the North Vietnamese beyond the killing zone of the mine staggering to their feet too late to do anything about it.

Some parting shots were fired, but the chase was over.

None of the survivors was willing to risk the threat of another Claymore waiting for him.

Pate and Bonn ran on, trying to catch Warner, having lived through the day by the very thin skin men always speak of their teeth having.

22

They caught Warner and untied him, and he could say nothing meaningful, still in a state of shock and disorientation. The enemy had roughed him up, but his injuries were not serious. They had spared him for his Judas role.

Bonn could not understand why Warner seemed to be afraid of Pate and himself. He showed as much fear of his friends as he should have his enemies, responding like a frightened animal. He even backed away from the food and water they offered, cringing from any sudden movement.

Warner's condition was not allowed to halt progress. Bonn and Pate made him forge on, terrified and babbling, and when night came, they had put many kilometers behind them.

Warner collapsed to his knees when Pate called a rest halt. Bonn unscrewed the top from one of his canteens and tried to give him a drink. The water made Warner choke, and he lay down, coughing and sniffling.

He didn't know what had really happened, what was really going on. There was a memory of the mission up to the target site, improbable men doing improbable things. Then the enemy had him. He reasoned he must have blacked out trying to get away, because he couldn't recall anything after the firefight.

The cushion the pills had made for him had crashed down when the NVA tortured him. The fear had come back, and it was too much. The Viet officer had asked him everything, and he had told everything.

Now, by some false miracle, he was back again with the men he thought were dead, so securely dead. They had to know what he'd done to them. They would want to kill him for sure, so he had to kill them all over again.

Bonn worked off his pack and equipment and sat down, rubbing his shoulders and back. Pate shed his load also, propping himself against a tree. "I never saw anything like what happened to us today," Bonn said.

"Me neither." Pate grunted. "We killed a passel of them sumbitches, didn't we?"

Bonn had his eyes closed. "How many do you think we got, I mean really?" he asked.

"Twenty, maybe more," Pate said. "That Claymore took out a lot."

Bonn laid his forehead on his knee. "I was firing straight into the middle of that platoon. I shot a few guys who were trying to run away. I wanted to—to kill them all," he said hazily.

Pate grinned and drank half a canteen of water in one long swig. "Yeah, we put a fuckin' to Charlie quick. I hope we can get back to collect the medals for it!" Bonn did not respond. Pate noticed, capping his canteen, and looked at him oddly. "You okay?" he asked.

Bonn raised his head enough to look Pate in the eyes. His gaze was emotionless but penetrating. "Yeah, I guess I'm all right," he said. "It's just that I've never felt that way. . . ."

Pate narrowed his eyes. "Take it easy, man," he told Bonn. "I know that wasn't your first firefight. You've killed gooks before."

"That's not it," Bonn said. "I had kills before I came on this mission. It was part of the job. Today it was different. The job didn't matter. I *wanted* to kill then. I even shot the wounded. I wanted them all."

Pate was inspecting his rifle and scope in the last light. "We gotta get outa here, buddy. I got one loony right there," he said, nodding at Warner. "I don't need two. You better get your shit together."

Bonn wanted no trouble. "Don't worry," he told Pate. "I'm okay."

Pate said nothing as he lay down and closed his eyes. Bonn knew Pate did not understand, and to a great degree, neither did he. If he had not killed those men, they would have killed him—he accepted that without question—but for the first time he had been affected by an overwhelming bloodlust. It had come and gone. Bonn did not feel like an out-of-control executioner. He felt confused.

He slept fitfully, every noise and movement waking him, and dreams haunted the sleep he did get. They were no more of a nightmare than what he lived, but his mental shield could not protect him in his dreams.

The *horror* was chasing him, had him in its gravity, slowing his legs, but he struggled and ran anyway. The *horror* was without form or shape, but it had a center, swallowing life and hope, a collapsing doom with a core of crushed graveyards and grief. It almost paralyzed him. He didn't look back because he was terrified that the *horror* might look like himself. Very soon he wouldn't be able to run anymore. He would fall and—

Pate grabbed him, and Bonn fought to get up, trying to cry out, but the poncho liner in Pate's hands smothered the effort. *"Easy!"* Pate said. "Easy, man!"

Bonn opened his eyes and stopped struggling. It was dawn. "Did I make much noise?" he asked fearfully.

Pate released him. "Naw, I just thought you might," he told Bonn, lying.

Bonn sat up. "I had a bad dream," he explained. "There was something dangerous after me, and I couldn't outrun it."

Pate was burning C-4 and boiling water for coffee. "What was it?" he asked, more to steady Bonn with talk than to find out about his dream.

"I don't know," Bonn answered. "I couldn't see it. It was trying to kill me."

Pate shrugged. "Well, you're okay now. No damn dream is gonna hurt you, but the NVA will, if they catch us."

Pate handed Bonn a hot cup of coffee, then prepared one for himself. The rolled metal edge on the canteen cup burned Bonn's lip, and he waited for it to cool.

Warner stirred, coming awake. Pate laid his cup aside, intent on Warner's actions, afraid he might do something to attract attention. Warner looked at Bonn and Pate, his facial bruises turning from blacks to reddish purples, sitting up very slowly.

"How 'bout some coffee?" Pate asked him, handing over his own cup.

Warner seemed surprised, then took it and drank from it. Bonn said nothing, wondering when Warner would speak.

Pate boiled more water and prepared them a ration each. Warner accepted his food and ate it, watching his teammates warily. "How do you feel?" Bonn finally asked, having taken awhile to develop the nerve to speak to him.

"Okay," Warner said, almost as a croak. Bonn waited for more, but there was none. He decided to drop the subject and let Warner talk when he was ready.

The iodine taste of the water was lost in the freeze-dried LRRP chili con carne rations, and the three ate with their small plastic spoons in silence. The jungle grew greener with the morning light, the coolness of the dawn giving way quickly to the promise of intense heat for the coming day.

Bonn brought his map out again, laying his compass beside it. He had no idea how far or in what direction they had traveled from the trail outside Lac Sao. "I need to go out and take some sightings," he said to Pate, who graciously extended his arm toward the jungle that surrounded them.

Bonn picked up his AKM and walked a short distance from the camp. He noticed a large clearing ahead. He crept to the edge of the clearing and looked across it. It was a natural open spot in the thickness of the rain forest, covering half a square kilometer, overgrown with knee-deep grass that lay heavy with the morning dew. The scene was as peaceful as an English dell.

He looked all around for major hilltops or a body of water to locate on the map sheet, but he was too low to see much. He was scouting for a good tree to climb when he heard the drone of an engine in the sky.

He looked up into the blue, hearing the aircraft engine more clearly now. The prospect of its being a search plane made hope soar in his heart.

Then he saw it. It was a distinct black speck moving across his view of the sky. The sun was just over the tree-tops. *The sun!* Bonn thought. *The sun!* He began to fumble into his pockets.

He found his metal signal mirror, sighted at the plane through the hole in the center, turning so the sun would reflect off the mirror, and began to flash it. The aircraft buzzed slowly on, a good three thousand feet high. He iden-tified it as a type SOG used, an OV-10 Bronco extended-range spotter craft.

He flashed until the plane was out of sight, although he could still hear it as it vanished over the trees. A massive sense of abandonment fell over him. Soon even the sound of the engine was lost in the wind.

He dropped the mirror, beyond words. The clearing sur-rounded him, localizing his despair into a concentrated dose that was too much to take.

He sat down, broken in spirit. A long time passed with Bonn contemplating the sky, before he could get the disci-pline to put the mirror back in his pocket and return to the team.

"Was that plane ours or theirs?" Pate asked.

Bonn squatted, the bitterness showing in his face. "A Bronco," he said. "I tried to get its attention with my signal mirror, but it's gone."

Warner listened to the news with no apparent interest. Pate squeezed his hands into white-knuckled fists. "Fuck!" he said with feeling. Bonn was about to tell him that he still did not know where they were when the hum of the engine returned.

It was louder this time and seemed to be coming right

over the clearing. Bonn ran for the open, carrying his rucksack. "They saw me!" he exulted, paying no heed to the
amount of noise he was making. Pate followed him. The
olive drab Bronco was passing over the far end of the field.
"Get a smoke! Get your marker panels out!" Pate yelled to
Bonn, who was already tossing ration packets out of his
rucksack, looking for the signaling equipment.

He found his panel and laid it in the grass, half folded
over, so both the orange and violet sides showed, giving the
prearranged code for "No Communication—Need Extraction!"

Pate took a hand flare and prepared to launch it if necessary. The aircraft came back, lower this time, and Pate shot
the flare, striking the base of the aluminum tube with the
palm of his hand to impact the built-in firing pin. It rocketed
up with a whoosh, burning a brilliant white. The aircraft
changed course and came roaring right over the marker
panel.

"They see us! They see us!" Bonn chanted, grinning uncontrollably. Pate slapped him on the back, jumping up and
down. The Bronco banked and dived back at the clearing,
the crew's faces visible through the side window.

Something fell from the aircraft on its next pass over the
clearing. Bonn raced out to recover the object while Pate
waved at the Bronco as it climbed steeply for altitude.

Bonn found a can of C ration fruit with a note rubber-
banded to it. He dashed back to the tree line and showed it
to Pate. It was a hand-printed message that read, "CHOPPER
ON WAY. STAY PUT."

The engine noise faded into the distance again. Bonn and
Pate hurried back to the camp to get Warner. "We're getting
out!" Bonn said the instant he saw the sergeant. "They're
coming for us!"

Warner looked puzzled for a moment, but he stood up.
"Give me your gun," he ordered Bonn, who almost handed
it to him out of habit, then stopped himself.

"No, Sarge," Bonn protested, fearing that Warner was
insane, "this is my weapon. I need it!" Warner laughed at

him, both hands locking on to the AKM, and Pate swung the butt of his sniper rifle into Warner's rib cage with crushing force.

Warner folded up and hit the ground, his eyes bulging. Pate snapped his Remington's safety off. "Don't give me any trouble!" he demanded.

Warner had to try several times to draw in any air. *"I'll kill you!"* he gasped, holding his ribs. *"I'll kill you!"*

Pate's expression altered, his hostility changing to a mask of professional calm. The barrel of his rifle moved to Warner's anguished face. Bonn kicked the stock of the Remington just as Pate pulled the trigger. The muzzle blast blew leaves and dirt into the air, the bullet intended for Warner's skull punching deep into the Laotian soil.

Bonn did not know at first if he had succeeded because Warner's body bounced, as if reacting to the impact of the shot. Pate jumped back, jacking a new round into the chamber, but Bonn's reaction was faster. Pate found himself looking straight into the muzzle of Bonn's AKM.

"Put it down!" Bonn said, hunching behind the assault rifle. Pate made an evaluation of Bonn's resolve and gently laid the rifle at his feet.

"Are you crazy?" Bonn asked, motioning for Pate to back away from the rifle. Warner looked up, almost deafened, frightened to the point of immobility. Pate stepped back, his hands at his sides.

"You don't know, do you?" Pate said, pointing at Warner. "He was the one who fired on us at the radar site! He got caught by the NVA trying to run away!"

"What are you talking about?" Bonn asked.

"I had an idea all along what had happened," Pate said. "That first burst of fire at the site came from right behind us, and when I looked around, Warner was gone!"

Bonn glanced down at Warner without moving his head, then back up at Pate. "Why would he do that?" he asked.

The flare and the shot were unexpected aids to the tracking team. The dogs had been good, if slow. They had followed every step the Americans had made for the last two days, and it promised to be over soon.

The patrol leader called a halt as the spotter plane buzzed the clearing, the flare falling slowly on its toy parachute, and the shot pinpointed the location of the Americans without a doubt.

The patrol leader evaluated the situation wisely, deciding to wait and bag the bigger game. It could not be too long before helicopters would be over the clearing.

He staked the dogs down far enough from the tree line so their barking or howling could not be heard by the Americans and ordered his men to dig in and wait. His one light machine gun, an RPD, was given the best field of fire, and his dozen men spread out as snipers.

The first warning was the distant clatter of rotor blades, the sound shifting with the wind, and every ear around the landing zone was aware of it.

"Get the smoke ready," Pate said, quelling the rise of excitement he felt in his throat. "We got to make sure they see us!"

Bonn held a smoke grenade in his hand, finger through the pin. "I'm ready," he said. The drumming of the chopper was getting closer. Bonn figured it must be coming in on the deck.

Warner sat behind Pate and Bonn, his wrists bound with Pate's belt. He could not hear out of his left ear at all, but his right picked out the helicopter, and he lifted his head, trying to see for himself.

"Throw smoke!" Pate ordered, and Bonn pulled the pin and heaved the grenade far into the field. A billowing plume of dirty white smoke spread into the air.

The helicopter made a pass over the clearing, engine laboring, making a check of the area. It was an old narrow high-cabined piston-engine H-19, vintage from Korea, part of SOG's obsolete air force, and its dark green paint was peeling badly. It was one of the first series of troop-carrying helicopters. The pilots peered out from flat windscreens over its bulbous nose. The cloud of smoke was whipped by the rotor wash into a murky haze that was driven across the LZ like artificial fog.

Bonn jumped out into the clearing, holding up his marker panel for the chopper to see. The H-19 turned and began its approach for the pickup. "C'mon!" Bonn shouted. "He's coming in!"

The grass was blown down by the windstorm created by the helicopter, the last of the white smoke swirling into the trees. The H-19 came in nose down, the pilot controlling the ship smoothly.

Pate came running from his concealment, his rifle slung and both hands firmly pushing Warner ahead of him. Bonn bent at the waist, dropped the panel, and lunged forward with them.

The helicopter hovered in, door gunners watching nervously on both sides. The big machine looked like salvation to Bonn, and he was grinning as he ran to it.

The RPD opened up from across the clearing, its pop-pop-pop almost diminutive in the roar of the hovering H-19. The gunner was accurate. His first burst tore out the old ship's windscreen, the brittle Plexiglas flying everywhere, and the copilot took mortal wounds in his chest and throat.

The pilot kicked left pedal, and the chopper twirled on its axis, the door gunners blasting into action, but the unseen machine gun had them zeroed like a floating bull's-eye.

Bonn heard bullets hit the chopper's sheet metal and saw it lurch out of control, and he dived into the high grass. The entire firepower of the ambush concentrated on the helicopter.

The H-19 hung there for a terrible moment, a din like sledgehammers beating tin roofs drowning out all else, the pilot fighting for control.

The chopper tilted, and the rotor blades dug into solid earth, disintegrating, and the fuselage hit the grass, going sideways at forty knots.

It flipped and bounced, panels and parts shedding, scattering dirt and roots until the fuel tank broke its mounts and doused the sparking electrical cables with aviation gas.

The explosion shook the trees, and a fireball ascended into the heavens to mark the spot of the aircrew's cremation. Bonn watched with disbelief, the helicopter burning hellishly too close to him, forcing him back with the heat. Until the first bomb hit in the forest just short of the LZ, no one knew the fighter-bombers were there, so fast did they drop out of the air. Pate and Warner looked up from the shallow gully where they had taken cover and stared wide-eyed at the smoke from the bomb.

A prop-driven Sky Raider, another Korean era veteran, under half throttle made a strafing pass down the trees, its cannon crackling wickedly, and released another bomb as it pulled out. The impact shook the earth, tree trunks and limbs showering for the length of the clearing.

Bonn heard the long, screaming dive of the first plane coming back. He was petrified because he knew the air strike could kill him just as easily as the enemy.

Exploding cannon fire ripped across the LZ and into the trees, cutting them down like a scythe. The aircraft jettisoned its bomb and climbed, the five-hundred-pounder slamming into the forest with a thunderclap that gave concussive nosebleeds to those far away enough not to be made deaf or dead.

The NVA commander had made a predictable mistake. He had planted his men in the edge of the forest, just where the experienced fighter-bomber pilots expected them to be.

Bonn, Pate, and Warner survived only because they were in the middle of the clearing, not on its border. The planes machine-gunned doggedly, twisting and diving, shredding the jungle from the clearing on out.

The NVA troops held, crouching in their holes, firing back, their light weapons not affecting the Sky Raiders.

The machine-gun ammo in the flaming chopper was cooking off, belts of it dancing crazily out onto the scorched earth, bursting like strings of firecrackers.

A gristly black column of smoke climbed jaggedly into the

sky from the inferno of the H-19. Bonn had pivoted on his stomach and started to crawl back through the tall grass when he was arrested by the sight of another H-19 coming in over the treetops, machine guns chattering.

The chopper barreled in, taking no chances. Both door gunners sprayed the tree line with tracers, and even the co-pilot had his window open and was pumping out fire from an M-16.

The pilot saw Pate waving and coasted across the sky, settling in for a landing. Bonn had seen the angel of mercy fall before him once, and a second chance to get out was more than he had ever expected.

Pate and Warner leaped up and ran for the helicopter, Bonn adding his AKM's support to the battle, firing into the places he suspected of concealing the NVA.

Several things happened at once. The fire and smoke from the burning ruin of the first H-19 was sucked into the down-draft of the hovering ship, and the LZ became blanketed with thick, oily smoke, blinding the pilot and crew. Next, the surviving North Vietnamese rallied to concentrate their remaining fire against the helicopter, and last, the grass fire started by the downed chopper reached Bonn.

Bonn felt intense heat on his legs and looked over his shoulder. He jumped away from the flames, beating at his legs and back, fighting out of his equipment. His rucksack was on fire.

A bullet hit Warner, and he thudded to the ground. Pate strode right over him, going for the helicopter. The pilot and copilot witnessed Warner's fall, and shots began to hit the ship at the same instant.

The smoke kept anyone from seeing Bonn.

Pate reached the ship, threw his rifle to the door gunner, and was attempting to get into the craft when the crew chief was hit, his nearly red-hot machine gun barrel falling forward on the swivel. The copilot screamed, *"Go,"* but his message was conflicting with the gunner's shouts over the intercom that the pickup was not yet complete.

A piece of the nose cowling covering the engine was torn

away before the pilot's eyes at that very moment by a burst
of automatic-weapons fire, and panic ensued in the cockpit.
The pilot grabbed the collective, twisted the throttle, and
climbed at full power.

Pate was halfway in the door when the ship took off as if
it had been catapulted. The G forces were too much, and he
was knocked to the landing gear strut, hanging into space
outside the doorway.

A hasty elevation of the light machine gun rained a handful of green tracers into the helicopter, but only one of them
did any real harm. The bullet entered Pate's back, blasted
through his chest cavity and into the airframe.

The shock took all of his breath, and blood spewed from
his nose and mouth as lung viscera filled his windpipe. He
tried in blank numbness to draw a breath but could not.

The door gunner was leaning out of the ship, trying to
save him, as the helicopter passed six hundred feet. The
gloved hand of the airman stretched out to Pate, who only
looked at him helplessly, choking on his own blood. *Just like
my old man,* the sniper thought.

The gunner watched Pate give up and let go, hands slipping off the suspension strut.

Bonn saw it all and screamed for Pate and for himself, in
the apocalypse of the fire and the moment. He found Warner
lying wounded and, with his smoldering pack again on his
back, picked up Warner's limp body, not knowing if he were
alive or dead.

Bonn ran for the forest, clutching Warner tightly, and
vanished into the heavy smoke.

The North Vietnamese patrol leader was dead. His second-in-command ordered a sweep of the clearing, and the
soldiers who could still function searched the burned-out
helicopter and the smoke-hazy surroundings. Most of the
grass was gone, burned into ashes.

The dogs were useless, the odor of the fire masking any
scent they might have found. The visibility had been so poor
during the brief, fierce encounter that the natural assump-

tion was that the remaining Americans had escaped on the
helicopter.

Bonn ran southward, Warner's weight dragging him
down, the death and disaster at the PZ behind him. He
looked back only once, overwhelmed with grief and fear at
the pall of acrid smoke hanging in the air over the jungle.

He cried openly, the tears streaking his grimy cheeks, jog-
ging deeper into the sanctuary of the jungle, not knowing or
caring where he was going.

Warner's blood was wet on his hands and arms, soaking
into his shirt. Bonn's AKM was slung on his shoulder, forgotten in the inner world he had entered. He did not feel the
burns on his legs or the ground under his feet.

His sense of security, the human belief in death only for
others, the untouchable sanctity of self, had toppled around
him. He knew his frailty, and the pain was too much. So he
ran.

23

The office door swung open. "We finally got the word on Tango," the MACV intelligence officer announced. The duty staff stopped their paperwork and looked expectantly at him. "They got zapped during extraction," the young officer began. "CCN lost a chopper trying to get 'em out."

"When did this happen?" an NCO asked, a file folder still in his hand, halfway inserted into a drawer.

The officer looked at his watch. "About ten minutes ago," he informed them. "I just got word from Da Nang."

A clerk picked up a field phone. "I'll call operations and tell them to call off the air search," he said.

"They had two radios, and we lost commo with them not three days into the mission; they had two monitors, and we've never received a signal from either of them; and when the spotter picked them up visually, they were only a few miles outside Lac Sao!" the officer said. "It kind of makes you wonder what goes on out on an operation like that, doesn't it?"

Bonn opened his eyes and realized he was not moving anymore. Pain brought him back to reality. He was lying beside Warner, his face in the sand. He had to make himself get up and look around.

It was daylight, but what time he didn't know. His watch had stopped, and the crystal was broken. It might have been the same day of the battle, but it did not feel like it. He was sure he had been asleep for a long time.

He looked at his hands. The blood on them was dried and caked. Was it his own? He examined his body and found cuts, bruises, and minor burns, but no bad wounds. It had to be Warner's blood.

Blood, he thought, *Warner's hit. He may be dying; he may be dead!* Bonn examined Warner, looking for the holes. He found them in Warner's left thigh, a direct hit in the fatty part of the leg.

A trickle of red blood coursed out of the torn exit wound with each weak heartbeat. Bonn found a bandage compress in his tangled mass of personal equipment and firmly bound the leg, his fingers obeying his brain poorly.

It was then he realized he had collapsed near a stream and the sand was part of the banks. Thirst conquered everything else, and Bonn left mercy to wait until his body had been appeased.

He struggled out of his gear and crawled to the water, which looked pure and flowed fast. He splashed cool water on his face, washing the dirt from his eyes. The bracing chill helped dispel the vortex of emotion that gripped Bonn's heart. He drank deeply, purging his agony with the infusion of new life.

He crawled back to Warner, moved his wounded leg, and decided it wasn't broken. An extensive bruise discolored the knee joint. Since Warner was still alive, Bonn knew the all-important femoral artery had not been ruptured, or Warner would have bled to death hours ago.

He loosened the bandage compress to make sure it was not cutting off the circulation and checked the pulse and body temperature. Both were very low.

The heart rate had slowed down, and the flesh was cold to the touch. Bonn dragged over a piece of log and elevated Warner's legs, then reached for his rucksack to get his poncho liner.

He was stunned to see an entire pocket and part of one side of the rucksack burned away. He had lost items vital to his survival. He pulled the charred poncho liner from the blackened hole in the side of the rucksack and covered Warner with it, staring at the rucksack with hate.

The hole in his rucksack disgusted and angered him, and he sat very still, trying to keep calm. He had to do something to deal with his state of fatigue and self-pity. His body still demanded rest, and he knew the stress he was under distorted everything. He lay down and allowed nature to take its own healing course.

He slept deeply, his emotional and physical reserves recovering, and the reverie brought him a measure of peace. He awoke in late afternoon, his eyes opening fully and clearly.

With a start he remembered the morning. He looked frantically around and found his weapon and shook the sand from it. Warner was still unconscious. *God,* Bonn thought, *I'm all alone!* He looked quickly to the jungle around him, the AKM barrel moving with his head. *I wonder if I lost them,* he asked himself hesitantly.

Everything's fucked up, Bonn groused to himself, gathering his web gear and rucksack. He dumped the contents of the rucksack on the ground, taking stock of what he had remaining.

The *map and compass were gone,* some rations were missing, the camera was nowhere to be found, and his signal flares had been lost. He beat the sand in frustration over the loss of the map sheet and the compass, the discovery of that particular loss bringing on another attack of depression.

He cursed himself, knowing if he had not run blindly through the forest as he had, he would not have torn open his pockets and pouches, smashed his watch, and the gear wouldn't have fallen out of the burned rucksack!

He took off the expensive Accutron. Maybe the concussion from those MK-82 five-hundred-pound bombs had fatally twanged its little sonically regulated heart before he'd backhanded a tree with it. He threw it away in disgust. All the special equipment was gone: the Starlight scope; the fancy camera with its precision lens; the sophisticated radios. Even Warner's drug kit, with all its science, was no longer in the team leader's pocket, obviously taken by the NVA.

Why did I come on this idiot mission? he asked himself, and suddenly it almost seemed funny, and he chuckled at being the only whole survivor.

He giggled, thinking how crazy his buddies back in the LRRP company would think him, and how ridiculous trying to operate with such a fouled-up team had been.

If he could write Linda now, if she could somehow get the letter, what would he say?

> Sweetheart:
>
> Everybody is dead or wounded but me. I've lost almost all my gear. All that invincible, superior soldier crap is just crap. I'm hurt and I'm scared, but we're never supposed to admit these things to anybody. I can't even tell you good-bye. Nobody will ever find our bodies out here in this jungle. I swear if I ever get out of this, I'll never do it again. I just want to get home to you.

He asked himself for help and came to his own rescue.

He'd been told what to do in cases like this in Recondo school. You could lose equipment, but you always had yourself.

He calmed himself, slowing down to think. He would use what he had. He would tell direction by the sun. He would remember the map, working out of his memory. He would rely on himself and do it.

He *would* make it.

Warner tried to raise his head, returning to the realm of the living. "Aghhh! My leg," he groaned. "Do something!"

Bonn forgot his troubles and jumped to Warner's side. "You're not hurt bad, Sarge," he said. "Just rest and take it easy!"

Warner felt the pressure bandage with trembling fingers. "Medic do this? Where are we?" he asked weakly.

Bonn bit his lip. "We're—we're still in Laos," he said under his breath. "They hit us at the PZ. Pate's dead. I carried you here."

Warner attempted to rise up on his elbow, to see what was around him. He could not get his back off the sand. "Shit," he said, and passed out again.

Bonn looked for the villain Pate had described in Warner's face, but all he could detect was pale skin and dirt, belonging to an injured human being. He could not conceive of one of his own men doing what Pate had flatly stated Warner had done.

"If just one of us gets back alive," Pate had told him while standing before his assault rifle, *"he has got to see that son of a bitch pays for this!"*

It had been easier to believe then, with Pate's conviction to lean on, but at the moment he felt responsible and protective for the bruised, bleeding sergeant. There had to be a more reasonable explanation for what had happened at the radar site. Bonn decided to set the decision aside for later.

The pain roused Warner again. He blinked his eyes, clenching his fists. "You gotta get help!" he whined. "Don't let me die out here!"

Bonn laid his hand on Warner's shoulder, finding strength in comforting someone else. "Don't worry," he told Warner. "We're gonna be fine. I got it all figured out. Just don't worry."

Warner started to speak again but choked on his words. Bonn offered his canteen to him, and he drank thirstily from it.

"You say Pate got killed?" Warner asked, seemingly a bit more lucid. Bonn acknowledged him with a nod. Warner handed the canteen back and closed his eyes again.

Bonn checked the bandage, gratified that the bleeding had indeed stopped, but he knew the blood lost already had so weakened Warner that it might be days before he could walk.

Meanwhile, what do we eat? Bonn wondered. If he held it down to one meal a day for the two of them, the rations he had left would last only four days. Warner would need the food just to build his strength up to make an effort at getting out.

Bonn drew a rough map of his section of Laos in the sand, with North Vietnam on the right and Thailand on the left. *We've got a hell of a walk ahead of us,* he thought professionally and without despair.

He figured they could make ten kilometers a day on the average, even with Warner's bad leg. *If I was by myself, I could do it in less than a week,* Bonn thought, *but with a lame man, I'll be lucky if it just takes twice as long.*

Bonn cleaned his weapon and magazines and straightened and repaired his other equipment, preparing to travel. Then he cooked up one ration of chicken and rice to split with Warner. He woke Warner as the sun was going down to give him the warm food, and Warner ate it all.

The fact Warner had an appetite seemed to Bonn a good sign. He finished by giving Warner aspirin for the pain in his leg and made him as comfortable as possible for the night.

Bonn cut camouflage from the bushes with his knife, distributed it around the campsite to screen out prying eyes, and set out his last three grenades by his side. He lay down in the leaves and slept with his AKM in his hands, with no plan on what to do except fight if the NVA caught them.

24

Bonn was up before daylight, making instant coffee, listening to the forest, feeling settled and confident. He was finding maturity in the tempering of war, and it was welcome assurance. He knew he could make the eighty-mile hike to Thailand, come Pathet Lao, Vietcong, or the North Vietnamese Army, and he'd carry his team leader all the way if it were necessary.

He filled a cup for Warner and touched his arm. "Wake up, Sarge. How do you feel?" he asked.

Warner grimaced before he opened his eyes. "B-bad . . ." he whispered, but Bonn had expected that. Warner took the cup and sipped hungrily at the coffee, and Bonn set a LRRP ration cornflake bar beside him for breakfast. "Do you have any cigarettes?" Warner asked.

"No," Bonn said. He examined Warner's leg. The swelling and discoloration around the knee had gone down. "Think you might try to stand up?" Bonn asked, encouraged by the improved appearance of the wound.

"I can't," Warner said, "my leg! Goddamn, I just got hit yesterday!"

Bonn was not going to be put off. "You've got to try!" he admonished Warner. "It's the only way we can get out of here!" Bonn's expression was very firm. He walked around behind Warner and lifted him by his underarms. "C'mon," Bonn insisted, "try it!"

Warner came stiffly to his feet. Bonn supported him.

"How is it?" Bonn asked. Warner's face was turning white. "Take a step," Bonn said, releasing him.

Warner swayed. "It's hurting like a son of a bitch," he managed to say, hobbling only a step or two forward before he fainted, falling to the stream bank and landing with a heavy thump.

"Good try, Sarge," Bonn said, talking to himself. He knelt beside Warner and turned his face out of the sand so he could breathe. It was awhile before Warner moved again.

Bonn waited for a sign of life from his team leader. "Ready to try it again?" he asked as soon as Warner looked up.

Warner reached down and coddled his leg. "You bastard!" he cursed, the insult meaning nothing to Bonn. He didn't hold Warner responsible.

"Best thing you can do is use that leg or it'll stiffen up on you," Bonn said calmly. Warner would not let his eyes meet Bonn's. "Sarge, I ain't trying to be hard on you," Bonn said, "but the only way we can get out of here is to walk out."

He allowed Warner to rest while he selected a tree branch for a crutch just outside the rim of the camp and cut at it with his knife. Warner sat and pouted like a punished child, watching Bonn with malice. The base of the branch was thick, and Bonn was taking his time sawing it with the serrated reverse edge of his survival knife.

Warner only had to lean over slightly to reach the AKM. He raised the weapon, pointing it into the woods at Bonn's back. His thumb quietly slid the fire selector down from safe to full automatic, avoiding the telltale click. His heart began to beat faster. If only he had a cigarette. The need gnawed him.

The assault rifle was heavy in his weakened state, even when he held it with both hands. Warner squinted across the sights and knew Bonn could be dead with no more than the slight pressure of his finger on the trigger.

The hammer was cocked back inside the receiver, the firing pin nested ready in the bolt, and the bullet in the chamber waited for the chance to be let go.

Warner considered many things in that long moment, all of them directly related to his own safety. It would not help right now to kill Bonn. *Let him do the work of getting me out first,* Warner thought. *Then I'll take care of him.*

Before Bonn finished the walking stick and returned, Warner placed the safety back on and laid the weapon down where it had been. "I've got you a crutch now," Bonn said, presenting the branch to Warner. "It'll help you get around."

With that pronouncement, he reached down, bodily lifted Warner again, and handed him the stick. Bonn backed away. "Now come to me," he instructed, holding out both arms.

Warner moved his bad leg first, but only a few inches, supporting his weight on his stick. He brought the other leg up, pain tightening his lips. Bonn stepped back again. Warner took another deep breath and hobbled forward six more inches.

"I think I could do better if I had a splint for my knee," Warner said shakily.

"No, you've got to use that knee!" Bonn argued. "If it gets so bad we have to bind it, we will. I want you to exercise it."

Warner made progress slowly, dragging his wounded leg, both hands on the walking stick. In five minutes he was exhausted and sank to the ground, dripping with sweat. Bonn was pleased anyway. "Good going!" he praised. "A little more of that and we can get on the way!"

Warner noticed fresh blood on the bandage. "Look at this!" he cried. "I'm bleeding again! I can't walk, not now!" Bonn knelt and made sure the bandage was in place and doing its job.

"The wound stopped bleeding by itself yesterday," Bonn said. "I didn't stop it. That means it's only a flesh wound. I don't think it even got any muscle."

Warner pushed him away. "Who made you a goddamned doctor?" he spit. "I can't walk in this condition, and that's that!"

Bonn's capacity for forgiving Warner suddenly evaporated, Warner's insult cutting to the quick this time. He almost hit the pale sergeant. *"Look,"* Bonn said through controlled rage, "you're wounded, and you're my team leader; but if you don't get up and try to walk, *I'll leave your ass right here!"*

Warner shrank back. He had never seen Bonn display any open temper. He had always been such an easy mark for manipulation. "I'm sorry," Warner said, lowering his voice.

The apology did not impress Bonn. He examined Warner with a critical glint in his eyes, Pate's words echoing in the back of his mind. *"He's a treacherous son of a bitch,"* Pate had said while they were waiting for the choppers at the PZ. *"Don't believe a thing he says or does!"*

"Get up right now and learn how to use that leg," Bonn said icily. Warner had no choice. He got to his feet and stomped around the stream bank, picking his steps as if he were in a minefield.

Bonn saw past the facade of helplessness to the genuine agony in Warner's movements. *He's really hurting,* Bonn thought, *but he* can *walk.*

"Enough?" Warner begged after ten minutes of the drill.

Bonn nodded, and they both sat. "We need to get clean," Bonn said, looking at the stream. "You bathe first, and I'll stand guard," he told Warner. "I've got a clean bandage to put on your leg when you get out. We'll wash out our clothes, too. Christ, they need it!"

Warner bathed, sitting on a rock beside the water, using a scrap of cloth to wash himself. There was no soap, but the water and the scrubbing from the rag worked well enough to dissolve the collection of blood, grime, and sweat that had accumulated on his body in the jungle. He couldn't get cigarettes off his mind. Or a green bomb. Just *one.*

Warner slept again while Bonn took his turn in the cool stream, his weapon within quick reach at all times. The burns on his legs had blistered and burst, and the water seemed to help the sores. He appreciated the water, standing there in the stream, enjoying it more than any other bath he had ever had.

Bonn made a promise to himself. If he lived, if he got out, he would keep his discoveries about the simple things alive within himself and never again in his life take for granted a plate of food or a good night's sleep.

He wrung out the uniforms, hung them to dry in the hot sun, and sat down to wait out the day and give Warner time to recoup for the next lesson. He was hungry, but there would be no more food for himself until nightfall, when he cooked. He figured the ration consumption at one meal a day, divided between them.

Bonn guarded while Warner slept and later prepared the night ration. Warner never uttered a sound while he lay there, curled up like a child. He hugged his walking stick in his sleep. The team leader might have been thoroughly unlikable, but before Bonn passed judgment on him, he wanted evidence.

"Wake up," Bonn finally said, and Warner did, so easily that he might not have been asleep at all. Bonn handed him the food. "Eat this," he told Warner, "and get all the rest you can. We're moving out tomorrow."

"Do I have to walk again today?" Warner asked meekly.

Bonn frowned. "No. You did fine. You don't need more practice."

For a reason not understood, Bonn felt guilty about being strict with Warner. He hid the feeling within himself, knowing what he had to do. The jungle darkened with quickening night. He ate his half ration in silence, not wanting any trouble. Tomorrow it began. He saved his strength for the morning's trip.

25

There were many times that first day of the journey out that Bonn truly wondered if Warner was going to make it. The jungle conditions were routine, meaning it was hot as hell, the terrain was a killer, and thousands of stinging insects and sucking leeches were after them for a meal.

Warner limped, hobbled, and crawled, hating Bonn for the pain, plotting the death of the only man who could save him. Warner constantly swore he was unable to travel, but Bonn never let up on him. The walk was hard going for a man with all his facilities, much less a partial cripple. Bonn knew that, and it was the reason he would not allow Warner sympathy. Warner might not have the will to get moving again if he could stop.

It took almost as much effort for Bonn to keep going as it did Warner, because he had to be there to steady Warner when balance was critical through rocky streams or over log crossings, to push and pull him up hills and out of ravines, to carry him through swamp, and to threaten him not to stop when the ground was firm and the obstacles were nowhere but in Warner's mind.

It seemed impossible for Warner to walk quietly. He caught himself in vines and thornbushes, broke bamboo, splashed in shallow water, and griped and groaned out loud during it all.

Bonn often had to recon ahead to see if an area was safe

before allowing Warner to cross it, because Warner had no speed at all and would slow or stop at the worst times.

By the fourteenth hour of the first day's walk Bonn estimated they had made a disappointing seven kilometers. He found an overhanging embankment for them to stay under during the night and prepared a ration to soothe their aching stomachs. After they ate, they went to sleep, exhausted from the beating Laos had given them.

Bonn dreamed again, the pain of the day robbing him of the pleasure of sleep. In his dream he was still out in the jungle, trudging on, legs failing, sweat burning his eyes, but alone instead of with Warner.

He had to rest, but knew he could not. The horror was too close, too deadly, ready to overtake him if he should stop. He pushed through the jungle, afraid to look back, afraid he would see it. He was terrified he would see himself.

When he finally did wake, it was hard to know where the dream stopped and reality began. The jungle was still there, just as it had been with his eyes closed. Bonn shuddered, the fear lingering in his brain, and the darkness of the forest began to break gray.

He damned the nightmare. There were no monsters. A werewolf was a poor second to a napalm bomb for sheer horror. The bloodletting bite of a vampire was nothing to the kinds of holes a machine gun makes in flesh. War took lives, but it took souls, too, claimed them like wailing ghosts trapped in hell for what they had done. Man killed, maimed, and tortured to infinite varieties, extracting more gore than all legend blamed on mere ghouls. War was the true horror, and man was the true monster.

Bonn pinched off a bit from his dwindling ball of C-4 plastic explosive and boiled a canteen cup of water for coffee, wondering what he would do when the supplies were gone. The coffee at least made the dawn bearable.

He shook Warner to life, giving him the first cup, and Warner took it without comment, dragging himself out from under the overhang to sit in the new sun and warm away the chill of the night. Warner's face was pinched and drawn, and he drank his coffee with his eyes closed.

"Sarge," Bonn said, "I know this is hard on you, but you have to do it. There's no other way out. I'm sorry it's like this."

Warner didn't answer. Bonn rolled the poncho liner and stuffed it into the rucksack so that it covered the burned hole and tied the flap down so nothing could fall out. Spots on the AKM had rusted overnight in the dampness, and Bonn rubbed them off with his oily cleaning rag.

"How do you feel this morning?" Bonn asked neutrally, trying to ease the tension between them.

Warner gave him a hateful glare. "What the fuck do you care?" he said bitterly. "All you want to do is to get me back, right?"

"Yeah, I want to get us *both* back!" Bonn said, irritated.

Warner looked him straight in the eye. "I'll see you dead first!" he said, his threat as vile as a curse.

The thing in his dream flickered in the back of Bonn's mind in that moment, urging him to kill Warner, to turn the AKM on him, but sanity drove it down.

"You're not responsible for what you're saying," Bonn said. He intended for the statement to show he was tolerant, but it came out defensive and tinged with apprehension.

"It doesn't matter if we get back or not," Warner said. "Do you think anybody really knows what's going on over here? Do you think anybody really *cares*?"

Bonn didn't answer, bewildered at Warner's unexpected questions.

"God, they're right," Warner said, agony and desperation radiating from his sunburned face. "We shouldn't be fighting a war here. What good are we doing? I know what they chant in the States. *Ho-Ho Ho Chi Minh, NLF is gonna win!* Our own people say that!"

"Those are jerks who don't know—" Bonn began, but Warner cut him off.

"We march around the jungle and get killed! They killed everybody in my squad in one ambush! I had to carry their bodies! I told the chaplain, I said I *can't* do this! I *can't* carry any more bodies! He told me to have courage! That hypocritical bastard!"

"Easy," Bonn said, gesturing with open hands.

"You just don't get scared, do you?" Warner asked, nearly in tears. "Don't you think? Don't you see what's right under your nose? This isn't our war! Let the gooks have it. Let them all kill each other! We're getting killed, and those greedy bastards at home are getting rich! I *can't* take this, *I've got to get out of here,* get me *out—*"

"We're going," Bonn said. "Just calm down. We're going."

Warner broke into sobs, staring helplessly at Bonn, who could only close his eyes and hope.

They started the day by climbing a steep hillside. Warner soon was tired and refused to go any farther than halfway up the slope. Bonn tried to persuade him to go on, promising the downgrade on the other side would be easier, but Warner was stubborn.

In disgust and anger, Bonn left him, climbing on up out of sight, and Warner sat alone. A half hour passed before Warner realized Bonn was serious. There was no noise of anyone returning. Warner panicked, his fear of being abandoned stronger than that of his being brought back by a man he believed was a witness to his crimes.

He climbed the rocky slope, scraping and bruising himself anew, making animallike sounds of terror and pain as he clutched and struggled.

His wound broke open, and blood began to dribble down his leg again. Warner was a shambles when he reached the top. He crawled over the edge and grabbed sideways on to a flat rock. Bonn was cooling off, sitting in the shade of a big tree.

"Why did you leave me down there?" Warner gasped.

Bonn made no attempt to move to help him. "I figured you'd make it on your own sooner or later," he said.

Warner held his hand out for a canteen. Bonn pulled one from its cover and tossed it to him. "I'm tired of this shit,"

Bonn said. "You're putting the whole thing on me. You're gonna help or you're not gonna get back."

Warner drank and handed the canteen back to Bonn, but there was no outstretched hand to take it. "You're starting by carrying your own water," Bonn announced, throwing the canteen's cloth drawstring bag to him.

The cover landed beside Warner. "You can't do that! My leg! I'm not able—" he protested.

Bonn took a deep breath. "You'd better do it," he said, "because I'm not going to do it for you."

Warner's face flared red, and he slammed the plastic canteen to the rock. Water arced through the air from its open neck, and the canteen bounced and tumbled down the mountain.

"Go ahead and shoot me!" Warner cried. *"Shoot me!* It's the same as leaving me here!" Bonn was surprised by the force of Warner's outburst, even though he was accustomed now to his strange moods.

"Why don't you stop pretending?" Warner shouted. "Why don't we get it out in the open?"

"Quiet!" Bonn commanded. "The NVA'll hear us!"

"They'll hear me and come kill *you*!" Warner said, and turned to face the valley. *"Hey!"* he screamed. *"He's up here! He—"*

26

Bonn covered the ten feet between them with one jump to slap Warner down and muffle his mouth with both hands.

Warner fought back, clawing at Bonn's face and biting his fingers, and Bonn discovered he could not hold him. Warner got his feet against Bonn's stomach, kicked him off, and, in the free moment, twisted and grabbed the AKM.

Bonn was quicker and rebounded, pinning Warner before he could bring the weapon around. Warner squealed like a pig, trying desperately to hold on to the assault rifle as Bonn beat at his hands with clenched fists.

The weapon was knocked aside, and Warner went for Bonn's eyes, a savage sneer distorting his face. Bonn lost control and stopped fighting a hostile invalid and began to combat a dangerous enemy. He used the power of the horror from his dreams, the stalking horror he had felt but not seen, and it felt good, the way killing the men had in the ambush.

It is one thing to cause death. It is another to *be* death, to be the all-consuming unstoppable taker of life, to be the fury and the destroyer, to be pure and have no other purpose but to rip the life out of a body. Life was helpless before death. Life fed it. Death was the victor.

When he realized Warner was no longer moving, Bonn saw his own hands clamped around Warner's neck, his thumbs dug deeply into the sweaty flesh. He jerked his hands back, his rational senses returning. The power left him.

Warner lay under him, tongue slightly protruding, dark bruises on his throat, bloody skin under his fingernails where he had scratched and torn at Bonn. He was not breathing.

Bonn felt Warner's chest and could detect no heartbeat. He had killed him! He had lost his mind and his temper and killed him! Bonn was aghast at himself.

He quickly pressed down on Warner's chest twice with both hands so hard ribs cracked at the sternum joints, then felt again for a heartbeat. Nothing. He pushed down again, trying to stimulate the stilled heart. Air wheezed feebly from Warner's nostrils, expelled by the pressure.

Bonn placed his hand under Warner's neck and lifted his head slightly, then touched his mouth to Warner's lips and blew. Warner's chest expanded as air filled his lungs.

He continued the mouth-to-mouth, not stopping to rest, and the better part of an hour passed with Bonn mildly pumping at Warner's lungs and pressing his chest to try to force a heartbeat, trying to revive him, to forestall brain damage.

Bonn had lost track of the time, following the lifesaving steps he had been taught in Recondo school, performing like a robot, when Warner finally drew his first breath on his own. Bonn rejoiced at the heaving of Warner's chest, wet a rag with cool water from another canteen, and wiped the blood and soil from Warner's sunken cheeks.

Life returned in irregular gasps to Warner's body, and when Bonn was convinced that the struggle was over, he crawled off to the side and sat down, staring up into the Laotian sky.

He had managed to stay just ahead of the horror in his nightmare; but it had finally caught him, and now they were one. The horror was infused into him. It left no room for fear. Everything else feared the horror. To be the horror was to be invincible, but it was too great to stay for long in him. It would burn him out like an incandescent flare. Flesh and bone could contain it for only so long. He was less than an observer when the horror came forth. He was it, and it was he. Only after could he reflect and feel mercy, something the horror, in its singularity, did not know.

The wind blew across the hilltop, moaning in the trees. The hill was a pinnacle, thrust into the sky, like the apex of a pyramid.

At last Bonn knew himself. *This is what I was born for,* he thought. *War.*

Warner sat up, his hands at his throat. His first attempt at speaking didn't work. He found his voice only after the third try, and it was odd and strained.

"Bonn?" he asked, looking around the hilltop, finding the silent young man sitting on a stump and blindly watching the valley. Bonn turned his head to look at him, then resumed his contemplation, without a word.

Warner was afraid to bother him if Bonn did not want to talk. He waited almost an hour for Bonn to recognize him, and in the meantime, his breathing became regular and the firefly spots he was seeing before his eyes went away.

Bonn stood up. "We're leaving," he said in a quiet voice.

Warner felt like a whipped dog. "You think I'm crazy, don't you?" he asked Bonn, as if the answer would declare him so or not.

"Warner," Bonn said bluntly, "all of us are crazy." Then he started down the hill, his movements plainly indicating he didn't care if Warner followed or not.

27

There were other hills and mountains and jungle so dense it had to be cut to pass. There were large and small streams and flooded swamps and bamboo brakes that barred their way.

Bonn found a way around, through, or over all of it. Warner stumbled along behind, getting help only when he could not make it at all, and the first seven kilometers became fifteen, then twenty-two, then thirty, and by the time the food gave out, five days and nights had slipped out of their lives, and thirty-six kilometers had been covered in perpetual walking.

Bonn buried the last ration bag. "That's it. We eat what we find now," he said. Warner's heart sank, but his expression didn't change. In his rotting uniform, with sandals made from pieces of Bonn's web gear, Warner was a study in despair. His gaunt, bearded face could have belonged to a death camp inmate.

His limp had worsened, and Bonn knew the wound was turning bad but said nothing. There was no point in adding to Warner's misery. The livid red and purple veins that ran up Warner's leg were streaked with infection.

Bonn cleaned the pus every day from the bullet wound, knowing that Warner's fever would be getting severe soon. He had given Warner all the B complex tablets there were in his medical kit and had used all the iodine and antiseptic ointment. He was reduced to tearing up the poncho liner for bandages.

The small jungle medical kit Bonn carried had been designed for minor cuts and infections, and the puny quantities he had to work from disgusted him. He wanted penicillin; he wanted clean, sterile bandages; he wanted food; he wanted a helicopter back to Vietnam.

What he had was a sick man with no shoes and a hundred kilometers more to walk through enemy territory.

There had been a time that the responsibility would have crushed him, but that was behind him now, in another life that Bonn could remember but could no longer identify with himself. He matched the odds with all he had, and that was nerve. Bonn would not consider being the loser. If something went wrong, he righted it. If he got lost, he found himself. If he was pushed, he pushed right back. He would not stop.

Several times he saw aircraft, and he flashed his signal mirror; but they flew away and did not seem to notice, and Bonn only pocketed the mirror, cursed, and waited for the next opportunity.

Warner questioned his sense of direction, his judgment, and his leadership, with foundless doubts about time, speed, and distance. Bonn ignored them. He knew where he was and where he was going. It was Warner, not Chris Bonn, who suffered from disorientation.

Bonn estimated that in their weakened condition a few days' walk without food would be all they could stand. They would have to make a camp soon and find something to eat. There was no choice.

He led Warner on, sharp fronds cutting bayonet-point pricks through their tattered trousers. He took frequent breathers to check the bindings on Warner's feet and to secure his bandage.

They slept in a tree to be out of the water in a mosquito bog at nightfall, suffering for the circumstance that placed them there, the insects sucking their blood until dawn.

The next day brought higher and drier country and the first human being they had seen since the battle at the PZ.

It was a man sitting in a field, as if on guard. Bonn watched him for a long time, trying to see if the man had a weapon or just a stick across his knees. His clothing was unmilitary, but that was meaningless. The enemy was everywhere and everyone.

Bonn chose a route behind the man, forcing Warner and himself to crawl five hundred meters to get past him without being seen.

That afternoon a forest fire that was burning across the horizon forced them to detour far afield, costing precious energy, a commodity neither of them could spare.

There had been no food along the way that Bonn had seen. Certainly some of the plants had been edible, but he was concerned more with fruits or small game.

He was just putting one foot in the front of the other to keep going. Warner was moving as if in slow motion. The lack of nourishment was responsible for it, Bonn knew. His hunger had grown from being intense to only a dull hurt in his abdomen. He had stopped thinking clearly the day before.

Warner looked like a living corpse, and Bonn was glad he could not see himself. He did not understand how Warner was managing to continue.

Time blurred in the march. The jungle was green and dense. In the open spots the temperature burned cruelly, and they trekked those shadeless spots of hell rather than go around, because to move off a straight line took effort, and there was none to spare.

Bonn looked for animals but saw only small birds, and they were too far away and too light to warrant a bullet from the AKM. He was willing to risk a shot the enemy might hear if the reward was food.

There was not even a good stream to fish in, and Bonn briefly considered going back to the last one they had forded days prior, but the idea of turning back was unthinkable.

Such was his stupor that he passed two banana trees before he realized they were there. Bonn stopped and leaned against one of them, mouth open, looking up at the heavy stalks of greenish fruit. "Food," he said to Warner, and fell to his knees.

They ate the soft, sweet bananas and rested for the remainder of the day, strength slowly flowing back into Bonn's arms and legs as the natural sugars pumped energy into his blood.

Warner did not recover so readily. "Can you walk?" Bonn asked him.

Warner tried to sit up, but he was not able. "Do we—do we have much farther to go?" he whispered.

"No." Bonn lied in a positive way, the very promise easing Warner's pain. "Sleep right now," Bonn said. "We won't try again until tomorrow."

Warner gratefully surrendered and went limp against the soil. Bonn stayed awake for a while, thinking fatal thoughts, as the sun set behind the hills.

The facts were obvious. Warner was not going to make it out of the forest on foot. The time was coming when he would have to carry Warner or leave him behind, and it would be soon.

Bonn did not know exactly where they were that night, except somewhere in the middle of the Laotian panhandle. He was traveling south by southwest, but he knew he was not maintaining a true course. *I'm probably weaving and straying off to the flank,* Bonn thought, *adding miles to this trip. We might be anywhere in a one-hundred-mile arc from Lac Sao to Thailand.*

He considered making a camp and trying to attract the attention of an aircraft, giving Warner a chance to recover, but the threat of the NVA's finding them before a rescue craft did prevented him from doing that.

The morning shed light on the full misery of their situation. The greener of the bananas had wrought havoc with their imbalanced digestions, bringing cramps and diarrhea, the illness preying on their already weakened systems.

Even ill, Bonn would not allow them to stay. If they were

to be sick, at least they could be sick while making progress. He wrestled Warner to his feet, forcing him to walk. Warner obeyed, beyond doing anything but plodding along when told to do so.

Bonn carried a few of the riper bananas in his rucksack to feed them until something better could be found. He damned the bad luck that seemed to keep him from discovering more food.

Warner was reaching the point of hopelessness. He would simply stop and sit, and it took more threats and promises each time to get him going again. His fever increased, and his contact with reality faded as the degrees of heat built in his brain.

Bonn resorted into tricking him into false goals, by telling him that there was a better place to stop and rest just ahead. Warner did not see through the trick, and the meters gained became kilometers.

Bonn did find some wild cabbage he boiled with salt in his canteen cup, and it fed them for a day, the vegetable matter reinforcing their tender stomachs. The banana illness was thankfully gone, and the push went on.

Warner developed a raging thirst, his fever and the tropic sun frying him alive. He stalled at streams as long as possible to cool off, but Bonn allowed only so much time for the breaks in progress.

The ritual wound inspection and cleansing on the eighth day of the walk used the last of the poncho liner. Bonn covered the whole thigh so Warner would not see the truth. The entire lower leg had become infected, each tiny cut or nick festering, and the pain Warner endured because of it chipped away at his quickly diminishing will.

Bonn had tried to stop the spread of the infection, using a tourniquet above the wound, but the bloodstream was carrying the gangrene up into the body, killing Warner from within.

The moment Bonn had anticipated came during the hottest part of the day. Warner sighed and collapsed into a fern bush, and Bonn could not revive him. He pulled Warner to a level spot and bathed his face with warm canteen water.

Warner's eyelids fluttered. He reached up and laid his hand on Bonn's shoulder. It was a dead weight. "Don't leave me here!" he begged.

28

"Take it easy," Bonn said. "I'm not going anywhere."

"No!" Warner whimpered. "You're going to leave me! I can go . . . let me rest a little . . . I can walk!"

Bonn was too tired to argue, and he felt no pity anyway. "I'm not going anywhere," he said firmly.

Warner lay there with tears in his eyes. Bonn made him as comfortable as possible, tucking the rucksack under his head for a pillow, and Warner fell into a feverish sleep, twitching every few moments, as if he were still trying to walk.

Bonn had almost no reserves left. The escape and evasion ordeal had broken him down physically, and he sat listlessly beside his dying partner, swallowed by the vast jungles of Laos.

I just can't sit here, Bonn said to himself. *I've got to do something. My own life depends on it.* His body was not as ready to continue on as his mind was, and it took some compromise to get the two of them together.

He left the thicket where Warner slept and soon found a stream, the water winding its way through the rocks to the lowland. He searched for animal tracks, hoping for deer or monkey. He found some unidentified animal prints that led to the water and spent the rest of the day waiting for game, his AKM now a hunting rifle.

He gave up the vigil at dusk and noted a clearing on his way back. He decided to inspect it the next day. Warner was still asleep when he returned, and he was glad, hating to come back empty-handed to a sick man.

At least there was water nearby, so Bonn knew it could be worse. He took the magazine out of the AKM, to clean the weapon. He had been hungry so long it was difficult to remember anything but, and he knew he was succumbing to slow starvation. He pulled the AKM's bolt back, extracted the round in the chamber, then cleaned the rifle slowly.

The childlike belief that no matter what happens, everything will turn out all right had been extinguished in Bonn on the hilltop. There was no one to make things all right but himself. And if he didn't do it, he would die. It was that simple. He reassembled the AKM and reinserted the magazine.

Bonn did not particularly fear death. He knew death intimately, being its tool, and he used his familiar knowledge of it to avoid his own fate. He viewed the end of life with a detached eye unshaken by its threat. He could face the grim reaper without flinching now, his spirit as strong as the macabre clutch of eternity was inevitable.

He would let Warner die if it had to be. Bonn was now a survivor. That Warner did or did not deserve his fate was of no concern to Bonn. Many questions that had puzzled him before were now clear. He no longer worried about the question of right or wrong. Right was what helped him. Wrong was what hurt him. It wasn't complicated.

Bonn slept through the length of the night and did not dream.

The sun was climbing, and it was plain the day would be miserable with sultry heat before long. Bonn took a sip of the stream water from his canteen to start the day. There was no coffee now.

Warner was deep in a cycle of gaining and losing consciousness, the infection and fever finally victorious. Bonn made him drink a sip of water, still cool from the night, and laid a dampened rag over his forehead and eyes.

Warner began talking out of his head, and Bonn humored

him, uncertain when Warner was speaking from the depths of his sickness or was near the edge of normality.

"I don't know!" Warner said.

"Know what?" Bonn asked.

"I don't know!" Warner repeated. *"Don't! Don't*! I'll take you to them!"

"Take it easy," Bonn told him. "You're safe! The dinks don't have you anymore!"

Warner went silent. He took several deep breaths. "Is everything all right?" he asked.

Bonn rewet the cloth on his face. "Yeah, it's all just great," he said. He saw Warner's body relax.

"Are they all dead?" Warner questioned.

"Who?" Bonn asked.

"The team, they're all dead, I think they're all dead," Warner said.

"Hey, we're not all dead yet," Bonn said.

"I tried to get them back," Warner said.

Bonn knew then it was the fever. "Rest, man, don't talk," he said.

"I had to kill them. . . . They wouldn't obey orders," Warner said, and Bonn went sick. Had Pate been right? Had Warner fired on them?

"How did you kill them?" Bonn asked slowly, feeling as if he were taking part in a séance. "Where did you do it?"

"I shot them," Warner mumbled, "I shot them at the target site, I had to—"

"Why did you have to?" Bonn asked.

"They would have told," Warner said with clarity.

"Told what?" Bonn asked, trying to extract anything he could.

"About the snoopers," Warner answered. "They knew what I did with them. . . ."

"So you had to kill them, didn't you?" Bonn asked. "They would have told for sure, wouldn't they?"

Warner nodded under the cloth. "Sure . . . you understand . . . nobody would ever know what happened . . ." he told Bonn.

Warner was talking out of his head, but he was making sense. He was unknowingly exposing his guilt. The confession ripped into Bonn.

His memory raced back over the events of the last two weeks. The briefings, the airdrop, the firefights, Tan making a stand so his team could escape, Pate falling to his death from the helicopter, the fires, the running, the hunger, the pain.

The man responsible for all of it lay before him.

If I get him back, they might let the bastard live, he thought. Bonn picked up the AKM and held it, biting into his lower lip.

I've been wrong all this time. Pate was right, he thought, and clicked the safety off on his weapon. *I've saved his life too many times; he belongs to me now.* Bonn touched the AKM muzzle to Warner's temple.

Good-bye, you son of a bitch, he thought, and pulled the trigger, but heard only the click of the action. The chamber of the AKM was empty.

Bonn jerked the bolt back, furious at himself for his error. He had cleared the weapon earlier and forgotten about it! What if he had run into the enemy? He snapped a round into the chamber, and the noise of the impact of the bolt seemed to continue even after it was closed.

Bonn looked up. The clatter was coming from helicopter rotor blades. By the sound, it was flying low and fast. Bonn crouched in the grass, his head raised, searching for the helicopter.

29

He saw it coming from the south. It was a Huey, clipping along at maximum cruise. *I've got to get his attention,* Bonn thought with excitement, running out of the high grass toward the clearing.

The ship was going to pass right over him if it held its course. He had no smoke grenades, no marker panel, no radio, no flares, but he did have his signal mirror. He ran through the brush and elephant grass and into the clearing, the mirror already out of his pocket.

The chopper came on steadily. *We might be closer to Thailand than I thought,* Bonn hoped. He aligned the mirror with the sun and began to flash.

As the Huey approached, he could actually see the spot of light his mirror was throwing on its nose and belly. He directed the reflected sunshine to the footwell windscreens, whipping the mirror from side to side.

The ship suddenly banked away, as if avoiding a missile. The move puzzled Bonn. The pilot changed the bank into a wide, shallow turn. Bonn did not stop signaling. He could not flash the ship for a full circle, so he waved his arms, standing out in plain view.

The goddamned pilot might be setting me up! Bonn realized. *He might think I'm the NVA!* He knew the door guns would be fixed on him, waiting for him to move. The gunners would not need an excuse to blast him, Bonn thought. All they would have to do was see him.

Bonn's courage was at odds with his experience. Thai aviation wouldn't be taking any chances out in the Laotian panhandle. The NVA had used every dodge in the book to lure rescue ships down, so he rightfully expected a hail of tracers from above at any instant.

Shit, Bonn thought, *I've walked too far to be killed by an asshole gunner!* He held his ground, noticing the orbits of the helicopter were getting tighter. He dropped the AKM off his shoulder and opened his shirt, so his light skin would show. His face and arms had long ago burnt to a brown the color of his knife sheath.

Bonn saw the Huey was without Thai or even ARVN markings. One of the door gunners returned his waves, and a rush of elation overcame Bonn. *I'm found!* He rejoiced. *It's over!*

The Huey cut back on power, hovering in, and touched down. It had to be a SOG ship. Bonn ran madly to the waiting helicopter. The crew were Orientals and Americans. An American wearing a flight helmet and intercom headset helped him in, and the feel of the familiar metal deck and the presence of friendly faces seemed unreal. Surely he would wake up and discover this was a dream.

"What are you doing out here?" the American shouted as Bonn jumped in.

"Recon Team Tango! SOG out of Vietnam! Aren't you looking for us?" Bonn asked.

"We're after some Thai LRRPs! Seen any?"

"No!" Bonn said, having no idea the Thai military worked this deep into Laos. It was likely another branch of SOG.

"Anybody else?" The GI yelled over the hurricane created by the rotor blades. Bonn hesitated. Should he tell? He wanted Warner dead, but could he sentence him to a slow torture of starvation and gangrene? A bullet was a different story. It would have ended the agony quickly.

"Yes," he shouted back, "he's hurt bad!"

The crewman spoke into his throat mike to the pilot. "Where is he?" he shouted to Bonn.

"Back there," Bonn yelled, pointing toward the elephant grass. "He can't walk! We have to go get him!"

The GI relayed the information to the pilot again. "We can't stay!" the crewman bellowed.

Bonn looked at the American and then at the Oriental pilot, who had turned around in his seat. Before anyone could move, Bonn jumped off the ship. The GI flipped up the sun visor on his helmet. "Hey! Where are you going?" he bawled, but Bonn could hardly hear him from outside the chopper.

"Get me another ship!" Bonn yelled. "Tell 'em you found recon Team Tango!" The Oriental crew chief tossed an olive drab canvas bag over the GI's shoulder to Bonn as the Huey lifted off and powered for altitude. Bonn grabbed the pack and ran swiftly into the elephant grass.

He fought his way back through the foliage to where Warner lay. Bonn did not wonder why he was trying to save the life of someone he had intended to kill a short time before.

It was a matter of principle. He'd had his shot at Warner and failed. It was the same type of reprieve the condemned should get when the hangman's rope breaks. The Army could have him now.

He was the law in the area, and he could dispense mercy if it suited him. Warner was awake and aware and almost on his knees when Bonn found him. He had heard the helicopter and had been trying to get to it. "What is it? What's happening?" Warner croaked, falling back to the ground when he saw Bonn.

"They found us!" Bonn said. "Another ship's on the way to get us out of here!" He opened the bag and spilled a treasure in C rations before Warner, who tried to pick up a can but was shaking too hard.

Bonn laughed, slicing into the container with his knife and handing it to Warner. It was ham and lima beans, and Warner ate it with his fingers, smearing the cold, pasty food into his beard.

Bonn punched two knife holes into a can of applesauce

and sucked out the contents, too busy to talk. They filled their empty stomachs on C ration jam and cookies, spiced beef, chicken noodle soup, and spaghetti and meatballs.

In the condiment packs Warner found the little boxes of stale cigarettes and packs of damp weather-resistant matches. He lit a Winston with palsied hands, sucking smoke into his lungs.

There was instant coffee with powdered cream and sugar in the condiment packs. Bonn efficiently produced two cups of good hot coffee, and it did as much for their morale as the chow they had just eaten. Warner began to look like someone living.

"This has been a real motherfucker," Bonn proclaimed, dunking preservative-flavored vanilla cookies into his coffee.

Warner winced and shifted his leg to one side. "I gotta get to a hospital," he groaned, puffing steadily on his cigarette. "Goddamn, I wish they'd hurry up!"

Bonn guessed Warner did not realize he was going back to Long Binh jail and a general court-martial. It was easier that way, so he said nothing to make Warner suspicious.

The heat of the day, his confidence in Warner's harmlessness, and the fullness of his belly gradually overwhelmed him, and soon Bonn was dozing. Warner lay and watched him for a long time. The food and promise of rescue were sharpening his wits, unclouding his brain. He didn't know he'd confessed, but such a detail hardly mattered.

He had needed Bonn to stay alive, but that was different now. The time to do what was necessary was near. He carefully reached into the bag and withdrew all three of Bonn's grenades. The smooth hulls of the M-26 frags were cool and hard, like steel eggs. He put them into his pockets and smiled behind his sweat-matted beard.

Once Warner would never have had the courage to kill. He'd needed the pills to find the nerve to pull the trigger at the target site. That was all over. He'd been to hell now, and he could kill.

30

A movement attracted Warner's eye to the trees but was gone too quickly to tell what it was. A chill shot through him. Was it the NVA? Bonn was soundly asleep. Warner stopped breathing, lowering his head.

The sound of men walking became distinct. There were people out there. Warner couldn't see them, but he knew they were there close. Dread numbed his senses. He touched Bonn, who lifted an eyelid and saw the expression on Warner's haggard face.

Bonn stiffened with apprehension. He heard the steady footfalls and tightened his grip on the AKM. Warner did not have to say a word. The situation was clear. An enemy patrol was moving past them.

Bonn waited until the sounds went away. *Shit!* He swore inwardly. *Not now! Not again!* It was not fear that pumped the adrenaline into Bonn's bloodstream; it was anger. In sign language he ordered Warner to stay down, adjusted his sweatband, and, crouching so low he was nearly crawling, slipped out after the patrol.

Warner watched Bonn leave, conflicting emotions struggling in his heart. He wanted Bonn dead, but he wanted Bonn alive at least long enough to protect him.

Bonn had not gone far when he saw the last man in the patrol. He was a frail Asian with a graying khaki shirt hanging from his narrow shoulders and baggy trousers rolled up to his knees, revealing thin legs. A too-large pith helmet topped off his aging face, but the SKS carbine he carried was no joke.

They must be looking for where the chopper landed, Bonn figured, *but they don't seem worried that anybody might have gotten off. They're too careless.* The small patrol was treading off into the forest, in no particular hurry, although the men were carrying their weapons in their hands, not on their shoulders.

Bonn caught sight of two more of them ahead and could tell one thing for sure. They were regular army, real soldiers, not guerrilla troops or local militia. They were not on their most alert, but their movements and equipment marked them as veterans.

They were heading for the clearing. Bonn trailed along behind them, stopping when they did, then allowing them to move on before continuing his pursuit. He estimated there were fewer than ten of them in the patrol.

He was close enough to hear them talk, though they did in hushed tones only to pass information from man to man. None of them wore a pack. Bonn supposed that their main unit was not far away and that they had been sent to investigate the possible landing of the Huey but that they felt they had nothing actually to worry about.

Well, you've got something to worry about now, dink! You can't fuck up this extraction! The horror was rising in him.

The patrol stopped again, this time to leave a man behind. The sad sack sat down, and the patrol leader walked back to give him his instructions. He was a proud NCO, with a folding-stock AK-47 and a tan leather belt around his waist, its brass buckle emblazoned with a single star. His hair was military cut, and his high cheekbones gave him the appearance of a leader.

They're going to spread out as pickets, Bonn thought, *probably to stay here for a while, just watching and waiting.* He got a positive count on them as the NCO pointed each man to his place. There were only six.

Bonn took the first opportunity that presented itself to move in. As the rest of the patrol walked away, their feet crunching in the leaves, he advanced on the man with the SKS, depending on their noise to cover his own. He was only a tree away from the man when he stopped. The sad sack had not heard a thing out of the ordinary and was still watching straight ahead toward the clearing.

Bonn paused for a few slow breaths, noting the general placement of the other NVA men on ahead. He pulled his survival knife from its sheath and was suddenly reminded of Tan. He wished for a moment that he could have managed to save the razor-sharp carbine bayonet that had been the interpreter's deadly trademark.

Bonn propped his AKM against a tree. It was two long steps to the man. He rehearsed in his mind just what he had to do and, since there was no point in waiting, did it.

31

Bonn came from behind the tree and jumped for the reposing soldier, his canvas shoe touching the ground only once. He landed on the man, hitting him as hard as he could, knocking the SKS from reach. The two of them rolled in a tangle, Bonn's arm clamped around the guard's face, smothering him.

The little man was stronger than he looked. He tore at Bonn's arm with fingers as hard as talons. Bonn jammed the point of his knife in the pit of the soldier's throat and pushed it with all his strength.

In the jerking and fighting, the blade scraped into solid breastbone, but Bonn freed it and rammed it upward, cutting powerfully. The struggle quickly ended as the man kicked and twitched.

Bonn wrenched the blade right and left until the body went limp. He maintained his armlock on the man's head and eased him to the leaves on the ground.

He had killed a man with a knife, that most primitive weapon, and it fed the horror in him. He was ready to kill again.

He pulled the blade out and crawled back to his AKM. He was smeared with bright red blood, his hands sticky with it. It was soaking into his shirt and pants. He cleaned the knife off in the soil. Issuing from the gore, the distinct, special smell of the slaughter was on him.

He started after his next victim, slinking like a panther.

The unsuspecting picket was sitting cross-legged, eating a ball of cold rice, a green flop hat obscuring his eyes. The ground around him was mostly bare and laced with roots. Bonn decided to bypass him and go for the center of the patrol. He stepped lightly on the exposed roots, AKM trained on the sentry's back, passing right behind him.

The pickets had been placed regularly every twenty meters, all facing the clearing. The patrol leader was a man of the book, Bonn noticed.

He wondered briefly how to begin the killing. The decision took only a second to make. *I'll just hit the hornet's nest,* Bonn thought grimly, *fuck it!*

He took careful aim at the third picket, sighting on the bare temple of the lounging man. The range was almost point-blank.

The single shot was flat and loud in the quiet of the forest. The soldier's head burst, his body thrashing as his nerves reacted to the shock, and Bonn squatted in the bushes near the corpse and waited for whatever would come next.

He heard a voice. The words were in Vietnamese, and they seemed to be scolding, as if asking harshly if someone had fired an accidental shot.

Spouting sharp words, the patrol leader came stalking into the area where he had left the third man, and the sight of the slumped corpse with its lumpy, pulped skull and eyeballs forced out of their sockets choked him off in mid-sentence.

Bonn had the AKM on automatic and fired a burst of three that knocked the Vietnamese down, one of the bullets punching an oblong hole in his starred belt buckle. Bonn grinned wickedly and stayed silently in place, the NCO dying as he hemorrhaged massively from within, a main artery shot open under his heart, and he clutched the holes in his chest with both hands.

The pickets yelled desperately back and forth to one another, confusion in their voices. A rapid exchange of fire broke out from ahead, and Bonn realized with evil glee they were shooting at one another. *Go to it, you simple bastards!*

he chided them from the safety of his warren in the center of their line.

More gunfire crackled between the Asians, wild shots followed by angry screams, and a man dashed blindly through the woods.

They're really screwed up, Bonn thought with satisfaction. *They can't even panic right!*

Since the enemy would not come to him, he went out to find them. He crept toward the crashing of someone in the undergrowth. He discovered a dark-faced man who was unarmed and had stooped in the thicket, seemingly trying to find his lost weapon.

The man saw Bonn, pure terror in his face, and Bonn kicked him in the jaw. The second kick was to the throat. The man folded up in agony. Bonn stomped his head until the skull broke, driving his heel into the dying soldier's brains with savage force and precision. Blood gushed from the victim's mouth and nose.

A bullet skimmed a tree near Bonn, splintering the bark. He looked up and saw two running figures in the jungle coming at him, weapons flashing fire. He was too involved now to worry about being killed. He bellowed a hoarse battle cry and faced them, firing back.

Bonn caught a burst, the stunning impact taking all his breath, and he dropped to the ground. Dark and light stars spun before his eyes, but the foremost thing in his mind was to keep going and kill the enemy. He lifted himself up and saw one of them charging between the trees, closing in.

Bonn's finger clamped on the trigger of his AKM and burned out the rest of the magazine, his blurry vision catching the trees coming apart in the fury of the fire and the punch of the multiple hits dropping the attacker.

Then he felt the first wave of pain and cried out loud, racked in a spasm of convulsions. Even in his state of crippling agony, he released the empty magazine from the AKM and clicked in a new one from out of his ammo pouch. He fell beside the body with the stomped skull, chambering a round into his AKM.

I can't stop. He commanded his body to continue, the severity of the bullet wounds pulling his left arm into his side, the tendons contracting on their own. He didn't want to know how bad his wounds were. All he wanted was to live to see the chopper and to kill anyone trying to keep him off it.

The determination within Bonn was great, and death granted him an extension for services rendered. He lived on the horror. He squinted into the forest. There was movement.

Bonn must have seemed out of fight to the soldier who warily approached, covering him with an SKS, coming to get a better look at the dying American.

Bonn let him get close, not trusting his ability any more to aim. The soldier was young and scared and was taking no chances. He aimed his rifle muzzle at Bonn, to put another bullet into him for security.

Bonn snapped his AKM up and fired all in one motion, the reports of both weapons blending thunderously together. The bullet intended for Bonn took a wooden peg flap fastener off his Chinese chest pouches, hit a steel AK magazine within, glanced, and punched into the dirt.

The burst from Bonn's AKM stitched the soldier up the chest and face, knocking him back with the combined force of the rounds he caught, and his body landed prone in a thornbush, unable to fall the rest of the way to the ground.

Bonn massed all his will and stood, torn rib muscles making him tremble with pain. He could not seem to use his left arm anymore. The wound in his side prevented him from standing up straight, and it was bleeding.

He tried walking and found he could just manage, even though each step felt as if a knife were stabbing into his abdomen.

He finally wondered how much he'd been opened up and if he'd live to see the rescue ship. It was important to do that. For Tan, for Pate, and for himself. He could not stop now.

Bonn heard the unmistakable cracking of a Huey's leading rotor blade slapping the air. "Here," he gasped to the helicopter, his voice barely a whisper, "I'm down here."

There was an explosion.

It felt as if he had been hit by lightning. He couldn't hear or see for a moment. The small part of his mind that was still functioning made him roll over and open his eyes. He saw the trees as if through a lens out of focus. His ears rang.

"How do you like it, you son of a bitch?" Warner said jeeringly from somewhere, his voice distant but identifiable. Bonn opened his mouth to speak, but his breath had not come back, so there were no words.

The drumming of the helicopter became more insistent.

Concussion faded from his senses enough to let him see Warner. He was kneeling, hiding in the trees. Bonn watched Warner pull the pin from an M-26 grenade and throw it toward him in a smooth underhand. *This is it,* Bonn resigned sadly, *this is what it all comes to.* He could not get away.

The frag fell just short of landing directly beside Bonn's head. It thumped to earth two feet away, but part of that distance was blocked by a heavy fallen log. It made all the difference.

The force of the explosion splintered the log as it absorbed most of the brittle fragment wire that had been wound within the hull of the grenade.

Bonn was still alive. He reached and grabbed a stout limb and pulled himself to his feet, catching sight of the big olive drab helicopter as it descended into the clearing so close the wind from the rotors blasted through the trees and fiercely whipped his ragged clothing.

"Warner!" he screamed. Warner was lurching toward the helicopter and almost fell when he stopped to look around and saw Bonn.

Bonn pointed his AKM at him and tried to fire, but nothing happened. He glanced at the receiver. A chunk of grenade had bent the steel. The bolt was forced partly open.

Bonn threw the AKM down and pulled his knife with his right hand, intent on killing Warner any way he could.

Warner had one last grenade. He tore it from his pocket and twisted the pin out, holding the safety handle down.

Bonn rushed him, his wounds slowing him to a limping gait.

A shattering rip of small-arms fire halted his attack. He looked over his shoulder, not surprised to see NVA soldiers coming out of the jungle.

Warner dived for cover. Bonn did not. He turned and hobbled straight for the clearing, using the last of his strength. The chopper was hovering, and a sprinting crewman was out of the ship, CAR-15 in hand, coming into the trees toward him.

The big flight-helmeted GI grabbed Bonn as they met, picked him up bodily, and ran back for the ship. Automatic fire was breaking out from the flanks. The chopper's door gunner returned the fire.

"Where's your buddy?" the door gunner yelled as they tumbled into the helicopter.

Bonn heard the concussive crash of a grenade exploding.

"Dead," he gasped, and collapsed.

The Huey roared into the air, and on the ground the shooting continued.

32

He remembered the medics taking him off the chopper in what he guessed was Thailand, and later he had a brief impression of suddenly coming to on a stretcher, in what seemed to be a big transport plane. He was alarmed and disoriented, wondering where his weapon was. Someone told him he was going to Japan. Then there was an anesthesia haze of green-gowned people, lights, the smell of antiseptic, and blurry glimpses of corridors. It was a hospital.

Bonn finally woke up, realizing he was in a real bed, but his arms were somehow tied down. His side was numb where he had been shot. Plastic tubes drooped down to him from bottles on racks. His mouth was very dry.

"You're going to be all right," a woman said in matter-of-fact English. He hadn't heard an American woman's voice in a long time. He couldn't quite focus his eyes on her, but she was in white. A nurse.

"We've got you on glucose, antibiotics, vitamins, and a sedative. You've been out of surgery since this morning. Try to rest now."

Pain woke him next. Someone was complaining about a drainage tube, and Bonn opened now-focusable eyes to see a doctor changing bandages on his injured side. It hurt. The doctor stopped when he realized Bonn was conscious.

"How bad am I hit?" Bonn asked, his voice thin and weak.

"You must have done some fancy dodging," said the doctor. He had a slack face and weary eyes. "A group of seven-six-twos grazed your rib cage. You've got broken ribs, lacerated muscle tissue, and bone fragments in one lung. I've cleaned out all the bullet jacket metal, but the bone we can leave alone. You've also got superficial grenade splinter punctures—they'll work out on their own—concussion, dehydration, exposure, and galloping fungal infections on your feet and legs. Is that enough?"

"Warner!" Bonn blurted out, remembering. "Did anyone go back—"

"Take it easy. They don't tell us anything. We just pass out the Band-Aids. And we get enough business without guys like you who go out asking for it. Do you feel like having some visitors?"

"Sure," Bonn said.

"There're some people here with pretty heavy credentials who want to talk to you. One came in with you on the plane, and one even stayed with you in the operating room. That's the rules, you know, so he can warn us to shut our ears in case you tell state secrets under sedation."

"Okay," Bonn said, and noticed for the first time a captain in crisp khakis sitting quietly on one of the chairs in the private room, assuming such elite accommodations were a local luxury. The captain wore a Ranger tab on his sleeve and a set of silver jump wings over his left shirt pocket, but no Combat Infantry Badge. His hair was crew-cut so short he seemed almost bald. A grin stretched across his ruddy face as he picked up a phone and spoke quietly into it.

"We'll check on that drainage later," said the doctor as he left.

The captain came to the bedside and shook Bonn's somewhat limp hand. "Glad to see you made it," the captain said. "I've been briefed on your mission. Looks like you ran into a world of hurt out there."

"Yeah—I mean, yes, sir," Bonn said as two men in civilian Windbreakers, sport shirts, and slacks entered the room. Both were in their late twenties, with neat, close haircuts and identical briefcases. Except that their clothes were different colors and one man was slightly taller than the other, to Bonn's still marginally groggy perception they might have been twins from the same career mold. They maintained appropriate sympathetic expressions for a hospital visit.

"These gentlemen are going to debrief you," said the still-smiling captain, "and I'm going to make a coffee run. Anything I can smuggle back for you?"

Bonn realized he was hungry, and his throat was still very dry. "Milk," he said. "A *milk shake,* if you can smuggle in one." The captain winked conspiratorially and briskly walked out.

From their briefcases the men took out map sheets, large air recon photographs, and a few pages of typed notes, all stamped SECRET in red ink. They placed these on the nightstand, pulled chairs close to the bed, and sat down.

"I'm with Army Intelligence," said the taller of the two, then indicated his partner, "and this guy is a civilian, but I think we can trust him." Bonn nodded, unaware the agent was trying to put him at ease. He guessed the civilian was probably CIA.

"We've got a list of routine questions to ask," said the civilian, notebook in hand. "They'll get our after-action report started. We can always come back later for clarifications, so if you feel too tired to continue, let us know, okay?"

The debriefing lasted an hour. The captain did come back with an unauthorized milk shake, and Bonn slowly drank it, staying alert through the whole session. He told the truth about Warner and noticed how it made the captain frown. Frequently the intelligence agents asked careful, precise questions, pointing to places on the maps or photos, and Bonn paused and thought out his answers before replying. The mission was being confined to dates and places and acts failed or accomplished. The interviewers never displayed an emotion or gave an opinion about anything Bonn said.

At the end the agents apologized for the intrusion, packed their briefcases, and, with a formal wish to Bonn for his rapid recovery, left without looking back.

"Jesus, I'm sorry," said the captain. "I've heard about some god-awful missions, but this one takes the prize. SOG owes you, soldier." Bonn shrugged and closed his eyes. "Is there anything else you need?" asked the captain. "Anything at all?"

"Can I have another milk shake?" Bonn asked.

They replaced the empties as the bottles drained into Bonn. He slept a lot during those first few days, while they swabbed his feet and legs with ointment to stop the fungus, but he awoke whenever his bandages were changed. The staff told him how well he was healing.

He ate the bland diet they gave him, began to read magazines between naps, and begged to get up and around as soon as possible to escape the catheter and bedpan. One morning a nurse and orderly came in, unhooked and unplugged him, and wrote an order for a new diet on his chart.

Bonn discovered that getting off the bed and to the adjoining bathroom was slow agony, but he did it and managed to shave and sponge-bathe even though the effort exhausted him. The black stitches under his arm looked frightening.

A radio played down the hall, the Rolling Stones snarling out a fuzz-boxed "Satisfaction." Bonn hummed along as he listened. There really wasn't any satisfaction. He felt uneasy, empty. Then Paul Revere and the Raiders sang "Kicks," a different song but with a similar message. Kicks keep getting harder to find. What do you do next when you've done the worst and survived it?

Bonn was lying and listening to the music when an orderly brought in his mail. By the stampings and scrawls on the envelopes, they had gone to half a dozen places before reaching Japan. All of the letters were from Linda. He sorted them by date, opened them, and, with a twinge of anticipation, began to read.

> Mom and I went shopping today. You wouldn't believe how hot it was. We were just exhausted, and the air conditioner in the station wagon doesn't work.

[*What does she know of real exhaustion or heat?*]

and:

Dad said you could get a job with his company sell-
ing insurance like he does. It's good, steady work.
[*Right. Buy this policy, lady, and make your old man
worth more dead than alive.*]

and:

Dot has female troubles, something to do with her
tubes. She's going to Mom's doctor. Dot thinks I
should get a checkup, too.
[*Great. She'll always be at one doctor or another now.*]

and:

Hazel invited me to the Students Against the War
rally. I went just to hear the music. You have to tell me
something. Our GIs don't really kill children over
there, do they?
[*Rage at the implication. Rage that it happens. Rage
she went. Rage.*]

and:

Why haven't you written? You know I worry about
you so. The least you can do is write.
[*I was busy. You were out shopping. I was trying to get
the hell out of Laos.*]

Bonn, disgusted, sadly folded the letters. Linda was like
someone he didn't know. She was more far away now than
ever.

There was a knock on the door, and Bonn looked around
as a white-haired full colonel, the silver eagles of rank on his

trim dress green uniform, stepped into the room. The colonel had a face age had fortified, as if he had learned some secret truth about life long ago and it had strengthened him, made him a survivor. He carried an expensive leather attaché case, and his artfully blocked billed uniform cap was tucked neatly under one arm.

The colonel wore a Combat Infantry Badge with two stars topping its wreath, indicating its third award, master's jump wings, a Special Forces patch on his right shoulder, and a MACV patch on his left. Row above row of colorful ribbons were pinned across his chest, more than Bonn could recognize.

"How do you feel, son?" asked the colonel.

"Fine, sir," Bonn said, even though it hurt to breathe.

"Mind if I sit down?"

"No, sir," said Bonn. He wouldn't have objected if the officer had asked permission to do handstands. Enlisted men didn't object to bird colonels.

The door opened again, and an orderly looked in. "Anything I can get for you, sir?" he asked.

"Coffee suit you?" the colonel asked Bonn, who nodded. The orderly hurried away as the colonel sat down on a chair by the door, having placed his hat on the nightstand and his attaché case out of the way against the wall.

"I'm Colonel Ben East," said the officer. "The doctor told me those AK rounds just busted your ribs. You're lucky. We need lucky people."

"Are you with SOG, sir?" Bonn asked.

"You mean, What am I doing here? This isn't an official visit. Your debriefings are over. I just thought you deserved to know a little more about the mission you've just finished."

"It was a total screwup," Bonn said flatly.

"Any mission you come back from is a good one. Anyway, the screwups weren't your fault. They were ours. Premission intel was bad; the team selection was wrong; even the mission support and planning were crossed up. It happens from time to time. I want to apologize for all of it."

The colonel had Bonn's attention. He'd never heard a ranking officer admit to much less short of perfection if command decisions were the subject.

"The CIA boys had that radar site figured wrong," the colonel continued. "The reds didn't have any science-fiction gadgetry out there. They were using some new tactics, changing bands or frequencies—I don't know much about radar—and switching their set on and off quickly so our ECM was apparently taking it as a false positive. They'd get an early fix on our incoming aircraft and vector MIGs on them before our people were even looking for trouble. They were pretty slick with those ambushes, but we've changed our own tactics now. It won't work for them anymore."

"We lost two teams because of that site," Bonn said.

"An Arclight took it out a few days ago," the colonel said. "Once we were sure of its tricks, we put it on the target list."

"What about Warner?" Bonn asked.

"Radio intercepts heard an NVA report that they had one GI body at your pickup zone."

"Pate? Tan?"

"Nothing. We have to presume both of them dead, from your own report."

"Warner just flipped out on us."

"It happens, son. Some people aren't cut out for this."

The orderly brought the coffee and left. Bonn tasted his. It was strong and bitter. Colonel East let his sit on the nightstand. "I wanted to ask you," East said, "what your plans are. I understand in a few months you'll be out of the Army."

"Too early to say, sir. Depends on if they send me home now or not."

"If they do?"

"Get out. I might get married."

The colonel smiled. "I did the same thing after the war. I was with the Marauders, a brand-new shavetail. Saw all my action right in Southeast Asia. I went home after V-J day, married my high school sweetheart, and got a job."

"How did you get the stars on your CIB?"

"Well, the marriage didn't work. I was too restless. I ended up back in the Army, joined the Rangers, and did a combat tour in Korea. That gave me my first star. Then I joined the early Special Forces. They were a rough bunch back then. The second star was for the little fracas in the Dominican Republic in '65. They say I'm entitled to another for Vietnam, but there's no point in triple gilding the lily."

"You've been with Special Forces all this time, sir?"

"Since before Kennedy awarded us the green beanie. I'm with MACV now. I was with the old MAAG group before. My time's up. I retire soon."

Bonn studied the colonel's ribbons, three wars' worth of valor, wounds, and duty reduced to a color code.

"I've read your records," East said, "and I want to talk to you. I've been in this business for a long time. I think I know when I find a man right for the job."

"Another mission?"

"More than that. I can get you a permanent assignment to the Special Operations Group."

"What do I have to do?"

"Extend for six months. Take a couple of schools."

"I've got leave time coming up at the end of this tour. Can't I go home first and—"

"In my experience, son, if you go home, you'll change your mind. A soft stateside billet will look pretty good for a while, and then being a civilian will look even better. But it'll start wearing at you. The wife starts to bitch; the kids cry; the rent has to be paid. . . . I know what I'm talking about. It happened to me."

To gain a moment to think, Bonn took a drink of the bad coffee. It was as if the colonel had known exactly what was worrying him.

"Colonel, why—"

"You've been here over a week. Christmas is coming up. You haven't asked for a call to the States. You received mail. You haven't even tried to answer it."

"I don't know what to tell anybody," Bonn admitted.

"Why did you volunteer for SOG?"

"They asked me to at Recondo school in Nha Trang."

"And you agreed because down deep inside you *wanted* to run missions like these, didn't you? And not for God or LBJ, but because the job pulled you to it like a magnet. I found out I needed to do it when I was hunting Japs in Burma."

"I volunteered for my own reasons," Bonn said, even more uncomfortable because he realized the colonel understood him. "For myself."

"The very best always do it for themselves," said East.

"You can't admit that to everybody," Bonn said. "Why me?"

"Because there're damn few of us," said the colonel. "We've got a new operation in the planning stage. It's just right for you. If you go home, you'll miss it." The colonel's eyes were dark, intense, as if he wanted Bonn to go *for him,* because he was retiring. "And if you wait," he said, "SOG won't take you. No more casual volunteers. Make your deal with the devil. I've got the papers with me. Use them, and then beat the bastards—who think *they're* using us—at their own game. *Are you in or out?*"

Bonn was still for a long moment. He wavered. Life with Linda, a job, a home, all he'd thought he wanted beckoned like the road untraveled. It led to a different future. But the dreams of Linda that had sustained him in the jungle were only dreams. The reality of the letters proved that. The worst was how she was waiting for him, depending on him. She didn't know he didn't belong in her world anymore.

The answer came up out of him without his full assent, on its own.

"I'm in," Bonn heard himself say.

33

It was his favorite daydream, a dream he could see and feel. It always began with his picking Linda up on a bright summer Saturday morning, his red convertible Monza so highly waxed it gleamed in the sun.

Linda would come out with her picnic basket, a white terry-cloth beach jacket over her ocean green bathing suit. Almost seventeen, with thick auburn hair, stand-up breasts, firm dancer's thighs, and trusting blue eyes, she always made him take a deep breath when he saw her like that.

Bonn stared at the paper, holding the pen with unwilling fingers, preparing to write what he must write. He wanted to go home. He wanted to go back into the jungle. He wrote, and every word was pain.

> Dear Linda,
>
> I'm not coming back. I can't marry you now. I can't explain. Go on and live your life. Just think of me if you go to the beach again. That's where I remember you best. We can always be together that way if we don't forget.
>
> I should never have come here!

He sent the letter, and it arced in its trajectory across the world and struck on target, wounding her heart, creating one more casualty of the war.

34

Bonn walked out of the hospital and stepped into the jeep that had been waiting to take him to the airport. He still favored his left side, holding his arm close to it.

In his handbag were a Silver Star and Purple Heart and orders assigning him permanently to Special Operations.

Both Pate's and Warner's caskets had gone back to the United States empty except for mortician's weights, with instructions for sealed casket funerals. The official letter of condolence to each family stated simply that their relative had been killed in action, not specifying the location or circumstances.

A posthumous Silver Star award accompanied each box.

The South Vietnamese government claimed Tan's few personal belongings. There was no funeral for him, mock or otherwise.

The Boeing 707 Bonn boarded took off from Japan and pointed its nose toward Southeast Asia. Bonn relaxed in his seat, watching the South China Sea below through the cloud cover.

They needed him back.

There was another mission.

THE END

GLOSSARY

The U.S. military in Vietnam spoke its own language of acronyms and slang. In case you weren't there, here is a dictionary of terms used in this novel.

"A" CAMP: Special Forces camp manned by an "A" team. "B" teams were support and organizational units not in the field.

AIR COMMANDOS: Air Force ground combat and close air support liaison unit.

AK-47: Automatic Kalashnikov, model of 1947. Soviet-designed assault rifle. AKM (automatic Kalashnikov modernized) was updated version of 1959. Both fire the 7.62 mm x 39 "Russian Short."

AO: Area of operations.

ARCLIGHT: Code for B-52 bombing strike.

ART: Automatic ranging telescope.

ARVN: Army of the Republic of Vietnam.

ASAP: As soon as possible.

AZIMUTH: A compass direction expressed in degrees.

BAC SI: Vietnamese for doctor or medic.

BANGALORE TORPEDO: Explosive warhead on a long pole.

BEAUCOUP: French for *many*. Pronounced *boh-koo*.

BLOOD EXPANSION KIT: Intravenously administered field substitute for whole blood or plasma.

BMNT: Beginning of morning nautical twilight. Opposite is NT, or end of evening nautical twilight.

BUCK SERGEANT: Slang for *lowest grade of sergeant*. Three stripes.

C&C: Command and Control. Headquarters for various Special Operations sections. After 1966 they were:
   CC North, headquartered in Da Nang, for missions into North Vietnam
   CC Central, out of Kontum, for Laotian missions
   CC South, out of Ban Me Thout, for Cambodian missions

CARBINE, .30 CALIBER: U.S. World War II weapon M-1 (semiautomatic) or Korean-era M-2 (full and semiautomatic) that was light and handy.

CAR-15: Commando short version of M-16 rifle, officially the XM-177E1 and E-2.

CHARLIE: Slang for *Victor Charlie*, the NATO phonetic alphabet words representing *Vietcong*, which actually means "Vietnamese United." (The official name of the Republic of South Vietnam during the U.S. support of that nation was Viet Nam Cong Hoa.) Other popular names for Charlie were slope, gook, dink, and zip.

CHOI OI: Vietnamese expression about equal to English "Good grief!"

CLACKER: Slang for Claymore detonator. It was a plastic squeeze-handle device that made a clack when used.

CLAYMORE: Mine type of weapon capable of blasting more than seven hundred ball bearings in one direction when exploded, like a giant shotgun.

CLICK: Slang for *kilometer* (pronounced *ke-lo-me-ter,* not *kil-om-me-ter*). It originated from military weapons sights adjustment terminology, as "Right two clicks, down one click."

CO: See xo.

COMMO: Communications by radio or other means.

CORPS (AREAS): The military regions of South Vietnam from the DMZ southward. They were I (pronounced *eye*), II (Two), III (Three), IV (Four), and V (pronounced *vee*) Corps. Remember, *corps* is pronounced *core.* It's French.

COVEY: Code used in this novel for an ABCCC, an airborne command and control center. ABCCCs were C-130s kept up on rotating shifts for radio relay of Special Operations teams messages. Hillsboro and Moonbeam were two actual ABCCC code names.

C RATION: Combat ration, officially "Combat Ration, Individual." Cs were canned food packed as single meals, one dozen meals to the case.

CRYPTO: Technical term for codes and code use.

CYCLO: Man-powered two-wheeled carriage, with bicycle in front. Technology improves the ricksaw.

C-4: Composition 4 plastic explosive. White and claylike in appearance. C-4 could explode powerfully if detonated or burn hotly for cooking if simply lit, a use strictly against orders.

C-123: U.S. medium capacity twin-engine cargo aircraft.

C-130: U.S. heavy-capacity four-engine turboprop cargo aircraft.

DAI UY: Vietnamese for *captain*. Pronounced *die we*.

DELTA: The southernmost region of South Vietnam, wet, marshy, and flooded. Not to be confused with Project Delta, a Fifth Special Forces group unit that was performing reconnaisance and raid missions from 1964 onward. Later Project Delta was incorporated into the Special Operations Group.

DEFOLIATION: The infamous Agent Orange, a sprayable chemical that killed plant life, was used to *defoliate* areas, to deny them as concealment to the enemy.

DI DI MAU: Vietnamese slang for *doing something quickly*, such as running away.

DINK: See CHARLIE.

DMZ: Demilitarized Zone. The dividing line between North and South Vietnam. It was anything but "demilitarized."

DONG: See PIASTRES.

DROGUE: A small stabilizing parachute.

DUSTOFF: Code for medical evacuation by helicopter.

DZ: Drop zone. Intended target for parachutist.

EB-66: Electronics bomber. EB-66s were used in Southeast Asia in electronic countermeasure roles to detect or confuse enemy missile battery radar.

ECM: Electronic countermeasure. Equipment designed to detect radar scanning, detect missile approaches, jam enemy radar, etc.

E&E: Escape and evasion.

EXTRACTION: Removing a team from the field.

FIRST FIELD FORCE: In addition to the corps areas, South Vietnam was divided into First Field Force and Second Field Force, an across-the-middle split for administrative and command purposes.

FORCE RECON: Marine reconnaissance unit.

FRAG: Slang for *fragmentation*. Usually applied to a *frag grenade* and later in the war, as a verb (*to frag*), meaning to kill a disliked officer or NCO with a grenade.

FULTON RECOVERY: A special air rescue method originally designed to get pilots out of remote areas. A large balloon is part of the kit. It is inflated and rises to mark the spot for the recovery aircraft. A strong, light line runs from the balloon to the pilot, who is waiting, seated on the ground and securely strapped into a body harness attached to the line. The recovery aircraft snags the line with a V-shaped hook on its nose.

The pilot is jerked into the sky and carried off, dangling by the line under the aircraft, where he is then reeled inside. Quite a sight to see.

GI: Government issue. Slang for a *U.S. soldier*.

GOOK: See CHARLIE.

GP: General purpose. A term used a great deal in the U.S. military, such as for the twelve-man GP medium (-size) tent.

GREEN BEANIES: Unflattering name for the U.S. Special Forces, from their green berets. Not a friendly term.

HALO: High altitude, low opening. Parachuting out of an aircraft at extremely high altitude with a very low opening of the parachute so ground observers cannot even see aircraft or observe descending canopies. Oxygen masks and special insulated clothing are part of HALO equipment.

HOOCH: Slang for *a small hut, shack,* or *tent.*

HUNTER-KILLER: Operation in which finding and eliminating the enemy are the main purpose.

HUEY: UH-1 helicopter. UH stands for *utility helicopter. Huey* is slang. Huey UH-1B and D models were widely used in Vietnam.

H-19: Obsolete piston-engine cargo helicopter used mainly by the United States in Korea and in the early stages of U.S. combat support in Vietnam.

INDIGENOUS: A fancy term for *local.*

INDOCHINA: What the United States calls Southeast Asia. Roughly, the countries of Vietnam, Cambodia, Laos.

INSERTION: Military term for moving a team into place.

LAI DAY: Vietnamese for *come here.*

LRRP: Long-range reconnaissance patrol. Small teams used for infiltration of enemy-held areas for intelligence-gathering missions. Later LRRP became LRP (long-range patrol) when the Army began to change its mission to include combat.

LZ: Landing zone or Lima Zulu, in NATO phonetic alphabet.

MACV: Military Assistance Command Vietnam. U.S. military headquarters in Saigon. MACV replaced the MAAG (Military Assistance Advisory Group) of the early days.

MATCH GRADE: Precision ammunition made for competition shooting.

MAU LEN: Vietnamese proper way of saying "go" or "hurry." See DI DI MAU.

MIKE FORCE: See STRIKERS.

MONTAGNARD: French term for mountain tribesmen of Indochina. The slang term was *yard*. The Montagnards (pronounced *mountain yards*) were racially different from the Vietnamese, negroid instead of oriental.

MPC: Military payment certificate. To discourage black-market trading, the use of U.S. dollars was forbidden in Vietnam, so MPC, or scrip, was issued to the U.S. troops instead of dollars. It was worthless outside Vietnam.

M-14: Selective-fire U.S. infantry rifle that replaced the semiauto-only M-1 Garand used in World War II and the Korean War. It was powerful and reliable, but too heavy for jungle warfare. In its full sniper version, it was known as the M-21 system. The M-14 shoots 7.62 mm NATO.

M-16: Lightweight 5.56 mm selective-fire rifle that replaced the M-14 as the basic U.S. infantry rifle in Vietnam as the M-16E1 but that developed a poor reputation for reliability until changes were made in the weapon and its ammunition; thereafter designated the M-16A1.

M113: Boxy, fully-tracked U.S. armored personnel carrier.

M-26: U.S. fragmentation grenade used in Vietnam. It made more fragments than the old Mark II fragmentation (pineapple) grenade it replaced.

M-60: Designation for both the U.S. 7.62 mm NATO machine gun and a U.S. main battle tank. The M-60 machine gun could be carried by one man and fired from the hip.

NATIONAL SECURITY ACT: Overriding U.S. security legislation that can eclipse any other U.S. civil or military legal procedures at any time. When the full force of the National Security Act is evoked, it has absolute power in a war or emergency, even to suspending individual constitutional rights. (NOTE: Until you run afoul of this broad act with its hidden capabilities, it's just another act or law. They can always come back later and apologize, but forget about due process if you are adjudged, in an *emergency,* to threaten national security.)

NCO: Noncommissioned officer. A leadership position beginning at rank E-4 (grade of corporal) and extending to E-9, the highest enlisted rank in the U.S. military, being sergeant major in the U.S. Army.

NDP: Night defensive position.

NKP: Military initials for U.S. air base at Nakhon Phanom in Thailand.

NLF: National Liberation Front. Vietcong political organization. *The Front* and *L* for short.

NUNG: Chinese tribe of mercenaries used by the CIA and SOG. Very capable and loyal men.

NVA: North Vietnamese Army.

OD: Officer of the day. The duty officer. Can also mean olive drab, the standard army color.

OJT: On-the-job training.

OP: Short for *operation.* Can also mean observation post.

PARKERIZING: Dull metal finishing process for military weapons.

PATHET LAO: Laotian version of the Vietcong in Vietnam.

PIASTRES: French term for Vietnamese money. The Viets called it *dong.*

PLF: Parachute landing fall. Technique used by parachutist to land safely.

PONCHO LINER: Lightweight quilted blanket with corner ties for attaching inside a waterproof poncho.

PRC-25: Backpack field radio used by U.S. forces. It replaced the PRC-10 of Korea and was later replaced by the PRC-77. All these radios use FM transmission and are battery-powered.

PUNJI: A sharp stake hidden in holes or in grass to injure infantry. Easy to make from bamboo.

PX: Post exchange. A military general store. In some services known as the BX, base exchange.

PZ: Pickup zone. Designated extraction point.

RA: Regular Army. RA troops enlisted.

RECONDO: *Recon*naissance Comman*do.* The Recondo school was operated by the Fifth Special Forces Group in Nha Trang, South Vietnam, from late 1966 to 1970, specializing in teaching small teams how to operate inside enemy territory.

REO: Radar and electronics operator. The "backseat" position in an F-4 Phantom fighter-bomber. The REO is responsible for monitoring the aircraft's ECM equipment and for taking over certain combat-targeting responsibilities from the pilot so he can fly the plane.

RF-4B: Recon F4 Phantom, camera-equipped, and unarmed.

ROCK AND ROLL: Slang for *fully automatic fire.*

RON: Remain overnight.

RPD: Soviet and Chinese Communist light machine gun. Normally belt-fed out of an assault drum attached to the weapon. It has a fixed barrel and is bipod-equipped. Fires 7.62 mm x 39.

RPG: Rocket-propelled grenade. Shoulder-fired recoilless anti-tank rocket, of the short-range Soviet RPG-2 (Chinese B-40) and longer-range RPG-7 type.

R&R: Rest and recreation.

RTO: Radiotelephone operator. The radioman, carrying one of the PRC (portable radio communications) series of backpack radios.

SAM: Surface-to-air missile. For this novel, the Soviet SAM-2, a radar-guided, high-altitude-reaching weapon pilots called the "flying telephone pole."

SAPPERS: Originally, soldiers who undermined a fort's walls and defenses by digging into and under them. Now infiltrators.

SAT CONG: Vietnamese slogan meaning "to kill communists."

SCRIPT: See MPC.

SEAL: Sea, air, and land. Navy unit for commando operations.

SF: Special Forces. Army unit basically for counterinsurgency operations and training of foreign nationals.

SHACKLE: A coded message and general term for certain codes.

SKS: Semiautomatic Soviet-designed "carbine" (rifle by U.S. standards) that fires same round as AK-47.

SITREP: Situation report.

SKY RAIDER: Single-engine, propeller-driven fighter-bomber put into U.S. service in Korean War. Its large bombload and low fuel consumption (compared with a jet) allowed it to stay over a target longer.

SLOPE: See CHARLIE.

SOG: Studies and Observations Group. Cover name for the CIA Special Operations Group. The mission of the SOG was to conduct covert action and intelligence missions inside enemy territory.

SPECIALIST: When the U.S. Army stopped making corporals at enlisted rank E-4, it made the E-4s Specialist 4s, not actually an NCO leadership position like corporal. To make Specialist 5, you would have to stay in a technical field. Most people went on to E-5, "buck" sergeant.

STABO: Acronym (related to designer's names) for body harness sewn from nylon strapping, equipped with D rings and snap links for helicopter winch extraction. Some load-bearing equipment could be attached to harness.

STATIC LINE: The nylon line attached to the plane, which automatically opens the parachute.

STARLIGHT SCOPE: Night-vision device that electronically amplifies available light thousands of times.

STAR SHELL: An illumination shell from the mortars or artillery.

STICK: Group of paratroopers.

STRIKERS: Mike Force, officially Mobile Strike Force. ARVN units working with U.S. Special Forces at "A" camps and field operations.

S-2: Brigade intelligence office. G-2 is division level. *Two shop* was used to indicate any intelligence office.

TAC AIR: *Tactical Air* Support.

TARGET AREA: SOG term for *patrol area.*

TDY: *Temporary duty.* A short-duration assignment with another military unit.

TIGER FATIGUES: Vietnamese copies of original French camouflage uniforms. They were called tiger because of the black stripes printed on them.

TOC: *T*actical *o*perations *c*enter.

TRACKER: Short for the Royal Malaysian Tracker School. This was an elite British jungle school operated in Malaysia and attended by U.S. and other allied military personnel.

TWO SHOP: See S-2.

U.S.: *U*nvoluntary *s*ervice, if it appeared as the prefix to a soldier's service number. It means draftee.

USARV: *U*nited *S*tates *A*rmy *R*epublic of *V*ietnam. High command of just American forces, as opposed to MACV, which was a separate command for the "military assistance" of the ARVN.

VHF NET: *V*ery *h*igh *f*requency. VHF radio net for high-security transmissions.

VIETCONG: United Vietnamese. See CHARLIE.

WEB GEAR: Load-bearing equipment (LBE), woven from cotton "webbing." This is a U.S. term and covered all LBE from World War I to Vietnam. (Now LBE is made from nylon.) Even enemy LBE, not true webbing, was "webgear" in GI slang.

XO: *E*xecutive *o*fficer. Second-in-command, as opposed to the commanding officer, or CO.

ZIP: See CHARLIE.

NUMBERS

3.2 (beer): Low-alcohol beer for military sales or distribution.

82 mm (mortar): Chinese mortar that will actually fire the U.S. 81 mm shell.

105 mm (howitzer): U.S. medium-range field artillery piece.

175 mm (howitzer): U.S. long-range field artillery piece.

201 (file): Record of military service file for U.S. troops.

5.56 mm: Caliber of M-16 rifle. The 5.56 mm bullet is a high-velocity lightweight projectile that can do massive tissue damage.

7.62 mm NATO: Caliber of U.S. M-14 rifle and M-60 machine gun. A long-range powerful cartridge standard for all NATO nations.

7.62 mm x 39: Shortened version of standard Soviet rifle and machine-gun cartridge, used in the AK series, the SKS, and RPD light machine gun.